THE BACHELORS

Muriel Spark

Introduced by James Campbell

4 17 23 86 21

This edition published in Great Britain in 2018
by Polygon, an imprint of Birlinn Ltd.

Birlinn Ltd
West Newington House
10 Newington Road
Edinburgh
EH9 1QS

www.polygonbooks.co.uk

3

ISBN 978 1 84697 429 8

  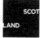

The publisher gratefully acknowledges investment from
Creative Scotland towards the publication of this book.

Supported by the Muriel Spark Society

British Library Cataloguing-in-Publication Data
A catalogue record for this book is available
on request from the British Library.

Typeset by Biblichor Ltd, Edinburgh
Printed and bound in Malta by Gutenberg Press

Foreword

Muriel Spark was born in Edinburgh on the first of February, 1918. She was the second child of Cissy and Bernard Camberg, an engineer from a family of Jewish and Lithuanian extraction. Her early life is recalled in loving and meticulous detail in her autobiography, *Curriculum Vitae*, published in 1992. Hers was a working-class upbringing, but while money was tight she was in no way deprived. Her mother was gregarious and extrovert, always singing songs and telling stories, and wearing the kind of clothes that made her unmissable among other, more dully dressed women in the Bruntsfield neighbourhood.

When she was five years old Spark began her education at James Gillespie's High School for Girls where she remained until she was sixteen. It was a period she remembered with great fondness. She was anointed the school's 'Poet and Dreamer' and many of her early verses appeared in its magazine. In 1929, she first encountered an inspirational teacher, a spinster called Christina Kay, who was to have a formative effect on her life. It was Miss Kay, for example, who took her and her friends – 'the crème de la crème' – on long walks through the city's Old Town, to exhibitions, concerts and poetry readings, and who insisted that she must become a writer. 'I felt I had hardly much choice in the matter,' Spark wrote later. In her sixth and most famous novel, *The Prime of Miss Jean Brodie*, the main character was modelled closely, if not actually, on Miss Kay. Like the unorthodox Miss Brodie, Miss Kay was an Italophile and a naive admirer of Mussolini, of whom she pinned a picture on a wall together with paintings by Renaissance masters.

On leaving school Spark enrolled in a course for précis-writing at Heriot-Watt College. She then found a job as secretary to the owner of a department store in Princes Street, the Scottish capital's main thoroughfare. At a dance she met Sydney Oswald Spark, a lapsed Jew, whose initials she felt in hindsight should have warned her to steer clear of him. Like her father's parents, 'SOS' had been born in Lithuania. She was nineteen, he was thirty-two. He planned to teach in Africa, and Muriel, eager to leave Edinburgh and launch herself at life, agreed to become engaged. In August 1937, she followed him to Southern Rhodesia (now Zimbabwe) and the following month they were married. Their son, Robin, was born in 1938. Soon thereafter the couple separated.

The outbreak of war the following year meant Spark could not return home as she had hoped and she had no option but to stay in Africa. In 1944, however, she obtained a divorce and returned to Britain on a troop ship. Having settled her son with her parents, she headed for London where the devastation of the Blitz was everywhere evident. She boarded at the Helena Club, the original of the May of Teck Club in *The Girls of Slender Means*, and found work in the Political Intelligence department of the Foreign Office, whose *raison d'être* was to disseminate anti-Nazi propaganda among the German population.

In the years immediately after the war she attempted to make a living as a writer. In 1947, she was appointed General Secretary of the Poetry Society and editor of its magazine, *Poetry Review*, but she fell foul of traditionalists, including Marie Stopes, a pioneer of birth control. It was a pity, Spark remarked, 'that her mother rather than she had not thought of birth control'. Her first book, *A Tribute to Wordsworth*, was co-written with her then lover, Derek Stanford, and published in 1950. A year later she won a short story competition in the *Observer* newspaper with 'The Seraph and the Zambesi'. In 1952, she published her debut collection of poetry, *The Fanfarlo and Other Verse*.

Her conversion to Catholicism in 1954 coincided with her beginning work on her first novel, *The Comforters*, which finally appeared in 1957. Praised by Graham Greene and Evelyn Waugh among others, it allowed Spark to give up part-time secretarial work and devote herself to writing. Four more novels – *Robinson*, *Memento Mori*, *The Ballad of Peckham Rye* and *The Bachelors*, and a collection of stories, *The Go-Away Bird* – followed in quick succession and enhanced her reputation for originality and wit.

It was with the publication in 1961 of *The Prime of Miss Jean Brodie*, however, that Spark became an international bestseller. It was turned into a play and a film for which Maggie Smith, who played the eponymous teacher, won the Oscar for Best Actress. Indeed, remarked Spark, so closely did Smith become associated with the part that many readers seemed to assume that she was her creator. The novel, which Spark liked to refer to as her 'milch cow', was a critical as well as a commercial success and continued to sell well throughout its author's long career. In America, it was first published in the *New Yorker*. Its editor, William Shawn, gave Spark an office in which to work. There, she wrote her next two novels, *The Girls of Slender Means* and *The Mandelbaum Gate*, which was awarded the James Tait Black Memorial Prize.

In 1967, having grown tired of the clamour and claustrophobia of life in New York, she moved to Italy and Rome.

That same year she was made an OBE. It also saw the publication of her first collected volumes of stories and poems. Novels continued to appear at regular intervals. *The Public Image* appeared in 1968 and was shortlisted for the Booker Prize. *The Driver's Seat*, which Spark believed to be her best, was published in 1970. In 1974 came *The Abbess of Crewe*, an inspired satire of the Watergate scandal, which she set in a convent.

In the mid 1970s Spark left Rome for Tuscany, settling in a rambling and venerable house deep in the countryside, owned by her friend, Penelope Jardine, an artist. Surrounded by fields of vines and olives, she was able to work without fear of interruption. *The Takeover*, *Territorial Rights* and *Loitering with Intent* – also shortlisted for the Booker – were among the first novels she wrote in the place that would be her final home. Among the many awards she received were the Ingersoll Foundation TS Eliot Award, the Scottish Arts Council Award for *Reality and Dreams*, the Boccaccio Prize for European Literature, the David Cohen British Literature Prize for a lifetime's achievement, and the Golden PEN Award from PEN International. In 1993, she was made a Dame.

Though in her later years she was often beset by illness, she never stopped writing. It was her calling and she pursued it with unfailing dedication. She always had a poem 'on the go' and she never wanted for ideas for novels and stories and plays. Among her later novels were *A Far Cry from Kensington*, *Symposium*, *Reality and Dreams* and *Aiding and Abetting*. Her valedictory novel was *The Finishing School*, the majority of whose characters are would-be writers, which was published in 2004. Spark died two years later at the age of eighty-eight and is buried in the walled cemetery of the village of Oliveto in the Val di Chiana. On her headstone, she is described in Italian with one simple word: *poeta*.

Introduction

James Campbell

The air of the city in *The Bachelors* is reminiscent of the atmosphere encountered in Graham Greene's 'entertainments', particularly those set in London and written before and during the war. In *The Confidential Agent*, *The Ministry of Fear* and other light novels, Greene seems determined to draw attention to the mundane particulars of existence, and Muriel Spark, having absorbed much else from her mentor, is happy to follow. In Ronald Bridges's bachelor flat, 'a heap of . . . unwashed laundry lay on the carpet', and when Ronald's friend Matthew Finch arrives, 'he stumbled over the laundry, put on his damp shoes, then went off to the lavatory'. Not everybody did, in novels of the time. It's perhaps no wonder. 'We had outdoor sanitation,' another character declares, in an effort to stress his working-class credentials, 'which we shared with two other families.' Life had its dreary side in the 1950s. It was F. Scott Fitzgerald who pronounced Sunday 'not a day, but rather a gap between two other days', and Spark catches the mood. 'Sunday morning, Sunday afternoon and the long jaded evening – the very clocks seeming to yawn – occurred all over London.' Especially, she adds, 'in Kensington, Chelsea, and Hampstead', the principal locations of the bed-sitting rooms where 'the bachelors stirred between their sheets' as daylight peeped through the curtains.

Spark began writing *The Bachelors* in Wales in the summer of 1959, and it was published by Macmillan in October 1960, one of two novels by her to come out that year (*The Ballad of Peckham Rye* was published in March). It appeared at a time when, in the words of her biographer Martin Stannard, she 'sensed the possibility of a radical change in the direction of her career – towards the theatre'. Her next book, *Voices at Play*, was to be a collection of short stories and 'ear-pieces', which is to say brief radio plays originally broadcast on the BBC's Third Programme. In a prefatory note, Spark acknowledged that her producer, Rayner Heppenstall, 'sometimes . . . clamoured for more visual bits to be written in', whereas her inclination was to entrust exposition and understanding to the voice alone. She was already at work on a full-length stage play, *Doctors of Philosophy*, which would be produced in London in 1962.

The theatrical infatuation cooled down, but *The Bachelors* bears its mark. It is a novel written largely in dialogue, inhabited by people fated to reveal themselves by what they say. The 'visual bits' – city streets and the journeys through them, drinking clubs and shivery bedsits – are sketched in to provide background to a tale that proceeds mostly by talk. Few other novelists would evoke seven separate London districts in the opening three sentences, without pausing to delineate their varied outlines. Spark was not a writer of 'scenery'. She happily admitted she didn't much care for it. Her narrative threads seldom lead her out of the city towards the banks and braes, unless by way of philosophy or a verse from a Border ballad, as in *The Only Problem* and *Symposium*. In an amusing story in *Voices at Play*, 'A Member of the Family', written at the same time as *The Bachelors* and originally published in *Vogue*, she gives her character Trudy a similar view. Arriving at an Austrian Alpine resort for the first time in her life (as her creator had, shortly before writing the story), Trudy suggests to the hostess, who is taken aback, that it is 'all rather like Wales'. Indoors, Spark was apt to disregard the furnishings in order to attend to the silent manoeuvrings of her characters' spiritual well-being (or ill-being). As Alan Taylor states in his memoir, *Appointment in Arezzo*, the kitchen was not her habitat. It was voices – inward voices as well as outward ones – which she paid attention to. 'Ever since I can remember,' she said in a radio talk in the year *The Bachelors* was published, 'I've had the habit of going over conversations which I have overheard, or in which I have taken part, recasting them in neater form.' The habit turned out to be just the thing for the writing of a novel.

The London of *The Bachelors*, set in the autumn of 1959, is depicted with minimal brush strokes. The odour of ration books and clothing coupons still clings to the surroundings. Not even Trudy would say that it is 'all rather like' this place or that one. At the time she wrote the novel, aged forty-one, Spark was familiar with just one other city in the world: Edinburgh. In Rhodesia, where she passed the unhappy interlude of her only marriage, she and her husband had lived in provincial small towns. Spark's visit to the Welsh-seeming Alps, where she went at the invitation of the novelist Christine Brooke-Rose, was her maiden voyage in what people still called 'Continental Europe'. I mention this because the sense of confinement is discernible behind the scenes of *The Bachelors*, in which little of the conversation is suggestive of the wider world. Few members of the cast, one might guess, have ever been to Europe, a common limitation among lower-middle-class people at the time. As much as they are marooned in unproductive bachelordom, of both male and female kinds, they are stranded in a metropolis with small-town features.

Is there no escape? Actually, yes, there is. Not to the enchanted land of 'abroad', but to another realm altogether. Spark once said that it was her ambition to make 'the supernatural' world seem part of the natural one. The supernatural was already a well-represented feature of her fiction. In *The Bachelors*, in which 'fraudulent conversion' – theft, in a word – is proposed as the MacGuffin of the story, the otherworldly part is given to spiritualism. Adherents of the 'Wider Infinity' sit round a table while a dubious medium lapses into a trance, conveying messages from a better place in which departed husbands continue to wear Harris Tweed suits and play golf. Memorable holidays are recalled from the hereafter, and even the enjoyable meals consumed on them. It can only be Harry getting in touch from the other side, Marlene Cooper insists. Who else could know about that lovely omelette they were served at the inn?

Ethnic variety in the London through which readers pass here is provided by Matthew Finch, correspondent of the *Irish Echo*, and the Scottish policeman, Detective-Inspector Fergusson. Resentment of foreigners is unlikely to go further than Ronald Bridges saying tactlessly to Matthew, 'I can't bear the Irish'. In addition to Mr Fergusson's presence, the novel contains a minor Scottish ingredient – always a pleasure to encounter in a work by Spark. Marlene is on the sleeper heading out of King's Cross, hoping to evade the responsibility of testifying in court against the feckless but strangely charismatic medium, Patrick Seton.

The train to Dundee was a rocky one. She stood up in her bunk and tried to adjust the air-conditioning equipment of the sleeping compartment, but failed. She pressed the bell. No one came. She wondered if Patrick might have some spiritual power over her, even in Scotland.

Surely granite-steady D.I. Fergusson will be up to the task of dealing with Patrick Seton (which half-rhymes with 'Satan')? The appearance of the policeman reminds me of one of my favourite Sparkisms, which need not be explained to Mr Fergusson's compatriots: 'It's better to be Scottish. Morally better, somehow.' It is often noted that *The Prime of Miss Jean Brodie* is Spark's only Scottish novel, but small northern dramas of the spirit realm turn up in others, notably *The Ballad of Peckham Rye* and *Symposium*. They usually involve a tussle between good and evil: not a soul wrestling with a haunting torment in the deep of the night, but a rehearsal of the contest fought by God and the Devil – good and bad, if you prefer – in the thick of everyday life, where it is most likely to be encountered.

Such a tussle is at the heart of *The Bachelors*. There is only one thoroughly bad person in the novel. For the others, it is a matter of choice. You can choose to be good, up to a point. In the absence of good, evil spies an opportunity. This is the central plank of the novel's theology, which Spark shared with Greene and others. Towards the end of *The Devil Finds Work* (for idle hands, needless to say), a book-length essay on film by James Baldwin published in 1976, the author leaves a cinema in the company of a friend, after a screening of *The Exorcist*. 'So we must be careful,' Baldwin's friend remarks, 'lest we lose our faith – and become possessed.' I can't say if Spark read Baldwin, or whether Baldwin knew *The Bachelors* or any other Spark novel, but the two are connected by a fundamentally religious, not to say Christian, outlook on life. Some members of the London circle at the seances held in *The Bachelors* are terrified of losing faith in what Patrick Seton relays from the other side, and of facing the unknown without a familiar figure for company, golf clubs, Harris Tweed suit and all. That's where the conman Seton (Satan was a conman too, remember) sees his chance.

It is easy to forget that Spark was approaching forty when her first novel, *The Comforters*, was published in 1957, and that she was already an experienced woman of letters. She had edited the *Poetry Review*, published poems of her own – *The Fanfarlo and Other Verse* (1952) – and co-written, with Derek Stanford, biographical studies of Emily Brontë and Mary Shelley, among others. By the time she came to write *The Bachelors*, in that miraculous feat of creativity that produced eight books between 1957 and 1961, the year of *The Prime of Miss Jean Brodie*, she was fully in command of a style that, notwithstanding its debts to Greene and Evelyn Waugh, was hers alone. Many writers envy the fluency of their own letters. Spark absorbed this lesson at the beginning of her fiction-writing life, and set it out as primary advice: Write as if settling down to compose a letter to a friend, using as few words as possible.

It is tempting to say that the London of *The Bachelors* no longer exists; but it does. Not so much in Kensington, Chelsea and Hampstead, as in the suburbs to the distant south and east of the city, some of the names of which are foreign even to other Londoners. In dimmed rooms, solemnity is imposed and seances are held; widows and widowers receive consoling messages; gurus, mediums and priests like Father Socket in this novel are believed in – often they believe in themselves. 'Fraudulent conversion' takes place in a variety of forms. The voices which Spark overheard and recast in neater form are all around, funny and grave at the same time.

I

Daylight was appearing over London, the great city of bachelors. Half-pint bottles of milk began to be stood on the doorsteps of houses containing single apartments from Hampstead Heath to Greenwich Park, and from Wanstead Flats to Putney Heath; but especially in Hampstead, especially in Kensington.

In Queen's Gate, Kensington, in Harrington Road, The Boltons, Holland Park, and in King's Road, Chelsea, and its backwaters, the bachelors stirred between their sheets, reached for their wound watches, and with waking intelligences noted the time; then, remembering it was Saturday morning, turned over on their pillows. But soon, since it was Saturday, most would be out on the streets shopping for their bacon and eggs, their week's supplies of breakfasts and occasional suppers; and these bachelors would set out early, before a quarter past ten, in order to avoid being jostled by the women, the legitimate shoppers.

At a quarter past ten, Ronald Bridges, aged thirty-seven, who during the week was assistant curator at a small museum of handwriting in the City of London, stopped in the Old Brompton Road to speak to his friend Martin Bowles, a barrister of thirty-five.

Ronald moved his old plastic shopping bag up and down twice, to suggest to Martin that it was a greater weight than it really was, and that the whole business was a bore.

'Where,' said Ronald, pointing to a package on the top of Martin's laden bag, 'did you get your frozen peas?'

'Clayton's.'

'How much?'

'One and six. That's for a small packet; does for two. A large is two and six; six helpings.'

'Terrible price,' said Ronald, agreeably.

'Your hand's never out of your pocket,' said Martin.

'What else have you got there?' Ronald said.

'Cod. You bake it in yoghurt with a sprinkle of marjoram and it tastes like halibut. My old ma's away for a fortnight with the old housekeeper.'

'Marjoram, where do you get marjoram?'

'Oh, Fortnum's. You get all the herbs there. I get a bag of stuff every month. I do nearly all the shopping and most of the cooking since my old ma's had her op. And old Carrie isn't up to it now – she never was much of a cook.'

'You must have it in you,' said Ronald, 'going all the way to Piccadilly for herbs.'

'I usually work it in with something else,' Martin said. 'We like our herbs, Ma and I. Come on in here.'

He meant a coffee-bar. They sat beside their bags and sipped their espressos with contented languor.

'I've forgotten Tide,' said Ronald. 'I must remember to get Tide.'

'Don't you make a list?' said Martin.

'No. I depend on my memory.'

'I make a list,' said Martin, 'when my ma's away. I always do the shopping at the weekends. When Ma's at home she makes the list. It's always unreadable, though.'

'A waste of time,' said Ronald, 'if you've got a memory.'

'Do you mind?' said a girl who had just come into the

coffee shop. She was referring to Ronald's bag of shopping; it was taking up the seat which ran along the wall.

'Oh, sorry,' said Ronald, removing his bag and dumping it on the floor.

The girl sat down, and when the waitress came to serve her she said, 'I'm waiting for a friend.'

She had black hair drawn back in a high style, dark eyes, and an oval ballet-dancer's face. She returned the two bachelors' sleepy routine glance, then lit a cigarette and watched the door.

'New potatoes in the shops,' Ronald said.

'They're always in the shops,' said Martin, 'these days. In season and out of season. It's the same with everything: you can get new potatoes and new carrots all the year round now, and peas and spinach any time, and tomatoes in the spring, even.'

'At a price,' said Ronald.

'At a price,' Martin said. 'What bacon do you get?'

'I make do with streaky. I grudge breakfasts,' said Ronald. 'Same here.'

'Your hand's never out of your pocket,' Ronald said before Martin could say it.

A small narrow-built man came in the door and joined the girl, smiling at her with a sweet, spiritual expression.

He sat side by side with the girl on the wall-seat. He lifted the menu-card and spoke to her soundlessly from behind it.

'Good gracious me,' murmured Martin.

Ronald looked towards the man, whose body was now hidden by the girl at his side. Ronald observed the head, unable to see at first whether his hair was fair or silver-white, but soon it was plainly a mixture. He was thin, with a very pointed, anxious face and nose, and a grey-white lined skin. He would be about fifty-five. He wore a dark blue suit.

3

'Don't stare,' Martin said. 'He's on a charge and I'm prosecuting him. He's coming up again before the magistrates next week. He has to report to the police every day.'

'What for?'

'Fraudulent conversion and possibly other charges. Somebody in my chambers defended Seton ages ago. Not that it did either any good. Let's go.'

Ronald put down the newspaper in his hand.

'Tide,' said Ronald in the street. 'I really must remember Tide.'

'Which way are you going?'

'Across to Clayton's.'

'I'm going there too. I haven't got a lot of groceries on the list, I'm dining out four times next week. Where do you go on Sundays?'

'Oh, here and there,' Ronald said, 'there's always somebody.'

'I go to Leighton Buzzard if anyone comes home to keep Ma company,' said Martin. 'It's rather fun and a change at Leighton Buzzard. But if Isobel stays in London I go to her in London.' They had crossed the road.

'I've left my paper in the café,' Ronald said inexpertly. 'I'd better go back and fetch it. See you some time.'

'Feeling all right?' Martin said, as Ronald turned on the kerb to cross back over the road.

'Yes, oh, yes, it's only my paper.'

'Sure?' – for Martin was touchily aware of Ronald's epilepsy.

'Bye.' Ronald had crossed over.

He found the paper. He sat down again in a seat opposite the one he had recently occupied so that he could the more easily see the silver-yellow-haired man as he spoke in low tones effortful with convincingness, to the black-haired girl.

4

Ronald ordered coffee and a cream cake. He opened his paper, from the side of which, from time to time, he watched the man who was deeply explaining himself to the girl. Ronald could not decide where he had seen the man before; he could not even be sure of having done so. 'I'm becoming a prying old maid,' he said to himself as he left, to explain his return to the café, preferring to call himself a prying old maid than to acknowledge fully his real reason: that he had been simply testing his memory; for he could not leave alone any opportunity to try himself on the question whether his epilepsy would one day affect his mental powers or not.

'No,' the American specialist had said, irritable with the strain of putting a technical point into common speech, 'there is no reason why your intellect should be impaired except, of course, that you cannot exercise it to the full extent that would be possible were you able to follow and rise to the top of a normal career. But you ought to retain and indeed expand your present mental capacity. The seizures will be intermittent; let me put it that your seizures concern the brain but not the mind. You will learn to prepare for them physically in some degree but not to control them. They won't affect the mind except in so far as the emotional psychological disturbances affect it. That's not my department.'

Ronald had retained every one of these words importantly in his memory for the past fourteen years, aware that the specialist himself would possibly remember only the gist, and then only with the aid of his record cards. But Ronald held them tight, from time to time subjecting the words to every possible kind of interpretation. 'Let me put it that your seizures concern the brain, not the mind.' But he believes, Ronald argued with himself at times throughout the years, that the mind is part of the brain: then why did he say 'Let me put it that . . .'? What was his intention? And anyhow, Ronald would think, I can manage. And anyhow, I might never have been able to follow and rise to the top of a normal career. What is a normal career? The law: closed to me; – but, his friends had said, you need not put in for Lord Chancellor, you could be a successful solicitor. Oh, could I? – You haven't seen me in a fit. The Civil Service: closed to me. No, not at all, said his advisers. Medicine, teaching, get yourself into a college, try for a fellowship, you've got the academic ability – you know what some of the dons are like, there wouldn't be anything odd . . .

'I could never be first-rate.'

'Oh, first-rate . . .'

He had been twenty-three, a post-graduate, when the fits started, without warning, three months after he had turned his attention to theology. The priesthood: closed to me. Yes, said his friends, that's out; and, said his theological counsellors, it never would have been any good in any case, you never had a vocation.

'How do you know?'

'Because, in the event, you can't be a priest.'

'That's the sort of retrospective logic that makes us Catholics distrusted.'

'A vocation to the priesthood is the will of God. Nothing can change God's will. You are an epileptic. No epileptic can be a priest. *Ergo* you never had a vocation. But you can do something else.'

'I could never be first-rate.'

'That is sheer vanity' – it was an old priest speaking – 'you were never meant to be a first-rate careerist.'

'Only a first-rate epileptic?'

'Indeed, yes. Quite seriously, yes,' the old priest said.

It was at a time when he was having convulsions three times a week that he had allowed himself to be taken by an itinerant specialist to a research centre in California, with the purpose of submitting to a two years' clinical trial of a new drug. He was one of sixty volunteers from five to twenty-eight years old. Ronald lived in a huge sun-balconied hostel. Some of the other fifty-nine were mentally deficient. Most were neurotic. None was highly intelligent. Of the total sixty patients three failed to respond to the drug, and of these Ronald was one. Of these three, Ronald succumbed to the dreaded *status epilepticus*, enduring fit after fit, one after the other in rapid succession, only four days after the treatment had started.

'This is due to emotional apprehension,' Dr Fleischer told him when, after a week, he lay partially recovered, thin and exhausted, in a cool green-and-white room with the sun-blinds down. 'You may withdraw from the experiment if you wish,' Dr Fleischer said. 'Or you may continue with profit.' Dr Fleischer's time and mind were largely occupied with the fifty-seven epileptics who had already begun to respond favourably to the new drug.

When Ronald was up and shakily walking about, drowsy from the effects of his usual drugs, he weighed up for himself the price of his possible cure. The patients who were responding to Dr Fleischer's treatment were all around him, they seemed even sleepier, drowsier than he – but, thought Ronald, this is not far from their normal condition, they were born half-awake.

'The new drug is successful,' the smart fresh-lipsticked young research woman told him. 'The drug has been found to have anti-convulsant and sedative effects on rats, and now it looks like being successful with the majority of patients here.' She smiled through her rimless spectacles with eyes far away, on the job, efficient, creamy-complexioned, first-rate.

7

'Well, your drug makes me worse,' Ronald said, feeling within himself, at that moment, the potentialities of a most unpleasant young man.

When he got the chance of another brief interview with Dr Fleischer he said, 'Do you understand what you are asking me to do when you urge me to persevere? I may have to undergo the repetitive fits again.'

Dr Fleischer said, 'I am not urging you to persevere. I suggest your failure to respond to the drug is caused only by emotional resistance.'

'Do you realise,' said Ronald, 'how long the few seconds of lucidity between the fits appears to be, and what goes on in one's mind in those few waking seconds?'

'No,' said the doctor, 'I don't realise what these lucid intervals are like. I recommend you to return to England. I recommend . . . I advise . . . No, there is no reason why your intellect should be impaired, except of course that you cannot exercise it to the full extent that would be possible were you able to follow and rise to the top of a normal career . . .'

'Perhaps,' Ronald said, 'I'll be a first-rate epileptic and that will be my career.'

Dr Fleischer did not smile. He reached for Ronald's index card and wrote upon it.

Before he departed Ronald's brain was tested by a machine that was now familiar to him, and which recorded the electric currents generated by his convulsions and which was beginning to be used in the criminal courts of some American States to ascertain the truth of a suspect's statement, so that it was popularly called 'the truth machine'.

While he was awaiting the convenience of the man who was to escort him back to England, Ronald deliberately ignored the scene around him. His fellow-patients, week by

8

week, busied themselves with tennis, bed-making, toy-making, and their jazz orchestra. It was only much later that these scenes, which he had made an effort not to notice, returned to Ronald again and again accompanied by Dr Fleischer's words – long after the specialist must have forgotten them – and mostly at the moments when Ronald, bored by his self-preoccupation, most wished to forget himself, clinics, hospitals, doctors, and all the pompous trappings of his malady. It was at these moments of rejection that the obsessive images of his early epileptic years bore down upon him and he felt himself to be, not the amiable Johnnie he had by then, for the sake of sheer goodwill and protection from the world, affected to be – but as one possessed by a demon, judged by the probing inquisitors of life an unsatisfactory clinic-rat which failed to respond to the right drug. In the course of time this experience sharpened his wits, and privately looking round at his world of acquaintances, he became, at certain tense moments, a truth-machine, under which his friends took on the aspect of demon-hypocrites. But being a reasonable man, he allowed these moods to pass over him, and in reality he rather liked his friends, and gave them his best advice when, in the following years, they began to ask him for it.

On his return from California he was surprised to find himself able in some measure to retain consciousness during his fits, although he could not control them, by a secret, inarticulate method which, whenever he tried to describe it to his doctors, began to fail him when next he practised it.

'I find it useful to induce within myself a sense,' Ronald at first told his doctor, '– when I am going under – a sense that every action in the world is temporarily arrested for the duration of my fit –'

'Seizure,' said the doctor.

'My seizure,' said Ronald, 'and this curiously enables me to retain some sort of consciousness during even the worst part. I find it easier to endure this partial consciousness of my behaviour during the fits than surrender my senses entirely, although it's a painful experience.'

Immediately he had said it, he felt foolish, he knew his explanation was inadequate. The doctor remarked, 'It's as I've said. There is always an improvement in the patient when he becomes used to his seizures. First he experiences the aura, and this enables him to take preliminary precautions as to his physical safety during the seizure. He learns to lie down on the floor in time. He learns . . .'

'No, that's not what I mean,' Ronald said. 'What I mean is something different. It is like being partly an onlooker during the fit, yet not quite . . .'

'The seizure,' said the doctor, meanwhile puzzling his brains with a frown.

'The seizure,' said Ronald.

'Oh, quite,' said the doctor. 'The patient might learn to exercise some control during the *petit-mal* stage to stand him in good stead during the *grand-mal* convulsions.'

'That's right,' Ronald said, and went home and, on the way, had a severe fit in the street; on which occasion his method would not work, so that he came to his senses in the casualty department of St George's Hospital, sick with inhalations which had been administered to him to arrest his frenzy.

Soon Ronald was obliged to earn his living. His father, a retired horticulturist, still mourning the early death of his wife, took fright when he realised that Ronald was incurable. Ronald reassured him, advised him to buy an annuity and go to live at Kew; the father smiled and went.

Ronald got a job in a small museum of graphology in the City, to which people of various professions had recourse as well as curious members of the public. To Ronald's museum came criminologists from abroad, people wishing to identify the dates of manuscripts, or the handwriting attached to documents of doubt. Some came in the hope of obtaining 'readings' by which they meant a pronouncement as to the character and future fortunes of the person responsible for a piece of handwriting, but these were sent empty away. Ronald gained a reputation in the detection of forgeries, and after about five years was occasionally consulted by lawyers and criminal authorities, and several times was called to court as witness for the defence or prosecution.

At the museum he had a room to himself, with an understanding that he could there have his fits in peace without anyone fussing along to his aid. He knew how to compose himself for a fit. He cultivated his secret method of retaining some self-awareness during his convulsions, and never mentioned this to his doctors again, lest he should lose the gift. He kept by him a wedge of cork which he stuck between his teeth as the first signs seized him. He knew how many seconds it took to turn off the gas fire in his small office, to take the correct dose of his pills, to lie flat on his back, turn his head to the side, biting his cork wedge, and to await the onslaught. It was arranged, at these times, that no one entering Ronald's office should touch him except in the event of blood issuing from his mouth. Blood was never seen at his mouth, only foam, for Ronald was careful with his cork wedge. His two old colleagues and the two young clerks got used to him, and the typist, a large religious woman, ceased to try to mother him.

After five years Ronald's fits occurred on an average of once a month. The drugs which he took regularly, and in extra strength at the first intimations of his fits, became gradually more effective in controlling his movements, but less frequently could he ward off the violent stage of his attack until he found a convenient place in which to lie down. Twice within fourteen years he was arrested for drunkenness while staggering along the street towards a chemist's shop. Twice, he simply lay down on the pavement close in to the walls and allowed himself to be removed by ambulance. As often as possible he travelled by taxi or by a lift in a friend's car.

The porter of his flats had once found him, curled up and kicking violently, in the lift, and Ronald had subsequently gone over the usual explanations in patient parrot-like sequence. And, on these out-of-doors occasions, wherever they might take place, Ronald would go home to bed and sleep for twelve to fourteen hours at a stretch. But in latter years most of his fits occurred at home, in his room, in his one-roomed flat in the Old Brompton Road; so that his friends came to believe that he suffered less frequently than he actually did.

Ronald had settled down to be an amiable fellow with a gangling appearance, slightly hunched shoulders, slightly neglected-looking teeth, and hair going prematurely grey.

'You could marry,' said his doctor.

'I couldn't,' Ronald said.

'You could have children. Direct inheritance is very rare. The risk is very slight. You could marry. In fact, you ought –'

'I couldn't,' Ronald said.

'Wait till you meet the right girl. The right girl can be very wonderful, very understanding, when a fellow has a disability like yours. It's a question of meeting the right girl.'

Ronald had met the right girl five years after his return from America. Her wonderful understanding of his fits terrified him as much as her beauty moved him. She was the

English-born daughter of German refugees. She was brown, healthy, shining, still in her teens and splendidly built. For two years she washed his socks and darned them, counted his laundry, did his Saturday shopping, went abroad with him, slept with him, went to the theatre with him.

'I'm perfectly capable of getting the theatre tickets,' he said.

'Don't worry, darling, I'll get them in the lunch hour,' she said.

'Look, Hildegarde, it isn't necessary for you to mother me. I'm not an imbecile.'

'I know, darling. You're a genius.'

But in any case the trouble between them had to do with handwriting. Hildegarde had taken to studying the subject, the better to understand the graphologist in her lover. Hildegarde took a short course, amazingly soaking up, by sheer power of memory, the sort of facts which Ronald had no ability to memorise and which in any case, if he was called upon to employ them, he would have felt obliged to look up in reference books.

Thus equipped, Hildegarde frequently aired her facts, her dates, her documentary references.

'You have a better memory than mine,' Ronald said one Sunday morning when they were slopping about in their bedroom slippers in Ronald's room.

'I shall be able to memorise for both of us,' she said.

And that very afternoon she said, 'Have you ever had ear trouble?'

'Ear trouble?'

'Yes, trouble with your ears?'

'Only as a child,' he said. 'Earache.'

She was by his desk, looking down at some handwritten notes of his.

'The formation of your capital "I's" denotes ear trouble,' she said. 'There are signs, too, in the variations of the angles that you like to have your own way, probably as the result of your mother's early death and the insufficiency of your father's interest in you. The emotional rhythm is irregular, which means that your behaviour is sometimes incomprehensible to those around you.' She laughed up at him. 'And most of all, your handwriting shows that you're a sort of *genius*.'

'Where did you get all this?' Ronald said.

'I've read some text-books. There must be something in it – it's a branch of graphology, after all.'

'Have you practised interpreting various people's characters from their handwriting, and tested the results against experience?'

'No, not yet. I've only just read the books. I memorised everything.'

'Your memory is better than mine,' Ronald said.

'I'll be able to remember for us both.'

And he thought, when we're married, she'll do everything for both of us. So that, when he remonstrated against her obtaining the theatre tickets, and told her he could perfectly well get them – 'I'm not an imbecile' – and she replied, 'I know, darling, you're a genius' – he decided to end the affair with this admirable woman. For it was an indulgent and motherly tone of voice which told him he was a genius, and he saw himself being cooked for, bought for, thought for, provided for, and overwhelmed by her in the years to come. He saw, as in a vision, himself coming round from his animal frenzy, his limbs still jerking and the froth on his lips – and her shining brown eyes upon him, her well-formed lips repeating as he woke such loving patronising lies as: 'You'll be all right, darling. It's just that you're a genius.' Which would indicate, not her belief about his mental capacity but her secret belief in the superiority of her own.

After the affair had ended Ronald took to testing his memory lest it was failing him as a result of his disease. On the Saturday morning when the small thin man, Patrick Seton, had been pointed out to him in the café as one who was coming up for committal on Tuesday, Ronald, having faintly felt a passing sense of recognition, and left the café, and gone home, began once more to think of the man. But Ronald could not recall him or anything to do with him. He wished he had asked Martin Bowles the man's name. In a vexed way, Ronald sorted out his groceries, chucking them into their places in the cupboard. Then he went across to the pub.

There, drinking dark stout, were white-haired, dark-faced Walter Prett, art-critic, who was looking at a diet sheet, Matthew Finch, with his colourful smile, and black curly hair, London correspondent of the *Irish Echo*, and Ewart Thornton, the dark, deep-voiced grammar-school master who was a Spiritualist. These were bachelors of varying degrees of confirmation.

Ronald was actually forbidden alcohol, but he had found that the small quantity which he liked to drink made no difference to his epilepsy, and that the very act of ordering a drink gave him a liberated feeling.

He took his beer, sat down at his friends' table, and soundlessly sipped. In nearly five minutes' time he said, 'Nice to see you all here.'

Matthew Finch ran a finger through his black curls. Sometimes a desire came over Ronald to run his fingers through Matthew's black curls, but he had given up wondering if he were a latent homosexual, merely on the evidence of this one urge. Once he had seen a married couple rumple Matthew's hair in a united spontaneous gesture.

'Nice to see you all together,' Ronald said.

'Eggs, boiled or poached only,' Walter Prett read out in a sad voice from his diet sheet. 'Sour pickles but not sweet pickles. *No* barley, rice, macaroni –' he read quietly, then his voice became louder, and even Ronald, who was used to Walter Prett's changing tones, was startled by this. 'Fresh fruit of any kind, including bananas, also water-packed canned fruits,' Walter remarked modestly. 'No butter,' he shrieked, 'no fat or oil,' he roared.

'I've got mounds of homework,' said Ewart Thornton, 'because the half-term tests have begun.'

Matthew went over to the bar and brought back two pickled onions on a plate, and ate them.

2

It was six o'clock in the evening of that Saturday in a third-floor double room in Ebury Street. Patrick Seton sat in a meagre arm-chair which, since he was narrow at the shanks and shoulders, he did not fill as people usually did. Alice Dawes was propped in one of the divan beds, still half-dressed. Her friend, Elsie Forrest, sat on the other divan and folded Alice's skirt longwise.

'If only you would eat something you would see the thing in proportion,' Elsie said.

'God, how can I eat? Why should I eat?' Alice said.

'You ought to build up your strength,' Patrick Seton said in his voice which seemed to fade away at the end of each sentence.

'What's the use of her building up her strength if she's going to lose it that way?' Elsie said.

'It was only a suggestion,' Patrick said, so that they could hardly hear the last syllable.

'Well, I'm not going to do it,' Alice said. 'You'll have to think of something else.'

'There's this unfortunate occurrence next week . . .'

'I don't see,' said Elsie, 'how they can bring you up on a charge if they haven't any grounds at all.'

'Not the slightest grounds,' Patrick said, more boldly than usual. 'I'll be acquitted. It's a case of a jealous, frustrated woman trying to get her own back on me.'

'You must have had to do with her,' Elsie said.

'I never touched her, and I give you my word of honour,' Patrick said. 'It's all her imagination. She took a fancy to me at a séance, and I was sorry for her because she was lonely, and then I took rooms at her place and gave her advice. Of course, now, she's made up this utter entire fabrication. That's my defence. An utter, entire, and absolute fabrication.'

'Funny the police are taking it up if they've no proof,' Elsie said.

Alice said from the bed, 'I've got every faith in Patrick, Elsie. The police wouldn't allow him his freedom if they thought he was guilty. They would have him under arrest.'

'Well, if he's so sure he's going to get off, why did he bother to tell you? It's a shame upsetting you like this in your condition.'

'I only,' Patrick said softly, stroking his silver-yellow hair with his thin grey hand, and gazing at Alice with his pale juvenile eyes, 'wanted to put it to Alice that after Tuesday and when this unfortunate occurrence is over we could make a fresh start if she would see the specialist and have something done before nature takes its course, and –'

'I won't have an abortion,' Alice said. 'I'd do anything else for you, Patrick, you know that. But I won't have it done. I'd be terrified.'

'There's no danger,' Patrick said. 'Not these days.'

'I would never risk it,' Alice said. 'Not with my disease.'

'He may be unlucky on Tuesday,' Elsie said.

'No question of it,' Patrick said.

'Oh, Elsie, you don't know Patrick,' Alice said.

Elsie said, 'Why don't you both skip off abroad this weekend, while there's time?'

Alice looked at Patrick, clutching her throat, for she had once been to a school of drama, and though she was not an insincere girl, she sometimes remembered to express those emotions which she wished to reveal, by certain miming movements of the head, hands, shoulders, feet, eyes and eyelids. So she clutched her throat and looked at Patrick to convey a vulnerable anticipation of his reply.

His reply was so low-voiced that Elsie said, 'What?'

'Difficulty about passports if one is discovered. It would' – his voice rose to loud assertion – 'look like an admission of guilt.'

'Patrick is right.' Alice's hand dropped from her throat and lay limp, palm-upward, on the divan-cover.

'You're going to leave Alice in a nice pickle if the case goes against you,' Elsie said. 'How long could you get at the outside?'

'Oh, Elsie,' said Alice. 'Don't.'

Patrick looked at Elsie as if this remark were sufficient reply.

'And when,' said Elsie, 'does your divorce case come up?'

'In a couple of months,' said Patrick, crossing his knees and looking down upon those knees.

'What date?'

'Twenty-fifth of November,' Alice said. 'I remember that date all right, because we'll be able to get married on the twenty-sixth.'

Patrick's blue eyes dwelt upon her affectionately.

'On the twenty-sixth,' he whispered and closed his eyes for a moment to savour his joy.

'I feel hungry,' Alice said.

'Put your skirt on,' Elsie said, 'and we'll go and get something. Don't eat anything greasy, you'll only bring it up again.'

Alice began wearily to get up.

'I'm starving,' she said.

Elsie said, 'Did you remember to take your injection this morning?'

'Of course,' Alice said. 'Don't be silly. Patrick gives me my injection every morning, regularly.' She pointed to the jug with the syringe stuck into it.

'Well, I only wondered, because you said you were so hungry. Don't diabetics always get hungry if they don't have their injections?'

'She's hungry because she brought up her lunch,' said Patrick defensively.

Elsie looked at him suspiciously. 'I hope you do give her the injection regularly,' she said. 'She needs taking care of.'

It was then Patrick's mind turned a corner.

But he replied meekly: 'Give her a good meal.' He stroked Alice's cheek. 'Don't work too hard tonight, darling.'

'I doubt if I can go,' said Alice who was standing shakily while zipping up her skirt. 'Elsie will have to ring up.'

'She'll have to get an easier job,' Elsie said. 'Coffee-bar work is too hard for a girl in her condition.'

'What do you see in him?' Elsie said.

Alice took her mouthful of omelette at slow motion to denote reflectiveness, although she knew the answer.

'Well,' she said, 'I'm in love with him. He's *got* something. You don't know how wonderful he can be when we're alone. He's so good on the spiritual side. He recites poetry so beautifully. He's a sort of a real artist.'

'I'll agree,' Elsie said, 'he's a first-rate medium. That I do admit.'

'And he's got a soul.'

'Yes,' said Elsie, 'I see that. But you know, he's a bit old for you.'

'I like an older man. I think there's something special about an older man.'

'Yes, but you wouldn't call him much of a man. I mean, if you didn't know him, if you just saw him in the street without knowing he was a medium, you'd think he was a little half-pint job.'

'But I do know him. He means everything to me. He loves poetry and beauty.'

'I'll tell you,' Elsie said. 'I've never really trusted him. He hasn't got a cheque book, you told me yourself. Now that's funny, for one thing.'

'He's not mean with his money. I've never said –'

'No, but he hasn't got a cheque book, the fact remains.'

'I think that's a materialistic way to judge. Patrick is not a materialist.'

'No,' said Elsie, 'I don't say he is. But I think he gets carried away and makes up a lot of these stories he –'

'Oh, Elsie, a man like Patrick must have had a remarkable life. He's been through it. You can see that. And his wife must have been hell. Do you know, she –'

'Funny thing about that divorce,' Elsie said, 'he doesn't seem much worried about it.'

'No, he's just waiting for it to come through, that's all.'

'You'd think he'd have a bit more to do with the lawyers than he seems to have. And she might claim on him –'

'She hasn't a leg to stand on in the case. He's divorcing her, she's not divorcing him.'

'What's her name?'

'I don't know. I wouldn't like to ask. It would be indelicate.'

'Seen a photo?'

'No, Elsie. Patrick isn't that sort of man, Elsie.'

'And about this at the Magistrate's Court on Tuesday,' Elsie said, 'well, I don't know what to think.'

Alice started to cry.

'You're only upsetting yourself,' Elsie remarked, while she ate steadily on as one who proves, by eating on during another's distress, the unshakeable sanity of their advice. Elsie also permitted herself to say, as she reached for another roll, 'And you're kidding yourself where Patrick's concerned. I don't believe half a word he says. I think he's in trouble. You take my advice, you could clear off now, have the baby in a home, get it adopted, and start afresh.'

Alice said, 'I'll never do that, never. I trust him.'

'He wanted you to get rid of the kid.'

'Men are like that.'

'Stop crying,' Elsie said, 'people are looking at you.'

'I can't help it when you call him a liar. What about the message he got for you from Colin that night at the Wider Infinity? You didn't say that was lies. You said –'

'Oh, he's a good medium. But when Patrick's under the control I shouldn't think he could help saying what comes to him from the other side.'

At eight o'clock Patrick Seton walked along the Bayswater Road, turned off it, then turned again into a cul-de-sac, at the end of which he mounted the steps of a house converted into flats where he pressed the top left-hand bell.

Presently the door was opened by a tall, skinny young man of about twenty-three, with a cheerful smile.

'Oh, Patrick!' he said, politely standing back to let Patrick pass into the passage.

'Well, Tim,' said Patrick as he climbed the stairs, 'and how's the Central Office of Information?'

'The Central Office of Information,' said Tim, 'is all right, thank you.' He cleaned his glasses with a white handkerchief as he followed Patrick upstairs to a modernly decorated flat. From the open door of a room came the sociable sound of voices. On the door of another room was hung a card on which were printed in blue Gothic letters the words

The Wider Infinity
'In my Father's house are many mansions . . .'
(John 14, 2)

Tim passed by this room on a frivolous tip-toe to conceal whatever awe he might feel towards it, and led the way to the room where the company was assembled. Patrick stood a moment in the doorway, looking round swiftly to see who was present. At his entrance the chatter ceased for two seconds, then started again. Several people tentatively greeted Patrick while Tim, with the restrained gestures of one who is not above playing the well-trained footman, fetched Patrick a cup of China tea from a side table.

A distinguished-looking woman with white hair and a lined face, the features of which were absolutely symmetrical, appeared. Patrick respectfully put down his tea and took his hostess's hand in silence except for the word 'Marlene'.

'Patrick,' she replied merely; and she rested her eyes on his, setting her head at a slight angle so that her long earrings swung as in a breeze.

Patrick's lower lip thinly began to tremble as he said in his almost inaudible voice, 'I nearly didn't come in view of the unfortunate occurrence. But I felt it was my duty to do so.'

'You were right, Patrick,' Marlene said, still gazing at his eyes intensely. 'There are naturally mixed feelings amongst us and she has been circulating rumours. But I have – and I know I can speak for the members of the Interior Spiral if not for the Wider Infinity at large – implicit faith in you. I'm only too grateful that we were guided to delay disclosing to her the existence of the Interior Spiral, that was fortunate. And had it not been for your powers as a great medium, and the warnings, we should most probably have issued the Communication to her last week. Oh – here she is.'

A dumpy much-powdered woman of middle age, wearing light-rimmed glasses, a grey felt hat, and a blue coat and skirt, had been ushered into the room by young Tim. She smiled brightly at her acquaintances by the door and even the lenses of her glasses seemed to glisten smilingly upon them. She had not noticed Patrick, who had resumed his tea-cup into which he was gazing with dignity. Marlene glided up to the newcomer, took both her hands, bestowed upon her a customary soul-to-soul gaze, kissed her upon the cheek, and said, 'Freda, you're just in time. I am about to proclaim the Commencement.'

'Tea, Mrs Flower?' Tim said to Freda, with the cup and saucer in his hand.

'The Commencement is about to start, Tim,' said Marlene, and as Tim hovered between handing the tea to Freda and not handing it to her, Marlene said, 'But of course you must have a little tea first, Freda, you must have your tea first.'

Marlene noticed, without truly observing, a large man with pink and white cheeks whom she had not seen at previous meetings. He was standing massively half in, half out of the room, and he had apparently arrived at the same time as Freda. But Marlene did not take great notice of him, since there were few meetings at which a newcomer was not present, having been brought along by someone or other. The pink-and-white-cheeked man looked rather like, possibly, a friend of Tim's. Tim had yet to learn to be reliable.

Marlene said to Freda, 'I shan't ring the bell till you've finished your tea. Don't hurry.'

Freda gulped her tea, with her eyes wandering over the rim of the cup. Suddenly she started at the sight of Patrick.

'So *he's* here,' Freda said.

'My dear Freda, mustn't we subordinate all our materialistic endeavours to those of the spirit?'

'It's most upsetting,' Freda said, 'and I'm surprised he has the nerve to show his face in here again. He's a fraud.'

Tim gave out a gentle cultivated noise from the throat as if he really were clearing it, and shifted himself gracefully to another group.

Marlene's ear-rings swung as she moved her head distastefully from Freda's remarks. 'The word fraud,' she said, 'is of the World. Freda, I don't think it should be voiced here. But I do see – I do understand – how a type of behaviour which is normal in our element may appear, shall we say, mysterious in yours.' She touched Mrs Flower's hand in absolution from all her dumpy limitations. 'I only hope,' she said, 'that nothing will happen to bring the Wider Infinity into disrepute. For myself, I don't care. I am thinking of – well, finish your tea, Freda dear, it is time for the Commencement.'

She moved away, and dark Ewart Thornton, who was one of the assembly, presently took her place, declaring deeply in her ear, 'I'm with you, Freda. A lot of us here tonight are with you. I meant to write to say so to you, but I've got such mounds of homework. The mid-term examinations . . .'

Freda's spectacles shone with gratitude. 'Does Marlene know your mind on the subject?' she said.

Ewart placed a finger to his lips while Marlene at the other end of the room proclaimed:

'The Circle will now enter the Sanctuary of Light.'

Tea-cups were placed down and a hush fell on the assembly. Marlene Cooper led the way, as she had done regularly since the year after her husband died, and she had taken to thoughts of the spirit. For how, she felt, could it be that Harry Cooper, who his worst business enemies admitted was sheer dynamite, could come to nought in the end? 'No,' she said, 'Harry is as alive as ever he was. He is communicating with me and I am communicating with him.' Certainly this was the case when he was alive, since they had then indulged in frequent noisy rows in different parts of the globe, she standing tensely clothed in her distinguished appearance, clasping and unclasping her long fingers, and shrieking; he sitting usually in an arm-chair answering her with short, loaded, meaningful words of power and contempt. He had been buried three months when, convinced of his dynamic survival, she had had him dug up and cremated, since this, it seemed vaguely to her, was more in keeping with the life beyond. To see his ashes scattered in the Garden of Remembrance was to conceive Harry more nearly as thin air, and since she had come to believe so ardently in Harry the spirit, she simply could not let him lie in the grave and rot.

Shortly after the cremation Marlene joined the Wider Infinity, an independent spiritualist group, proud of its independence from the great organised groups, and operating from a room in the region of Victoria. During the period of her initiation Marlene was impressed, the more and more especially when personal messages began to come through from Harry on the other side.

Patrick Seton was the first medium to get through to Harry.

'I have a message for our new sister, from Henry. Henry will not speak himself tonight but he will speak on another occasion when Carl is in control of Patrick,' said Patrick. 'But in the meantime Henry sends his affectionate regards and is thinking of you in his happy abode. He particularly wants to say you have been too generous and have stood by too long and let others take first place. You were born to be a leader but you have not yet fulfilled yourself. Now is the time to start living your true life.' Patrick moaned. His mouth drooped, the lower lip disappearing into his chin. He looked very ill by the dim green light, and even when he had come round and the full lights were on, his complexion was more grey and the lines on his face deeper than before he had gone under. He was genuinely shaken.

'Amazing,' Marlene whispered after the séance. For Henry was Harry's real name, and the Carl who was going to act as control in the promised future might very conceivably be that Carl, her boy-friend that was, who had been killed in a motor-race in 1938; and indeed Marlene had been moved to wonder as far as she dared how Harry and Carl were making out together in the land of perpetual summer. And it had been summer-time when Harry had found out about Carl. But the possibility of Carl's acting as the spirit control between Harry and the medium seemed to make everything all right, and indeed there was an authentic rightness in the idea, for although Harry's had been the more dynamic personality, there was no use pretending that Carl's had not been the rarer.

And she thought it very like Harry to urge her to push herself to the fore. It was exactly what Harry would advise, being now incapacitated, or rather released from materialistic endeavours. It was almost as if Harry were urging her to take his place in life. It was so true that she had always let others take place before her.

Marlene, in order to be fair, went and attended a séance of another spiritualist group on an island near Richmond. But this was a disappointment, for the people were not quite the reasonable, respectable sort one expected to find in the spiritualist movement. One young man had hair waving down to his waist. One middle-aged woman with a huge blotchy face wore a tight cotton dress although it was early March. The place was not heated, and Marlene shivered. The woman in the tight cotton dress told Marlene she was going to give clairvoyance. She told Marlene nothing about Harry, only advised her to be careful of false friends, and not to despair, she wouldn't end her life alone.

'I'm not despairing,' Marlene said.

The other members looked at Marlene with hushed hostile warnings, since she was interrupting the woman in her trance.

So Marlene remained with the Wider Infinity at Victoria. Soon, however, inspired by the dynamic spirit of Harry, she began to note this and that member who was perhaps unworthy of its high purpose. She led a purgative faction.

'We must,' she said to Ewart Thornton, that big sane grammar-school master, 'rid our Body of the cranks.'

'I quite agree,' Ewart said. 'They lower the tone.'

Two clergymen who were unembarrassed by wives or livings were retained; several women cashiers and bookkeepers who did not mind the journey from Wembley, Osterley and Camberwell on Monday and Thursday evenings; two middle-aged retired spinsters who were interested in art; one or two of Marlene's old friends who, however, were erratic in their attendance; a childless married couple in their early thirties; three widows; an Indian student who had been doing undefined research at the British Museum for fifteen years; a retired policeman whose wife, not a spiritualist, was a doctor's receptionist; Ewart Thornton, the schoolmaster; and Patrick Seton, who was, by common consent, the life and soul of the Circle.

'We must have a cross-section of the community,' Marlene declared. 'A sane cross-section. Why can't we have a labourer, for instance?'

No labourer who was worthy of his hire could be found. Ewart Thornton, however, was the means of introducing to the group a number of single schoolmasters and Civil Servants who, although interested in spiritualism, had never had sufficient courage to attend a séance. Some of these bachelors became regular members, others attended occasionally and compulsively when the desire to do so overwhelmed them. 'My bachelors,' Marlene called them.

'At least,' she said, 'we are all respectable now; we have no cranks.'

'I hate cranks,' Ewart said. 'Insufferable people.'

By the end of that year the Wider Infinity had moved its headquarters to Marlene's flat in Bayswater and Patrick and Ewart Thornton had so much become her closest intimates that very often this trio held private séances which were kept secret from the rest of the group. 'Carl and Harry,' Marlene said, 'definitely understand my nature now better than they did in the flesh. Carl of course was always more evolved. Why does he call Harry by the name of Henry, I wonder?'

Patrick said, 'I'm only the medium,' and his voice died away on the last syllable.

'But you're a genius, Patrick – isn't he, Ewart?'

'Absolutely. That was excellent advice that came through from Guide Gabi about my headmaster. Had his character to a T. He expects me to do mounds of homework. Well, I –'

'Señor Gabi is one of my best Guides,' Patrick murmured. 'But Henry is coming on. Through the influence of Carl, he –'

'Why doesn't Carl call him Harry?' Marlene said. 'He never called him Henry while in the flesh, he always called him Harry.'

'The name Henry represents his primary and more noble personality,' Patrick said gently. 'I'm sorry, Marlene, I'm only the medium, I can't say Harry when I get Henry.'

'Patrick, you're wonderful. It only proves your honesty.'

She put a great deal of money into the training of mediums, Patrick Seton being the principal trainer; she liked most of all to have the more intelligent members, or those rare few with university degrees, trained as mediums. It gave her a thrill to see these knowledgeable novices going into, and coming round from, their first and second feeble trances.

Eventually she recruited her young nephew, Tim, whom she had discovered to have no religion at all. Tim had not enjoined, but she, perceiving his mind, had promised secrecy about this activity where the family was concerned.

Meantime Patrick had made a tremendous advance in divining how matters stood between Harry and Carl on the other side, and in instructing Marlene, through Harry, how best to develop her personality.

At the first séance to be held by the newly constructed Circle in Marlene's flat, Patrick had gone under in style with a quivering of the lower lip and chin, upturned eyes and convulsive whinnies. A few threads of ectoplasm, like white tape in the dim light, proceeded from the corners of his mouth. Then, in a voice hugely louder than his own he announced, 'I am now coming in touch with the control. This is control. Henry will speak through Patrick under the control of Carl.'

Two or three of the Circle, as they had sat hand in hand round Patrick, shuffled slightly at this mention of Carl and

Henry, for that particular combine was, in the experience of the Circle, exclusively interested in the affairs of Marlene and did not seem aware of the claims of the Wider Infinity as a whole.

'Guide Henry speaking: my dear wife, there are two on earth who mean a lot to you. You can depend upon them and especially upon one who will never desert you unto death. Do not be deceived by appearances. I am well and happy. Do you remember the Loebl Pass where we stopped at an inn and ate a marvellous omelette?'

'Oh,' Marlene said.

'Control lifting,' Patrick said. 'Guide Henry is wearing leather shorts and an open-neck shirt.'

'Oh, how it takes me back!' said Marlene when the lights had gone up. 'Honestly,' she said to the newer members of the Circle, 'I have a photograph of Harry on that holiday wearing his leather shorts and –'

Later she said to Ewart and Patrick, 'I wish they wouldn't concentrate so much on me from the other side. I think some of the less evolved members may feel I'm getting more than my fair share.'

Ewart said, 'You are the most dominant personality in the room, Marlene. It stands to reason.'

'Stands to reason,' Patrick said, 'Marlene.'

'Well, I'll stay outside at our next séance. I definitely felt a hostile aura after Patrick returned to us during our last session. These people feel: you pay your money – pittance that it is – and you take your choice.'

'Not everyone feels that way,' Ewart said.

'Whom can we trust and respect?'

Ewart mentioned a few of the more docile and regular attenders, Marlene eliminated half of them, and it was thus that the Interior Spiral, their secret group, came to be formed within the Wider Infinity.

'We must keep the ramifications pure,' Marlene stated, 'we must exert a concealed influence on the less evolved brethren and the crackpots and snobs who keep creeping in.'

On the Saturday night before Patrick's appearance before the magistrates was anticipated, when Freda Flower had put down her cup, the company trod reverently into the Sanctuary of Light. Patrick ignored the widow, Freda Flower, exaltedly, as enemies do in church; but she glanced at him nervously. Marlene did not herself join them; this was now her habit on most evenings, since her presence so invariably attracted all the spiritual attentions available to the company.

Tim led the way and acted as usher, placing about twenty people with the conviction of extreme tact, the results of which, however, did not satisfy all. Some, who were placed so that they had an imperfect view of the medium's chair were restive, but nothing like a scene occurred in this velvet-hung dark sanctuary of light.

This room had previously been a dining-room in one wall of which was a service recess opening to the kitchen. The curtains that covered this recess were arranged to part imperceptibly at a point which admitted of Marlene's watching the proceedings from the kitchen, which she felt was only her due. And there she stood, in the dark, watching Tim's arrangements in the dim green-lit séance room.

She was furious when she saw Tim, as it were with the height of aplomb, place Freda Flower, the beastly widow who had gone to the police about Patrick, in the place of honour directly facing the medium.

All were seated except Tim who, before sitting down in the humblest position from the visual point of view, took off his glasses, wiped them, replaced them slowly and, with an elegant lightning sweep of the same handkerchief, dusted the chair on which he was to sit, at the same time replacing his handkerchief in his pocket. He then sat, joining tentative hands with his neighbour, as the others had done. Marlene, from her place behind the recess, watched her nephew closely and by an access of intuition despaired of Tim's becoming even teachable as to the seriousness of the Circle, far less a member of the Interior Spiral.

It was then she noticed once more the newcomer, seated in his massive bulk, beside Freda Flower, and in fact he was whispering something to Freda Flower. Marlene realised it was Freda who had brought him to the Circle and felt deeply apprehensive.

All hands were joined. The green light shone dimly. Ewart said, 'We will now have two minutes' silent prayer.'

Heads were bowed. Before Marlene had taken over the Circle this silence had been followed by a hymn to the tune of 'She'll be coming round the mountain' and which went as follows,

> We shall meet them all again by and by,
> By and by.

Marlene had found that this hymn was unaccountably not ease-making to the schoolmasters and clergymen and more educated members, and on reflection even herself decided that she did not in fact want to meet the whole of her acquaintance again by and by. And so, after trying several other hymns which, for reasons of association, seemed unsuitable to various members, she had eliminated hymn-singing altogether. So they had a silence.

After the silence Ewart said, 'Mr Patrick Seton will now unite the Two Worlds.'

Patrick had been bound at the arms and calves of his legs by canvas strips to his chair. He let his head fall forward. He breathed deeply in and out several times. Soon, his body dropped in its bonds. His knees fell apart. His long hands hung, perpendicular, over the arms of the chair. Not only did the green-lit colour seem to leave his face but the flesh itself, so that it looked like a skin-covered skull up to his thin pale hair.

He breathed deeply in the still dim room, second after second. Then his eyes opened and turned upward in their sockets. Foam began to bubble at his mouth and faintly trickled down his chin. He opened his mouth and a noise like a clang issued from it. The Circle was familiar with this clang: it betokened the presence of the spirit-guide called Gabi. Soon the clang was forming words which became clearer to the listeners in the circle round Patrick and to Marlene behind the hatch.

'A message for one of our sisters present whose name resembles a plant. It comes from a short man in a Harris-tweed suit through Guide Gabi who is speaking. The short man appears to be bearing on his back a long tube-like sack of faggots; no, they are golf clubs –'

Freda Flower cried, 'That's my husband – !' but was immediately hushed by the rest of the Circle.

'His name is William,' clanged the voice. 'He appears to be in a most disturbed state of mind. He looks very upset, and is trying to get a message through to our sister whose name is like a plant. He is extremely concerned about her.'

'Why is he going for a game of golf if he is so upset?' – This question crashed into the atmosphere; it came from the large newcomer sitting next to Freda Flower.

'Not now, Mike,' she said. 'Ask the questions later.'

The clanging voice had stopped talking through Patrick's lips. Patrick had begun to writhe a little in his bonds. His feet kicked with sharp clicks of the heels on the parquet wooden floor.

Ewart Thornton dropped his neighbours' hands and came over to Mike. He bent over him. He said, 'By interrupting the medium you may do him great harm. You may even kill him. If you interrupt again you will have to go outside.'

Freda said, 'I'm sorry, Ewart, but my friend, Dr Mike Garland, is a clairvoyant.'

'He must not give clairvoyance at this stage.'

Dr Garland smiled and joined hands once more with those on either side of him. Ewart returned to his place. Patrick had stopped writhing and was apparently sunk in a deep sleep. He snored for a while through his open mouth from which presently emerged once more the inarticulate clang of Guide Gabi's voice. For a while it repeated sounds which could not be identified. Eventually it said, 'The sister whose name is of a plant is troubled in spirit.'

Tears which she could not wipe away, since both her hands were engaged, spurted down Freda's cheeks.

'I see a man,' the voice said, 'in a Harris-tweed suit –'

'What colour?' said Dr Garland in a persuasive voice.

'A green or a blue,' the voice replied, 'I can't say exactly.'

'That's him!' said Freda, brokenly.

The voice from Patrick's lips said, 'His message to the sister with the name like a plant is this: Do not act against another of the brethren. If you do so it will be at your peril.'

Several of the group gasped or muttered, for it was known that a court case was pending between Patrick and Mrs Flower. Many peered forward to scrutinise Patrick's appearance, but not even the most shaken or the most easily prone to doubt could find evidence that he was faking his trance. His physical characteristics had plainly undergone a change.

The skin of his face appeared to cling even closer to the bone than when he had first gone under and the cheek-bones stood out alarmingly; his mouth had widened by about two inches, seeming now to reach almost from ear to ear as the clanging voice continued to proceed from it.

'Let the sister beware of false friends and materialistic advice. The letter killeth but the spirit giveth life. What shall it profit a man if he gain the whole world and loseth his soul?'

'He was so well-read in the Bible,' said Mrs Flower, weeping.

The large pink-faced newcomer announced aloud, 'I am going to give clairvoyance.'

'No,' Freda whispered, though all could hear, 'I feel, somehow, this is genuine after all. I'd like to think it all over –'

The newcomer shouted above Patrick's din, 'Nevertheless, I am going to give clairvoyance.'

Ewart came over to him again and said, 'Are you a trained clairvoyant? I've warned you about the danger to the medium of interruption.'

'I am a trained and authentic clairvoyant,' said Freda's friend.

'Guide Gabi,' Patrick clanged on, 'is about to give the initials of the spirit in the Harris-tweed suit. The initials are W.F.'

'William!' said Freda.

'I am a trained clairvoyant,' shouted Freda's friend. 'And I hereby give notice that I am about to give clairvoyance to the medium in the chair.'

'Señor Gabi speaking,' Patrick clanged; 'I hereby give notice that I reinforce the warnings given by the aforesaid spirit whose initials are W.F. to the sister among our members. These warnings can only be disregarded at the utmost peril to the sister whose name resembles a plant.'

The man beside Freda had thrown back his head and lifted his hands to his temples.

'No, Mike!' Freda moaned.

'I see,' bellowed Mike Garland to the ceiling, 'I see the medium in the public court, under a charge of fraud. I see the so-called medium exposed. I see –'

A small rustling hubbub had arisen amongst the audience.

'Señor Gabi speaking,' came the voice from Patrick. 'There is a hostile spirit among us who may cause infinite harm to –'

'Patrick Seton, you are a fraud,' boomed Mike to the ceiling. 'And I challenge you, if Señor Gabi is an authentic guide, to give the initials of my name.'

The small rustle amongst the audience immediately became a hush.

'Señor Gabi speaking: the first initial of the hostile spirit is M.'

'You are a fraud. You heard Mrs Flower calling me Mike,' boomed Mike. 'What is the second initial?'

Foam appeared at Patrick's mouth and bubbled for a few seconds.

Ewart murmured, 'This is dangerous to him. We must stop it.'

'The second initial,' Mike shouted.

'The second initial,' came the clang, 'is G.'

'He's right!' said Mrs Flower. 'Oh, Mike, I've been mistaken.'

'You are a fraud,' shouted Mike. 'You have heard my name. You heard Mrs Flower introducing me to a member.'

Patrick dribbled from the mouth and his head drooped with exhaustion, and the water from his mouth dripped down his coat. His eyes closed.

Ewart called out, 'This disruption must cease. The clairvoyant will kindly leave the séance room.'

But Mike, with his hands to his temples and head thrown back, began to intone. 'There will be weeping and gnashing of teeth. I see the prisoner brought to judgement and cast into outer darkness. There will be a trial. I see a young woman in distress and an older woman justified. I see –'

Patrick cast up his eyes. 'Guide Gabi warns the Circle of an evil influence present,' he said. He lifted his head high and tossed it like a war horse.

'You'll put him in a frenzy,' Ewart shouted, and the audience began also to cry out phrases like 'Too bad', 'Wicked', 'An evil influence', and 'Uncivilised'.

The room was in turmoil when Marlene flung wide the door. 'What is this turmoil?' she said, trembling with the impatience she had been repressing throughout her service-hatch vigil. She then switched on the lights.

The noise ceased except for a sobbing sound from Freda. Patrick drooped once more, and breathed as one in a deep sleep. Mike shook his head, covered as it was with sweat, brought it to a normal level and his eyes into normal focus. Patrick slowly came round and looked at the roomful of people in a dazed way.

Freda then collapsed with a thud on the floor, where she continued her sobbing, her legs moving as in remorseful pain and revealing the curiously obscene sight of her demure knee-length drawers.

'Throw some water over her,' ordered Marlene.

'Tim, fetch some water – Where's Tim? Tim, where are you? Where's that boy?'

But at some point during the dark and troubled séance Tim had slid silently away.

3

'Never again,' said Tim. 'It was absolute hell let loose.'

'Tell me a bit more,' said Ronald Bridges. Just then Tim's telephone rang.

'Oh, Aunt Marlene,' said Tim. 'Sorry I keep forgetting – *Marlene*. After all, you are my aunt and – yes, Marlene. No, Mar – Yes, it was just that I was *overwhelmed*, Marlene. Yes, I was just going to ring you.'

He made a sign to Ronald to fetch over his drink.

'No, Aunt – sorry, – No, Marlene. Yes. No. Of course. Of course not. Look, I've got a fellow here on official business. Yes, I do know it's Sunday, but this was urgent and he called – Tomorrow at eleven. Right, I'll ring you at eleven. Yes, at eleven. Goodbye, Aunt – Yes, at eleven. Yes. No. Bye.'

Tim took up his drink and subsided on to the sofa. 'As I was saying,' he said, then closed his eyes and slowly sipped his drink.

'I've often been tempted to go to a spiritualist meeting,' Ronald said, 'just to see.'

'I nearly died,' said Tim, opening his eyes behind his glasses.

'I thought you had actually joined the thing,' Ronald said.

'Well, yes, I suppose I had. But last night's show was something special.'

'How did it end?'

'I left after the second act.'

'Finished with it now?' Ronald said.

'Well, yes. But it needs caution.' Tim nodded over to the telephone as if the spirit of his Aunt Marlene, whose voice had a few moments before come over on it, still lingered there. 'She needs handling with tact,' said Tim.

'Whatever made you take it up?'

'Well, it was rather exciting to start with. And it's a fairly bleak world when all is said and done.' He rose and carelessly slopped more gin and tonic into the glasses, without, however, spilling any. 'And, you know,' he said then, 'there is something in it. This medium, Patrick Seton, isn't altogether a fraud, you know. He's got something.'

'Patrick Seton, did you say?' Ronald said.

'Yes. Know him?'

'A meek little thin-faced fellow with white hair?'

'Yes, do you know him?'

'I do remember him,' Ronald said, pleased with this functioning of his memory. For now he was able to place in his mind the man he had seen the previous morning in the coffee-bar. 'There was a case of forgery about five years ago,' Ronald said. 'I had to identify the handwriting. He was convicted.'

'I believe there's another case coming up against him,' Tim said. 'I'm not sure if it's forgery. It's the talk of the Circle. What a crowd!'

'Fraudulent conversion,' Ronald said.

'You seem to know a lot about him.'

'Martin Bowles is prosecuting counsel. He mentioned the case.'

'I can't believe he's entirely a fraud as a medium,' Tim said. 'I've heard him come out with the most terrifying true facts that he couldn't possibly have known about. He once

40

told me during a séance about a personal affair at my office that nobody could have known about except me and another chap. And the other chap hadn't any remote acquaintance with Seton.'

'The affair might have been on your mind, and he might have picked it up by telepathy. Do you believe in telepathy?'

'Well, yes, there seems to be evidence for telepathy. But it's odd that Seton keeps picking things from people's minds. He's got *some*thing.'

'I should like to have heard him,' Ronald said.

'You can go along if you like. Really, I mean it,' Tim said eagerly. 'There are meetings on –'

'No, thanks,' said Ronald. 'You'll have to make your escape some other way.'

'I only thought, if you wanted to see Seton in his trance –'

Ronald said, 'He'll probably be in prison before long.'

'Do you think so? What a pity, in a way,' said Tim.

'Of course I know nothing about the case. But that type doesn't ever stay out in the open for long.'

'I suppose he could be a genuine medium,' Tim said, 'and a fraud in other respects. It's a widow-woman who's taking action against him. I think he used to sleep with her and he got some money off her, and then he stopped sleeping with her and now she's furious. But she seemed pretty scared of him last night when he started to give out messages from her husband who's dead. She'll probably change her mind and withdraw the action.'

'Can she do that?' Ronald said. 'It's a police prosecution.'

'Oh, I don't know, really.'

Tim's telephone rang. 'Yes, Marlene. No, Aunt – No. Well, yes, he's still here. No, I can't manage lunch, I'm afraid, I – Don't be upset, Marlene. Listen. Don't. Yes. No. Hang on a minute.' Tim covered the receiver with his hand.

'Would you come with me to lunch with her?' he said, mouthing at Ronald. 'Not a séance, only lunch.'

Ronald nodded.

'Listen, Marlene,' Tim said, 'I think I can come. Can I bring Ronald Bridges? He's the chap that's with me. Yes, of course he'll be interested. No, I don't think so, no, he's R.C. Yes, I know I said he was here on business but now we've finished our business chat. But of course he's allowed to lunch with you, at least I think so. We're just going for a drink now. Yes. Quarter-past. Yes, thanks. No, yes. Bye.'

Then he said to Ronald, 'She's upset. She thinks I'm going to leave the Circle after what happened last night. She's right.'

Ronald said, 'Do you mind if I go home first to fetch my pills?'

'I'll come with you. I can't tell you how grateful I am that you're coming for support. I don't particularly want to *fall out* with Marlene.'

'I was going to fry bacon and eggs,' Ronald said.

'I was going to skip lunch,' Tim said. 'One can't afford two restaurant meals in one day. And yet one's got to eat, hasn't one?'

'There's something about Sunday,' Ronald said, 'which is terrible between one and three o'clock if you aren't in someone's house, eating. That's my feeling.'

'Same here,' said Tim. 'Funny how Sunday gets at you if you aren't given a lunch. Preferably by an aunt or a sort of aunt.'

'Yes, it's nice to see a woman on a Sunday,' Ronald said.

'I sometimes go down to Isobel's with Martin Bowles,' Tim said. 'She's a difficult woman but still one does like her company.'

'On a Sunday,' Ronald said.

'I know exactly what you mean,' Tim said. 'Funny. Now Marlene is difficult, too. But I'm rather fond of her in a way. She thinks I'm after her cash and comforts, the darling. But in fact I'm genuinely fond of her. They don't ever quite realise that.'

'What was so distressing,' Marlene said, 'was hearing all the noise and not being able to *see*.'

'There wasn't much to see,' Tim said, 'it was nearly all noise.'

'You shouldn't have gone away,' said his aunt. 'Why ever did you go away?'

'I was overcome,' Tim said.

'Another time,' his aunt said, 'go and lie down on a bed. Don't just go away.'

'Yes, of course.'

'I've found out the name of the man who came with Freda Flower. He's a Dr Garland. Doctor of what, I don't know. He has quite a reputation as a clairvoyant, but of course he's a fraud. So many frauds manage to get themselves good reputations. They prey on gullible women. Is all this boring you, Mr Bridges?'

'No,' Ronald said. 'It's very interesting.'

'Shall I call you Ronald, Mr Bridges?'

'Please do, I was going to suggest it.'

'I hope you don't mind eating in the kitchen.' She pointed to the shuttered hatch. 'The dining-room is now the Sanctuary. Please call me Marlene. I don't want you to think, Ronald, that what we're discussing is in any way a normal occurrence. It has never happened before at any of our meetings, has it, Tim?'

'Well, things have been working *up* to a row, haven't they?'

'Not at all. The deplorable behaviour of the Circle last night was quite unforeseen.'

Tim stretched his long legs and sprawled on the sofa. He took off his glasses and cleaned them with a white handkerchief, then put on his glasses again. He made a rabbit out of his handkerchief.

'Tim!' said his aunt.

Tim sat up, pulled the rabbit back into a handkerchief, and said, 'What?'

'You are not taking this seriously enough. I suggest that after lunch we all go into the Sanctuary for fifteen minutes for spiritual repose.' She pointed to the hatch to indicate the Sanctuary. 'I wish Patrick were here to guide us.'

Tim said, 'I shouldn't really like to go in there again. At least, not yet.'

'What do you mean? There's nothing wrong with the room – what was wrong was the evil spirit of that false clairvoyant amongst us.'

'We can't have spiritual repose while Ronald's here,' said Tim, looking desperately at Ronald, 'because Ronald is a Roman Catholic and not permitted to have spiritual repose.'

'I'm anti-Catholic,' said Marlene.

Ronald was used to hearing his hostesses over the years come out with this statement, and had devised various ways of coping with it, according to his mood and to his idea of the hostess's intentions. If the intelligence seemed to be high and Ronald was in a suitable mood, he replied, 'I'm anti-Protestant' – which he was not; but it sometimes served to shock them into a sense of their indiscretion. On one occasion where the woman was a real bitch, he had walked out. Sometimes he said, 'Oh, are you? How peculiar.' Sometimes he allowed that the woman was merely trying to start up a religious argument, and he would then attempt to explain where he stood with his religion. Or again, he might say, 'Then you've received Catholic instruction?' and, on hearing that this was not so, would comment, 'Then how can you be anti something you don't know about?' which annoyed them; so that Ronald felt uncharitable.

There were always women who confronted him with 'I'm anti-Catholic' as if inviting a rape. Men didn't do this. Mostly, Ronald coped with the statement as he did on this present occasion, when he said to Marlene, 'Oh, I'm sure you're not *really*.'

'Yes really,' Marlene said, as most of them did, 'I am.'

'Well, well,' said Ronald.

'But I don't mean I'm anti *you*,' said Marlene. 'You're sweet.'

'Oh, thanks.'

'There's a distinction,' Tim pointed out, bright with tact, 'between the person and their religion.'

'I see.' Ronald attended closely to his potatoes.

'But you don't like us,' said Marlene. 'In fact, you detest us.'

'Detest you?' said Ronald. 'Why, I think you're charming.'

'Now, now. You're avoiding the question. The fact is, you're not allowed –'

'Ronald's awfully interested in spiritualism,' Tim said.

'He doesn't believe in it,' Marlene said. 'He thinks it's all baloney. He's one of those –'

'I'm sure it's possible to get in touch with the spirits of the dead,' Ronald said.

'Are you?' said Tim. 'Now that's interest –'

'Catholics aren't allowed to do it,' Marlene said.

'We invoke the saints and so on,' Ronald said, 'and they are dead.'

'A very different thing,' Marlene said. 'That's idolatry. In Spain, for instance – well, perhaps I shouldn't say. I once had an Irish maid, she was most difficult. But anyhow, you don't *get through* to the saints, do you? They don't send you messages. Have you heard the actual voice of any one of your saints?'

'No,' said Ronald. 'You've got a point there.'

'I have indeed,' Marlene said. 'I've heard my husband's actual voice. Haven't I, Tim? I've heard Harry. His own dynamic voice.'

'Uncle Harry was always very dynamic,' Tim murmured.

'Have a bit more lamb,' Marlene said. 'It's got to be eaten up. You boys aren't eating anything.'

'Thank you, I will,' said Ronald.

'Thanks,' said Tim.

'Tim,' said Marlene, 'fill Ronald's glass and your own, for goodness' sake. What do you do for a living, Ronald?'

'I work in a museum devoted to graphology.'

'Handwriting,' said Tim.

'Throughout the ages,' Ronald said.

'Can you read handwriting?'

'I read it all day long.'

'Can you judge a person's character from their handwriting?'

'No,' Ronald said.

'That's exactly what I expected you to say,' Marlene said. 'I think you're killing.'

'Ronald,' said Tim, 'is sometimes consulted by the police on questions of forgery.'

'No!' said Marlene.

'Yes,' said Tim, 'he is.'

'How thrilling!' said Marlene. 'I do love to see a genuine fraud exposed.'

'Well, now,' Tim said, 'since you mention it, I did feel that last night –'

'Oh, Patrick completely exposed him,' Marlene said, turning to explain to Ronald. 'This fraud-clairvoyant Dr Mike

46

Garland who entered our midst during our séance last night was completely outwitted by our leading medium whose name is Patrick Seton.'

'No!' Ronald said.

'Yes,' said Marlene. 'Garland created a great disturbance, being in the pay of one of our members – one of our *former* members – Mrs Freda Flower, but Patrick gained the ascendancy. He was unshakeable – wasn't he, Tim?'

'I was obliged to leave,' said Tim, 'before the end.'

'Another time you must go and lie down on a bed, Tim. It was too bad of you to leave me with Freda Flower in hysterics. Did you notice the absurd pose that Dr Garland – doctor so-called – adopted during the séance when he was giving clairvoyance? I *knew* he was a fraud the moment he raised up his head to give utterance. Did you notice, Tim, how he raised his head with*out* relaxing in his chair? He didn't lean back in his chair, you see, he didn't lean back. And I knew right away he was fully conscious of all he was saying. I'm making further investigations about Garland. He ought to be exposed.'

Tim's eyes glanced briefly at the hatch. Marlene noticed it and realised she had betrayed her peep-hole. Tim's eyes returned to his soufflé and he said, 'This is delicious, Marlene.'

'I am rather clairvoyant myself,' Marlene said specifically to Ronald, with a tiny swing of her ear-rings, 'and this enables me to see through a fraud immediately. They can't get away with anything from me.'

'When is Patrick's case coming up?' Tim said.

'Freda will not proceed with the case,' Marlene said, 'if I know anything of Freda. She has too much faith in Patrick, although she won't admit it, to ignore the warnings which he transmitted to her last night from the other side. However, I have told Freda Flower that she is no longer welcome in our midst.' She looked at Tim who was still looking elsewhere. 'I feel bound, Tim,' she said, 'to *keep an eye* on things.'

'Oh, quite,' Tim said, wiping his glasses with his white handkerchief.

'It's all very well for you to stand in judgement,' she said.

'Who, me?' Tim said.

'But you are a comparative newcomer to the Circle. You know nothing of the inner workings. That was evident last night. Your seating arrangements . . .'

She rose and bade them come and see the Sanctuary. Glancing back she noticed Ronald taking his pills and washing them down with water.

'Aren't you feeling well?' she said.

'Ronald suffers from indigestion,' Tim said.

'My dear boy, was my cooking so frightful?'

Ronald could not reply. He stood gripping the back of his chair. His eyes were open and, for a moment, quite absent.

But his attack passed and he regained control of himself while Tim and his aunt were still staring at him, Tim fearing the worst and Marlene fascinated.

'Are you psychic?' she said.

'I don't know.'

He followed Tim into the Sanctuary, on the threshold of which Marlene took Ronald's arm.

'I do believe,' she said, 'that you are sensitive to the atmosphere of this flat. For a moment, just now, I thought you were going into a trance. I am psychic, you know. I'm certain you would make an excellent medium, if properly trained.'

On the way home, before they parted, Tim said to Ronald, 'I adore her, really.'

'A good-looking woman,' Ronald said.

'She was a beauty in her day. Of course, she's a bit crackers. There is some*thing*, you know, in her spiritualism, but she hasn't a clue how to cope with it. She cheats like anything herself – thinks it's justified.'

'It's a difficult thing to cope with, I should think.'

'I can't cope with it,' Tim said. 'The awkward thing is, how am I going to get out of it?'

'You'll find a way.'

'Oh, I'll find a way. Only I don't want to fall out with Marlene, you know. What did you honestly think of her, quite honestly?'

'Rather charming,' Ronald said, quite honestly.

Nevertheless, when Martin Bowles rang him up later in the evening and said, 'Come along to Isobel's for supper: she wants you for supper,' Ronald replied that he was engaged. One auntie, he thought, is enough for one Sunday. Enough is always enough.

'God save me,' said Matthew Finch, London correspondent of the *Irish Echo*, 'and help me in my weakness.' He was peeling an onion. Tears still brimmed over his eyelashes when the telephone rang. 'Let it not be an occasion of sin,' he said to himself or to God as he went over to answer it.

'Hallo,' he said, apprehensively, although he knew, really, who would speak.

'Elsie speaking,' said Elsie Forrest.

'Oh yes, Elsie. Hallo, Elsie.'

'You expecting me, Matthew? You said Sunday, didn't you?'

'Yes, Elsie, I want you to come. Will you find your way? A tube to South Kensington, then a 30 bus, and you get off at Drayton Gardens. I'll meet you at the bus stop. You'll be there by quarter to six.'

'Well, I was thinking of getting the Underground to –'

'No, no, the bus from South Kensington is better. I'll wait from quarter to six.'

'All right, Matthew.'

Elsie had not come to his flat before. He had really preferred the other girl in the coffee-bar, Alice Dawes, but she was tied up to a man. On the whole, he had been glad to discover Elsie. Not that he needed to have taken up with either of them. But, yes, he did want to know a girl again, since his previous girl had gone to America and he felt lonely in London without one. Alice Dawes with her black piled-up hair was the handsomer of the two, but Elsie Forrest was the more accessible.

'God help me with my weakness,' said Matthew as he went back to his onion. For he was weak with girls and had a great conscience about sex. It had been easier in Dublin where the bachelors protected their human nature by staying long hours in the public houses. He was not sure what he would do with Elsie. He had to prepare some supper, but she would do the cooking. He was not sure what to do with the onion, and he weighed up what the force of Elsie's attraction was likely to be, and how the evening would turn out. It was for this that he had prepared the onion. For he had found that the smell of onion in the breath invariably put the girls off, and so provided a mighty fortress against the devil and a means of avoiding an occasion of sin. Matthew was not sure, however, that Elsie called for the onion altogether. She was not very pretty. But you never knew when a girl might show the charm she had within her. And again, the onion might be useful for the supper, to mix with the mince-meat. There wasn't another onion left in the box.

Was there not another onion left in the box? Matthew decided that this would be the testing point: if there was a miraculous onion in the vegetable box which could be used in the supper he would, before he went to fetch Elsie from the bus, eat the raw onion he had peeled upon the table; if there was no onion in the box he would risk having Elsie to the flat with a clean breath. He looked in the box. A small shrivelled onion nestled in the earthy corner among the remaining potatoes. He lifted this poor thing, looked at it, pondered whether it was big enough for the supper. He thought perhaps he should peel and eat this little onion and leave the larger one for the cooking.

But then he recalled his previous lapses from grace, and the exact terms of the vow he had made before looking into the box. He thought lustfully of Elsie who would soon be coming back with him to the flat. He seized the peeled onion off the table, ate it rapidly like a man, dabbed his eyes and his brow with his handkerchief, and set off to wait for Elsie at the bus stop.

As if forewarning her, he gave her a breathy kiss when she alighted. She drew back only a little; in fact she took it very well.

He let her go first up the stairs to his flat and was filled with delight as he followed her small hips, which moved at his eye-level.

'Nice room,' she said. 'Is that your mother over there?'

'Yes, and this is my elder brother and that's my sister with her husband on their honeymoon. I'll put on the light, wait and you'll see them better. My sister's got three children. My younger brother is married, too, but my elder brother isn't.' He passed the photographs one by one. 'This is the National University of Ireland, Galway, where I was till nineteen fifty,' said Matthew, and then he poured out the gin. 'That's my cousin that was killed in the war, fighting for Great Britain.'

'Would you have anything in the gin?' Matthew said. 'There's orange juice or water.'

'I'll have it neat,' Elsie said, 'and by God I need it.' She placed the photographs aside. 'Alice was ill last night and I was on alone at the coffee-bar till twelve. Why didn't you come in?'

'I was on duty,' Matthew said. 'I'm always on duty on Saturday nights.'

'Well, before I left the shop I rang up Alice to see how she felt and she was in such a state I had to go round and see her. Patrick didn't come home.'

'What's wrong with her?' Matthew said.

'She's expecting a baby. She's got diabetes. And the man she's living with's no good.'

'Can't something be done about the diabetes?' Matthew said.

'She has to take injections every day. The man wants her to get rid of the baby.'

'She shouldn't do that.'

'She won't do it.'

'Yes, she looks a nice girl,' Matthew said. 'Who's the man?'

'Patrick Seton – he's the medium.'

Matthew thought she meant go-between, so he said, 'But who's the man?'

'He's the man – Patrick Seton, he's a medium.'

'Oh, a spiritualist?'

'Yes, he's a wonderful medium. But he's no good to Alice. Weak as water. He's supposed to be getting a divorce from his wife and then he'll marry Alice. But I don't believe he's getting a divorce. I don't believe there's any wife. And there's a case coming up against him on Tuesday for embezzlement or something like that. He's been up before the magistrates once already, but the police didn't have their evidence ready. Suppose he gets a sentence?'

'What a terrible fellow,' Matthew said. 'Alice should leave him, a lovely girl like that.'

'She's completely under his power. In love with him.'

'A terrible thing,' Matthew said. 'A girl like that taking up with a spiritualist. Aren't they a lot of mad fellows, spiritualists?' He was thinking of Ewart Thornton with whom he frequently had loud arguments on the Irish question. 'I know a spiritualist,' Matthew said, 'who's a schoolmaster, we both belong to a drinking club out at Hampstead. But he won't talk about spiritualism to me because he knows I'm Irish. He talks politics. He's mad.'

'Are the Irish against spiritualism?'

'Well, the Catholics, it's the same thing.'

'There's a lot in spiritualism,' Elsie said. 'I'm not a spiritualist myself exactly. At least, I've never joined a Circle. But Alice is a member. And I believe in it.'

'Do you really?' Matthew was interested with an eager mental curiosity in direct proportion as he was put off her sexually by the thought of her being a spiritualist. A deep inherited and unarguable urge made him move his chair a little bit away from her, whereas he had previously been moving it nearer; and he reflected, then, that he need not have eaten the onion. A spiritualist girl might dematerialise in the act, if it came to the act. But his mind was alert for knowledge. 'How do they summon up the spirits of the dead?' Matthew said. 'Would you have some more gin?'

She said, 'I need it, after a sleepless night.'

'There's some mince-meat and onion and potatoes and there's some custard and fruit. Or you could have bacon and eggs,' Matthew said. 'You just say when you're hungry. How do they call up the dead from their repose?' He poured the gin and gave it to her while she described the thrilling process of the medium's getting through to the other side.

'I had a friend called Colin that was killed,' she said, 'and Patrick Seton got through to him and he gave me a message, it was quite incredible because nobody could have known except Colin and me about this thing that he mentioned, it was a secret between Colin and me.'

'Can't you tell it to me?' Matthew said.

'Well,' she said, 'it's rather personal.' She looked at Matthew rather meaningly. Matthew felt himself slightly endangered and was grateful, after all, for the strong onion in his breath.

She drank down her gin. Matthew filled her glass, and moved his chair towards her again. 'Are you feeling like supper?' he said. 'Perhaps we'll just fry a couple of rashers and eggs. Or you'd perhaps prefer to come out, that would be simpler.'

She looked at him with quite a glow, and her face, haggard as it was, showed its youth. 'I'll just have my drink,' she said. 'I'm enjoying this rest and opening my heart to somebody.'

She came over and sat on the arm of his chair. She began to finger his black curls. He turned and breathed hard upon her.

'You remind me of Colin,' she said, 'in a certain respect. He used to be fond of onions and I minded at first, but I got used to it. So I don't mind your onion-breath very much.'

Matthew clasped her desperately round the waist, and sighed upon her as if to save his soul. But she too sighed and shivered with excitement as she subsided upon him.

At ten o'clock they went out to eat. Elsie then telephoned to see how Alice was getting on and returned to report that Patrick had still not come home and Alice was upset. And so Elsie took Matthew to the room in Ebury Street where Alice sat up in bed with her long black hair let loose, and her beautiful distress; and Matthew fell altogether in love with her.

After he had gone, Alice said, looking at Elsie in a special way, 'You've been to bed this afternoon.'

'Yes. He reminds me of Colin in a way. His breath –'

'Have you been foolish tonight, Elsie?'

'Well, you know,' said Elsie, 'that I don't mind a man whose breath smells of onions. Colin's always did.'

'Makes me sick, the thought of it.'

'Oh well,' Elsie said, 'I suppose there was something psychological in my childhood. It makes me sick too, in a way.'

4

Patrick Seton sat in his room in Paddington, about which nobody except Mr Fergusson knew anything, and thought. Or rather, he sat and felt his thoughts.

It was the unfortunate occurrence.

Freda Flower: danger.

Tomorrow morning at ten at the Magistrate's Court. Unless Freda Flower had changed her mind again . . .

Mr Fergusson would know. Mr Fergusson had taken his passport away from him.

Patrick brushed his yellow-white hair with an old brush in his trembling hand and went out to see Mr Fergusson. He walked hastily, keeping well in to the shop side of the streets. He hastened, for something about Mr Fergusson always brought him peace. Meanwhile, he felt his thoughts, and they began to run on optimistic lines.

A great many witnesses for the defence. They knew he was genuine. Marlene in the box.

Freda Flower: what a gross, what a base, betrayal of all she had held sacred!

You are acquitted, said the judge. After that: Alice.

Alice must be dealt with, and her unbelievable baby. For her own sake. He loved her. And always would. Even unto her passing over. The spirit giveth life.

He had come to the police station. The constable at the desk looked up and nodded. 'I'll tell Detective-Inspector Fergusson you're here,' he said.

Patrick sat and fidgeted until the policeman came to call him. Patrick dusted the lapel of his dark coat with a mothlike flicker of the fingers and followed the policeman.

Patrick's nerves came to rest on Detective-Inspector Fergusson, who stood sandy-haired, with his fine build, and spoke with his good Scots voice.

'I've come to see if there has been any development, Mr Fergusson,' Patrick said, 'in the unfortunate occurrence.'

'Mrs Flower has been here,' said Mr Fergusson. 'You must have got at her.'

'She's changed her mind, I presume?'

'Yes.'

'Oh!'

'But we haven't.'

'How do you mean?' Patrick said.

Mr Fergusson said, 'It's a police prosecution, you know. Witnesses can't change their minds.'

'Yes, but Mrs Flower's your chief witness. You'll want the best out of her. You'd want it given willingly.'

'You're right there.' Mr Fergusson gave Patrick a cigarette. 'The Chief is considering our next course of action. There will probably be a remand tomorrow.'

'I won't be sent for trial?'

'The case will merely be postponed,' said Mr Fergusson reassuringly. 'We've got your statement.'

'I could always deny it,' Patrick whispered absent-mindedly. 'I was in a dazed condition after a séance when I signed it.'

'That didn't get you very far the last time.'

'It made an impression on the court.' And Patrick waved the subject away as a wife does when reciting to a husband retorts that she has repeated on other weary occasions.

'Keep in touch with me,' Mr Fergusson nodded.

Patrick felt sorry the interview was over. He felt steadied-up when in the company of this policeman. One expected worldliness from Mr Fergusson. One did not expect it from people with an interior knowledge of the spirit, like Freda Flower.

'It's a very painful occurrence,' Patrick said.

'Very,' said Mr Fergusson.

'Is there any chance of the Chief deciding not to proceed?' Patrick said.

'A slight chance. If Mrs Flower remains reluctant to give evidence against you there's a chance we won't proceed. But Mrs Flower may change her mind again. We have to see her again and have a talk.'

Mr Fergusson rose and patted Patrick's shoulder, at the same time propelling him gently towards the door. 'Ring me every morning,' he said, 'or call round. I'll keep you informed.'

Then Patrick asked his usual question. 'If the worst comes to the worst,' he said, 'how long . . . ?'

The policeman said, as usual, 'It depends on the judge. Eighteen months, two years . . .'

'That's a long time.'

'They go by the antecedents,' said Mr Fergusson. 'Cheer up, you're lucky you're a bachelor. It's worse for a married man. Look on the bright side, Patrick.'

At the street entrance Patrick looked out on to the bleak pavements and immediately felt unhappy again. He stood for a moment under the protective porch, then took the plunge up the street. He felt within him a decision to go and see the doctor.

'He can look you in the eyes,' said Freda Flower to Mike Garland, 'and make you believe it's you that's telling the lie.'

'You don't be a fool,' Mike said. 'You go back to Inspector Fergusson and tell him you're going on with it, as you said in the first place. The whole of your savings gone. Remember that.'

'Oh, Mike, I was so good to him. You should have seen how he got round me with his interior decorations and his odd jobs round the house.'

Pink-cheeked Mike looked round the walls which were done with a pink wash. 'Didn't make much of a job of it.'

'He didn't do this room. He did the paint. And he did the kitchen. But I was good to him.'

'He's a fraud,' Mike said, 'and he ought to be exposed. For the sake of the Movement.'

'I can't believe it, Mike. I still can't believe, inside me, when I think of him that he's a fraud. He's given me such good advice from the chair, Mike, and last Saturday night –'

'That was a fake-up, clear enough,' Mike said. 'He wanted to frighten you.'

'No, Mike. He was really gone on Saturday night. You could see it.'

'Think of your money,' Mike said. 'What's happened to your two thousand?'

'I still can't believe it, Mike.'

'You know what Fergusson told you.'

'I don't know what to think, Mike.'

'There have been other cases in the past. There are two other women over the last two years.'

'I always feel somehow,' she said, 'that there's some expla-nation. I was the only woman for Patrick.' She saw in her mind's eye the grave thin face and blue eyes of Patrick as it were superimposed on the curtain.

She said, 'You don't realise how nicely he could talk. There was something about him lifted you up. He's a poet at heart.'

'And he lifted up your cash as well.'

'Perhaps there was some mistake.'

'He admitted it,' Mike said. 'And there's your handwriting he's forged.'

'Perhaps I did write the letter. I don't know. It could be my own signature, after all, if I didn't know what I was doing. I thought the money was for bonds, but perhaps the bonds were a dream, I don't know –'

'He frightened you by his warnings,' Mike said. 'Well, let me tell you, there's nothing in them. I'm a clairvoyant and I can *see* he's a fraud.'

She looked at Mike's pink face and his large frame. He failed to move her as much as Patrick had done.

'Two thousand,' Mike said. 'Come, put your hat on and I'll take you back to Inspector Fergusson. You were a fool to part with the cheque.'

'I think he said he'd buy the bonds, I don't know.' Desperately she looked at the white blossom on the green carpet, and at the curtains, fawn with a touch of pink to match the walls, and her fawn and green suite.

'Two thousand, your life savings,' Mike said.

'I've got the rooms all let,' she said. 'Thanks to you, Mike.'

'But nothing in the bank. Come on, let's go. Two thousand, remember. He should get five years' imprisonment.'

She said, 'It was worth the money.'

But she got ready, and accompanied Mike Garland all the way back to Detective-Inspector Fergusson, who had been so severe when she had called previously to withdraw her statement. When he spoke to her on this second occasion he was even more severe, for she was so very full of tears and doubts.

Patrick spoke to the receptionist from the telephone kiosk with a courteous smile, as if she could see him.

'If at all possible,' Patrick said.

'His appointment book is very full all day,' the receptionist said.

'Perhaps,' said Patrick, 'you could have a word with him and he'll slip me in. You remember me, don't you? A private patient – Mr Seton.'

'Oh, Mr Seton.' She went away and returned.

'Half past twelve, Mr Seton. He can give you some time.'

'Thank you,' Patrick said. 'I am so much obliged.'

Patrick was unaware what precisely was the deep secret in Dr Lyte's career, to which he had given unconscious utterance one night in the séance room, the only occasion on which Dr Lyte had attended a spiritualist meeting. Patrick, on coming round from his trance, had perceived the shaken stranger and had moved with fluttering obliquity towards him as a moth to the lamp.

The stranger was Dr Lyte. Patrick rapidly appreciated that he had said something in his trance which had truly got its mark. 'How exactly did you know?' Dr Lyte said in a way which was very different from his nice clothes.

Patrick bashfully screwed his head to the side and smiled.

When Patrick called on him the next day, Dr Lyte had pulled himself together.

'I only went there as an experiment,' he explained.

'By whom recommended?' Patrick said quietly.

'Chap called Ewart Thornton. A friend of –'

'That is correct,' Patrick said. 'Mr Thornton recommended you. You are speaking the truth.'

'I have no faith in spiritualism,' Dr Lyte said.

Patrick nodded like a man of the world.

'And what you described,' Dr Lyte said, 'in your so-called trance, was inaccurate.'

'No,' Patrick said, 'Dr Lyte, it was not inaccurate.'

'Where did you get this information?'

'I don't know what you're talking about,' Patrick said with mendacious truth. 'I'd rather not discuss the details.'

'What do you want with me?'

Patrick closed his eyes reprovingly.

'What can I do for you?' said Dr Lyte.

And so he never refused Patrick an appointment, or a piece of advice, or a drug to alleviate the effects of a trance. Patrick was not unduly troublesome. Dr Lyte even went so far as voluntarily to obtain the new drug which had been employed, for experimental purposes, to induce epileptic convulsions in rats, and which, taken in certain minor quantities, greatly improved both the spectacular quality of Patrick's trances and his actual psychic powers.

'What can I do for you, Patrick?' said Dr Lyte when Patrick was shown in at half past twelve sharp. Dr Lyte was untroubled: he had got used to Patrick, as one does get used to things.

'It's about Alice. She won't think of doing away with it. Not by an operation. I mentioned the address –'

'Well, she can get it adopted. Much easier if you don't marry her till afterwards. The State has arrangements for these girls.'

'Yes,' Patrick said. 'Alice,' he said, 'isn't too well.'

'Send her along.'

'I think perhaps she isn't taking her injections properly,' Patrick said.

'Oh, she's got to take her two injections every morning before breakfast. They need the regular insulin. Tell her she'll die if she doesn't take it.'

'How long does it take,' Patrick said, 'for a diabetic person to die if they deprive themselves of insulin?'

'She's not trying to take her life, is she?'

'I'm not sure,' Patrick said, his fingers interlacing each other in agitated jerks. 'But don't you think she might try to get rid of the baby by reducing the insulin and making herself really ill?'

'That would be foolish,' said Dr Lyte. 'Surely she knows – but why don't you see to the injections yourself until this trouble's over?'

'Oh, she won't let me touch them. She won't ever let me use the needle on her.'

'Do you watch her taking it?'

'No. You see, she won't let me see her doing it.'

'I'll have a talk with her. I'd better come along.'

'Well,' Patrick said, 'I don't think that's necessary. I'll tell her she'll die if she doesn't take her insulin. I'll say you said so. How long would it take?'

'It varies,' said the doctor. 'My goodness, if Alice really did get negligent she might die within a few days. But she *knows* –'

'Perhaps, on the other hand, she is taking too much insulin,' Patrick said. 'Would that account for her symptoms?'

'What are the symptoms? Exhausted? Hungry?'

'Yes.'

'Really, you know, I'll have to see her. What makes you think she isn't following her proper routine in the mornings?'

'Oh, it's only an idea I had,' Patrick said. 'I may be quite wrong.'

'Is she testing her urine every morning?'

'I don't know,' Patrick said. 'It's all just a stupid idea in my mind that she may be neglecting her insulin treatment. She's probably just off colour, with the baby and so forth . . . It's a worry for me. Tell me, if she took *too much* insulin, what might happen?'

'She'd die. I'll look in this afternoon,' said the doctor.

'Very well,' Patrick said. 'Good of you,' he said; and the doctor was vaguely disturbed by his docility. Patrick was saying, his voice trailing off, 'But my suspicions may be quite unfounded, and how am I to know what she does with the needle and so forth . . . ?'

'Feeling better?' said Patrick.

'Heaps better,' she said. 'I'm going to work tonight.'

'Did you miss me the last two days?' Patrick said.

'You know I did, darling.'

'I was worried about you all the time,' he said. 'I asked Dr Lyte to come and see you.'

'Oh! He hasn't been.'

'He's coming this afternoon.'

'Well, you can put him off. It's too late. I'm better.'

'He's anxious in case you've been forgetting to take your insulin.'

'I never forget my insulin. But I've missed you giving me the injection.' She took his hand. 'I've missed that little touch the last two mornings, Patrick.'

'Dr Lyte,' Patrick said, 'wondered if perhaps you were taking too much.'

'I never take too much. Does he think I'm an imbecile? I've been taking injections for six years.'

'Well, I'll ring and put him off,' Patrick said.

'*I'll* ring and tell him what I think of him,' she said. 'Suggesting that I'm negligent –'

'Now, Dr Lyte is a good friend. Better leave him to me. I'll tell him you're all right now.'

'And then we'll go out and celebrate,' she said, 'the collapse of the court case.'

'Well, it's only in abeyance. Of course Freda Flower hasn't

64

a leg to stand on. But she's a dangerous woman, and she could change her mind.' His voice faded away out of the window where he was looking.

'Hasn't she got a heart?' said Alice. 'Hasn't she got a heart?'

'The police want to proceed,' Martin Bowles told Ronald in the book-lined barristers' chambers. 'But the widow won't stand by her evidence satisfactorily. Seton has scared the pants off her with messages from beyond the grave.'

'Is it forgery, then? I thought you said fraudulent conversion,' Ronald said.

'Fraudulent conversion on one count. But Seton has now produced a letter by which he hopes to prove that the widow gave him the money. Of course, it's a forgery.'

Ronald looked at the letters and the sad second-hand-looking cheque with the bank's mark stamped on it.

'She wants them back,' Martin said. 'But the police are hanging on to them. We've got photostats.'

'I can't work from photostats,' Ronald said, locking the documents away in his brief-case. 'The widow will have to wait.'

'I'll give you a lift home,' Martin said. 'I'm going along to Isobel's.'

They walked through the Temple courtyard to Martin's car.

'What do you think,' Martin said, 'goes on in a man like Patrick Seton's mind when he looks back on his life?'

People frequently asked this sort of question of Ronald. It was as if they held some ancient superstition about his epilepsy: 'the falling sickness', 'the sacred disease', 'the evil spirit'. Ronald felt he was regarded by his friends as a sacred cow or a wise monkey. He was, perhaps, touchy on the point.

Sometimes he thought, after all, they would have come to him with their deep troubles, consulted him on the nature of things, listened to his wise old words, even if he wasn't an afflicted man. If he had been a priest, people would have consulted him in the same way.

'What goes on at the back of his mind?' Martin inquired of the oracle. 'Tell me.'

'I should think,' Ronald replied after a meet pause, 'that when he considers his past life he suffers from a rush of blood to the head, giddiness and bells in the ears. And therefore he does not consider his life at all.' And having thus described his own symptoms when a fit was approaching, Ronald fell silent.

Martin negotiated the traffic all along the Strand to Trafalgar Square. 'I think,' he said then to Ronald, 'that's a terrifically good piece of observation. Do you feel like coming along and cheering Isobel up?'

'All right,' Ronald said.

'Got your pills?' said Martin.

'Yes, I've got them on me.'

5

If there is one thing a bachelor does not like it is another bachelor who has lost his job.

The Hon. Francis Eccles, small, with those very high shoulders that left him almost neckless, leaned over the bar of the Pandaemonium Club at Hampstead, whose members were supposed to be drawn from the arts and sciences. No scientist had yet joined the club in its twelve years' existence, but the members at present in the bar were fairly representative of the arts side: a television actor, a Welsh tenor, a film extra who took peasant-labourer parts when they were available, a ballet-mistress, and a stockbroker who was writing a novel.

It was not only the Hampstead representatives of the arts who frequented this club: many who had left Hampstead occasionally returned to it. Walter Prett for instance, the mammoth art-critic of middle age and collar-length white hair, had come from Camden Town; and Matthew Finch, having sent off the last of his week's tidings for the *Irish Echo*, had come to meet Walter here on the early autumn evening that tiny Francis Eccles hunched necklessly over the bar so sadly, having lost his job.

'But you don't need a job, Eccie,' said Chloe, the young barmaid. 'I don't know what you want with a job anyway.'

Without exchanging a word or sign and by sheer migratory instinct, Matthew and Walter removed their glasses over to the window-seat where they were separated from the job-less nobleman by a grand piano.

'Tell me,' said Walter to Matthew, 'do I look any thinner?'

'No,' Matthew said, 'you look fine.'

'I've lost eight pounds,' Walter said confidentially, moving his snowy long-haired head close to Matthew's short blue-black curls.

'Don't worry, you look –'

'I've got to lose two stone,' Walter said very loudly. 'Simply got to. My heart won't stand up to it.'

Matthew shied a little. 'Were you not on a diet?' he said.

Walter's voice subsided. 'I was, but it insisted on no beer, wines, or spirits. I'd rather be dead.' Walter's eyes bulged redly from the inner circle of his face, for it was surrounded by outer circles of dark blood-pressured flesh. He sipped his wine daintily through his face-wide lips. Matthew thought perhaps the glass would be crushed in Walter's great hand. Walter was liable to sudden outbursts of temper for no reason at all. Matthew looked at him uneasily, his eyes peeping from under his black glossy eyebrows.

Walter, observing this effect, was dissatisfied. He smiled sweetly, and it was indeed a sweet smile, such as wide full mouths only are capable of.

'It's my birthday,' Matthew said. 'I'm thirty-two today. I come under the Sign of Libra, the scales of justice. I'm passionate about justice. Like all the Irish.'

'Do they all come under Libra?'

'No. I don't believe in astrology,' Matthew said, drinking down his wine in an anxious way.

'Well, well,' said Walter. 'Many happy returns. I could give you fifteen years.'

'Could you?' Matthew said with his mind on something else.

'Forty-eight next year,' Walter said, 'and what have I done with my life?'

'You've got your column.'

'I should have been a painter,' Walter said. 'I showed promise.'

'Did you ever think of getting married?' Matthew said.

'I showed tremendous promise,' Walter said, 'but my family was indifferent to art. They were interested in horses. My father kept three hunters in the stable and then he couldn't pay the milk bill.'

'Yes, you told me that before,' Matthew said, looking wistfully at a girl in a large jersey and tight jeans who had just come in and was now sitting up on one of the high chairs at the bar.

Walter stood up and roared, 'Well, I'm telling you again.' For he hated his family stories to be treated indifferently.

'Sit down, now, sit down,' Matthew said.

'Vulgar little fellows all over the place,' Walter observed, casting his inflamed eyes round the room. 'Especially in the art world.'

'Sit down,' Matthew said. 'Would you have a drink?' he said.

Chloe called over from her place behind the bar. 'Walter! What's all the noise about?'

Walter sat down broodily while Matthew edged round the room and up to the far end of the bar so that Eccie's hunched back was turned to him. When he had obtained the drinks he did the same detour on his return to their window-seat. On the way, however, he said 'Good evening' to the girl in jeans.

'I'm thinking of getting married,' Matthew said.

'Oh, are you? Who to?'

'I haven't anyone in mind,' Matthew said. 'Only my brother-in-law thinks I should get married. My sister wants me to get married and so does my uncle. Every time I go home to Ireland my mother's ashamed that I'm not married to a girl.'

'I got a young woman into trouble at the age of eighteen,' Walter said. 'Daughter of one of our footmen. He was an Irish fellow. The butler caught him reading Nietzsche in the pantry. To the detriment of the silver. Of course there was no question of my marrying his daughter. The family made a settlement and I went abroad to paint. My hair turned white at the age of nineteen.'

Matthew said, 'I know a girl who's expecting a baby by an old spiritualist. She's lovely. She's got long black hair.' He saddened into silence and gazed upon the girl in jeans dispassionately, recognising her as Ronald's former girl-friend.

'I went abroad to paint, but my cousin the Marquise –'

'I'll tell you this much,' Matthew said, 'there's no justification for being a bachelor and that's the truth, let's face it. It's everyone's duty to be fruitful and multiply according to his calling either spiritual or temporal, as the case may be.'

'Monet admired my work. Just before he died he visited my studio with his friends, and –'

'These are the figures,' Matthew said, and took from inside his coat a bundle of papers from which he selected one which had been folded in four, and which was split and grubby at the folds. He straightened out the sheet, following the typewritten lines with his finger, as he read out, 'Greater London, the census of nineteen fifty-one. Unmarried males of twenty-one and over: six hundred and fifty-nine thousand five hundred. That's including divorced and widowed, of course, but the majority are bachelors –'

'I can see him now,' said Walter, 'as he was when he was assisted into a chair before my easel. Monet was silent for fully ten minutes – the painting was a simple, but rather exquisite roof-top scene –'

'Unmarried males of thirty and over,' said Matthew: 'three hundred and fifty-eight thousand one hundred. Since nineteen fifty-one the bachelor population has increased by –'

'Put that vulgar little bit of paper away,' Walter said.

'Tim Raymond gave it to me,' Matthew said, putting it away very carefully. 'He works in the C.O.I. God help him.'

'You'd better get married,' Walter said.

'Do you think so? Why?'

'Because you obviously haven't got the courage to get your sex any other way.'

'There's more than sex in marriage.'

'But not in your mind.'

'Perhaps that's true. I often wonder if it's only sex when I think of getting married. Still, I feel I should be married and multiply. I feel –'

'Do you really want to get married?' Walter said.

'No.'

'I nearly got married,' Walter said, 'in nineteen tirty-two when I was out of work and the family had cut me off. The girl had a job. If a girl had a job in those days it was like a dowry. She was anxious to marry me. But I was really more taken up with her father. He was a carpenter, one of the last of the true English craftsmen. But I did not marry his daughter. She was a bourgeois little bitch with her savings in the post office. Her name was Sybil, if you please.' The memory of Sybil, though in fact she had never existed, was so fiercely implanted in Walter's mind through frequent elaborations of his imagined affair with her, that he was always thoroughly incensed by her.

'I wished her joy of her savings in the post office and departed,' Walter shouted. He rose and set down his empty

71

glass and fastened his black coat on one button across his huge stomach.

'Are you going to go?' Matthew said.

Walter clenched both fists as if to fight with Sybil.

'I'll walk with you to the station,' Matthew said.

Walter sat down again and made his lips into a long line.

'I'll have to be going,' Matthew said. 'My other brother-in-law has just come over and I've got to meet him at my uncle's.'

'My boy,' said Walter, 'you have much to bear.'

'Not my uncle at Twickenham. My other uncle at Poplar,' Matthew said, with his eyes on the brown bobbed head of Ronald's girl in jeans who was laughing with Chloe.

'I want a drink,' Walter said.

'I'm a bit short of cash,' Matthew said, 'this time of the month.'

'Fresh young Chloe will cash me a cheque,' Walter shouted.

'Chloe will not cash you a cheque,' Chloe called out, 'for the simple reason that Chloe is not allowed to cash cheques any more.'

Francis Eccles swivelled round in his high chair.

'Why, Walter!' he said.

'Why, Eccie!' said Walter.

'There's a very definite rule about cheques,' Chloe said.

Walter ambled over to the bar and said in a tone of dignified reproach, 'As it happens I haven't got my cheque book on me. But I'm surprised, Chloe, that you should take up this ridiculous lower-middle-class attitude.'

'I have my orders, Walter,' Chloe pleaded.

'What will you drink, Walter?' said Eccie.

'You have your orders, Chloe,' Walter said. 'Very well, you

have your orders. But really, my dear, this is dreadfully bourgeois of you.'

It worked quicker than usual. Chloe said, 'I'm not bourgeois, really I'm not. I'll personally cash you a cheque. It's only that I can't, I mustn't, cash cheques for the club.'

'Since when?' said Walter.

'Since last week,' she said. 'Honestly,' she said.

'First I've heard of it,' said the girl in jeans.

'I'll cash your cheque,' said Eccie, also anxious not to be bourgeois.

'It's of no matter,' Walter said. 'I only object on principle. As it happens I haven't got my cheque book on me.'

Eventually he accepted a loan from Eccie, and when the deal was done Matthew reappeared from the cloakroom. He took a high chair at the bar and helped himself to a pickled onion off a plate.

'Matthew,' said Chloe, 'meet Hildegarde. Hildegarde, meet Matthew.'

Matthew leaned forward and smiled across Walter's bulk at the girl in jeans. 'We've met before,' he said.

'Where?' she said.

'At Ronald Bridges'. Aren't you a friend of Ronald's?'

'I used to be,' she said.

'I know Bridges,' mused Eccie. 'I wonder if he could help . . . ?'

'No,' said Chloe. 'I shouldn't think so, Eccie.'

'Don't you?'

'No.'

'What is this secret conversation?' roared Walter.

'It's something Eccie and I were discussing,' Chloe said. 'It's private.'

'Common little creatures,' Walter shouted. 'Very bad behaviour.'

'I'm not standing for that, Walter,' Chloe said. 'Are you standing for it, Eccie?'

'Well, no,' said Eccie. 'I must say, Walter . . .'

'This is too much,' said Hildegarde. She swung her long legs off the stool and departed.

'Come on, Walter,' Matthew said, 'I've got to meet my brother-in-law –'

'I shall not be driven away by a barmaid and a snivelling middle-class younger son of an upstart earl,' Walter said.

'You're drunk,' said Chloe.

Walter laughed without noise or humour, but with a shaking of his flabby shoulders, chest, and stomach.

Eccie said sadly, 'Walter, Walter, I don't like this.'

'You are deriving a certain pleasure from lumping it,' Walter said.

'Walter, I'm out of a job, you know. The Institute is closing down.'

'Not before time,' Walter said.

'As an art school, I admit it had its weaknesses,' said Eccie. 'But I flatter myself I was able to contribute something useful with my lectures, especially on the country itinerary which I've been taking for the last two years.'

'Nonsense. You contributed nothing. You know nothing of art.'

'Oh, Walter, come!' said Eccie, Christianly.

'He's drunk,' said Chloe.

'I'll have to go and phone my sister,' Matthew said.

'Drunk,' said Chloe, 'and this time's the last. He can't come here insulting the members –'

Walter took from his pocket the five pounds that he had borrowed from Francis Eccles. 'I'll give you this back,' he said, 'before I'll admit you know anything about painting, Eccie.'

Eccie said, 'Goodnight, Chloe. Goodnight, Matthew,' in a tone of gentle reproach, and left.

'That was mean of you, Walter,' Chloe said.

'I am an honest man,' Walter observed, 'when treating of the few existing subjects to which honesty is due.'

'I'd better ring my sister,' Matthew said. 'My cousin will be on the telephone to her as I haven't turned up at my uncle's to meet my brother-in-law.'

'It was unkind of you, Walter,' said Chloe, leaning over the bar forgivingly. 'Poor old Eccie's upset at losing his job.'

'He doesn't need a job,' Walter said. 'He's got his private income and his basement. And he's an Anglo-Catholic. Anglo-Catholics always get jobs.'

'He hasn't got much income,' Chloe said. 'Have you seen the way he lives? That basement is going down and down. No one to look after him.'

'He ought to have got married,' Matthew said.

'He's not the marrying type,' said Chloe.

'He pees in the sink,' said Walter, 'not that I hold that against him.'

'He *doesn't*!' said Chloe.

'True,' said Walter. 'It's nothing. We bachelors all pee in sinks and wash-basins.'

'I don't,' said Matthew.

'You're young yet,' Walter said.

'Filthy beasts, the lot of you,' Chloe said, laughing towards one face and another as she leant over the bar.

Then she straightened up.

'Hallo, hallo,' she said, for Mike Garland, accompanied by an elderly man who wore a clerical outfit, had entered.

'Walter, Matthew,' she said, 'this is Dr Garland and Father Socket.'

'How do you do, Father,' said Matthew, jumping off his stool to shake hands.

'Not of our persuasion,' Walter informed Matthew, whereupon Matthew drew away his hand nervously and said, 'Pleasant evening.'

'These two are fraud spiritualists,' Walter roared.

'I beg your pardon, sir?' said Father Socket.

'I grant it with a plenary indulgence,' said Walter as he pushed Matthew before him out into the high autumnal winds of Hampstead.

'I'd have liked to talk to them a bit,' Matthew said. 'What was all your hurry? Alice Dawes, that pregnant girl with the long black hair, is a spiritualist.'

'These are fraud spiritualists.'

'Is there a difference, then?' said Matthew.

6

Ronald said, 'How long have you known her?'

'Since two weeks,' Matthew said. 'She's got long black hair. She has it done up on top when she's in the coffee-bar and she lets it go long when she's in bed.'

'I should think you've got a chance,' Ronald said. 'Seton isn't much of a rival, from what I know of him. But are you sure you want to marry this girl?'

Matthew hastily remembered that the last thing he had said might be misconstrued, so he told Ronald, 'I saw her in bed because she was ill and her friend Elsie took me along – Elsie's the other girl in the coffee-bar.'

'Have some tea,' Ronald said. 'Help yourself. Pour it out.'

'I hope you don't mind me consulting you like this?'

Ronald poured out tea, holding the teapot as high over the cup as possible without making a splash. This had been a habit of his for as long as he had been making tea for himself, and he did not notice now what he was doing as he raised the teapot, by habit, twelve inches above the cup, nor did he remember that the pretty sight of the long stream of golden liquid had once made the process of tea-making less of a bore than if he had poured it from a normal height.

'Be careful,' Matthew said, 'you don't spill it.'

'You will be thirty-two this month,' Ronald said, testing his memory.

'My birthday was last week,' Matthew said, aimlessly as a boy-seminar answering a tall black frock.

Ronald said, 'Everyone consults me about their marriages.' Three months ago Tim Raymond, before he had joined his aunt's spiritualist circle, had come to Ronald with the marriage question. He had said, 'Do you think everyone will say I'm marrying her for her money and she for my connections?'

'I don't know. I expect so.'

'Perhaps that's the truth of the matter.'

'Well, you've got good connections. It isn't every set of connections a woman wants to take on. And for your part, it isn't everyone's money you would touch, I daresay. There's an element of mutual respect involved.'

'There's something in that. Still, it would be tiresome if people said –'

'Do you love the girl?' Ronald said.

'Funny thing, you know, in a funny sort of way, she's *fun.*'

'Well, I don't see why you shouldn't get married. Does she love you?'

'I think so. Of course she says so.'

'What does your mother think?'

'Oh, she likes the idea. They all like the idea. And *I* quite like the idea. But –'

'Do you want to get married at all?' Ronald said.

'No,' Tim had said. 'I don't know why, but I don't.'

Ronald said to Matthew, as he poured tea from a great height, 'Do you want really to get married?'

'Well, I'm very much in love with Alice.'

'Are you sure you want to get married?'

'I'd like Alice for a wife if I was to marry.'

'Do you want to marry at all?'

'I can't say I do,' Matthew said. He drank down his tea which had become cold through Ronald's method of pouring.

'It's the duty of us all to marry,' Matthew said. 'Isn't it? There are two callings, Holy Orders and Holy Matrimony, and one must choose.'

'Must one?' Ronald said. 'It seems evident to me that there's no compulsion to make a choice. You are talking about life. It isn't a play.'

'I'm only repeating the teaching of the Church,' Matthew said.

'It isn't official doctrine,' Ronald said. 'There's no moral law against being simply a bachelor. Don't be so excessive.'

'One can't go on sleeping with girls and going to confession.'

'That's a different question,' Ronald said. 'That's sex: we were talking of marriage. You want your sex and you don't want to marry. You never get all you want in life.'

'I'll have to marry in the end,' Matthew said, gazing at the tea-leaves in the bottom of his cup. 'The only way I can keep off sex is by going to confession and renewing my resolution every week, and sometimes that doesn't work. It's an unnatural life if one's a Christian.'

'Find the right girl, then, and marry her.'

'Alice is the right girl.'

'Well, get her to marry you.'

'I don't *want* to get married, you know.'

Ronald laughed. He was rather surprised that the conversation was becoming rancorous.

Matthew said, 'Do you want to marry?'

'No,' Ronald said. 'I'm a *confirmed* bachelor.'

'Why don't we want to marry? It isn't as if we were homosexuals.'

Ronald greatly desired, as he sometimes did, to run his fingers through Matthew's black curls. He thought, well, isn't he right? We are not homosexuals. Repressed homosexuality is a meaningless term because no one can prove it.

Matthew said, 'I suppose most people would say the confirmed bachelor is a subconscious homosexual.'

'Impossible to prove,' Ronald said. 'You can only deduce homosexuality from facts. Subconscious tendencies, repressions – these ideas are too simple and too tenuous to provide explanations. There are infinite reasons why a man may remain celibate. He may be a scholar. Husbands don't make good scholars, in my opinion.'

'I'm only saying,' said Matthew, 'what people say. They say all bachelors are queers. Hee hee. Or mother-fixated or something.'

'Oh, what people say! They always look at what might be, or what should be, never at what is.'

'My trouble is this,' Matthew said, 'I have a mind to consider the lilies of the field. In other words, I'm a lazy Irish lout and I like to feel I can chuck up a job any time, and go off to Bolivia.'

'Are you thinking of going to Bolivia?'

'No,' said Matthew, 'not particularly.'

'Your shoes are wet,' Ronald observed.

'Yes, can I take them off?'

'You should have taken them off before.'

Matthew said, 'Are there any women who really don't want to marry?' He let his shoes fall with a plop. Ronald put them straight and at a shrewd drying point near the gas fire.

'Yes, very often, but those are the ones who marry.'

'They get married, not actually wanting to?'

'Yes. Like many men.'

'Why? Is it sex?'

'Not always, I think. It's probably a development in human nature. Something both conforming and unconforming. Otherwise, spinsters and bachelors would all be in religious orders.'

'Part of me feels they should be.'

'The whole of you should acknowledge that they aren't.'

'It's fear of responsibility that puts me off marriage. Responsibility terrifies me. Does it terrify you?'

Ronald considered. 'No,' he said. 'No one offers me much of it.' He thought of Hildegarde and her attempt to take him over as a whole burden for herself.

'I've got responsibilities,' Matthew said, twiddling his stocking-toes. 'I've got to send money home to Ireland to my mother and my aunt. There's only my mother and her sister on the farm and the farm's gone down. They want me to get married, though. I feel immoral as a bachelor. Do you ever feel immoral?'

'Not very often,' Ronald said. 'I've got my epilepsy as an alibi.'

'It used to be called the Falling Sickness,' Matthew said. 'Would you come out to the coffee-bar and have a look at Alice?'

Ronald could not forbear to say, 'I've seen her.'

'Have you? Where?'

'In a café in Kensington. She was with Patrick Seton.'

A heap of Ronald's unwashed laundry lay on the carpet. He had started to make a list which bore the words '3 cols'. This lay on the top of the pile.

'How did you know it was Patrick Seton? Have you met him?' Matthew said.

Ronald could not forbear to say, 'Yes, I gave evidence on his handwriting once. He was convicted of forgery. I have a

81

letter here in my desk,' Ronald rattled on, 'which will probably convict him again. So your way will be clear,' he said, 'to marry Alice.'

'She told me the case was off.'

'That hasn't been decided yet.'

'Will you come out and meet Alice?' Matthew said. 'She's working at the Oriflamme.'

'All right.' Ronald kicked the laundry.

'Of course, you know,' Matthew said, 'she isn't a Catholic. She's a spiritualist.'

'I don't suppose she'd let it stand in her way if she wanted to marry you.'

'I meant, from my point of view –'

'Yes, I know what you meant.'

'Well, as a Catholic how do you feel about –'

Ronald turned on him in a huge attack of irritation. 'As a Catholic I loathe all other Catholics.'

'I can well understand it. Don't shout, for goodness' sake –' Matthew said.

'And I can't bear the Irish.'

'I won't stand for that,' Matthew said.

'Don't ask me,' Ronald shouted, 'how I feel about things as a Catholic. To me, being Catholic is part of my human existence. I don't feel one way as a human being and another *as a Catholic*.'

'To hell with you, now,' Matthew said.

Ronald lifted one of Matthew's shoes, which he had placed so carefully to dry – neither too near the gas fire nor too far from it – and cast it casually at Matthew's head.

Matthew started to hit out, then stopped with his hand in mid-air. Ronald's arm, lifted for protection, was arrested for a second before he dropped it, and he realised that Matthew was sparing him on account of his epilepsy.

Matthew stumbled over the laundry, put on his damp shoes, then went off to the lavatory. When he returned Ronald was ready to accompany him to the coffee-bar where Alice was working.

'Her pregnancy doesn't show as yet,' Matthew said. 'I'd adopt the child as my own if I married her. Do you think, by the way, I ought to try to marry her? She's got long black hair, only you don't see it look so glorious when she piles it up as when she lets it fall.'

Time had come round for one of Alice's ten-minute rest periods, and she sat at the table with Ronald and Matthew while they ate tough salty pizza. She delicately picked a speck of tobacco from her tongue and sadly inhaled her cigarette.

'I love the man,' she said. 'I know he's innocent.'

Matthew immediately said, 'Ronald here is examining one of the vital documents in the case. Ronald is a hand-writing expert. He is often consulted in criminal cases – aren't you, Ronald? He's got this document that's supposed to be a forgery. It's a letter – isn't it a letter, Ronald?'

Ronald smiled as one who had only himself to blame.

Matthew went on, 'He puts these documents to all sorts of tests – don't you, Ronald? There's a test for the ink, and the paper, and all the folds. The most important thing is the formation of the letters – anyone can do the rest, but Ronald's the best man for detecting the formation of letters. And sometimes the forger has stopped to assess his handiwork and then retraced. That's fatal because there's an interruption in the writing which can be detected under the microscope, at least Ronald can detect it – can't you, Ronald?'

Alice was looking at her cigarette, which she was tapping on the edge of the ash-tray.

'I shall never believe he's guilty,' she said. 'Never.'

Ronald thought, 'How that second, histrionic "never" diminishes her – how it debases this striking girl to a commonplace.'

'I'll always believe in his innocence,' she said. 'Always. No matter what the evidence is.'

'I haven't yet looked at the document,' Ronald said. 'I am sure it will not be incriminating to your friend.'

She looked up at him. 'Why are you sure?'

'Because he is your friend,' Ronald said.

Something in his tone made Matthew collect his senses. 'I haven't been indiscreet in talking about the letter, have I?' he said.

'It's perfectly understandable,' Ronald said.

'After all, *you* told me about it.'

'That's right,' Ronald said, 'I did.'

Matthew kept looking uncomfortably at Ronald. But he chattered on, desperately, in his desire to depreciate the girl's lover.

'Ronald says Patrick Seton has been convicted of forgery before.'

'Well, I don't believe it. He's been abroad a lot of his life at famous séances. He was married at one time. His divorce is coming through shortly, and we're getting married. Colonel Scorbin, who's one of the leading spiritualists in Mrs Marlene Cooper's Circle, and a colonel, said to me, "Patrick is one of those rare persons who are born to do great things and to suffer injustice and persecution." I said to him, "I believe it," and I do believe it and I always will, always.'

She seemed not sure how to look at Ronald, whether to show a predominance of hostility which might frighten him, or of fear which might move him to pity; or whether to affect charm and win him over. She offered all three in a way, by holding her head loftily as she regarded him, by pleading with her eyes under their lashes, and by sitting with the elbow over her chair so that her breasts rose unmistakably towards him.

Matthew realised that he had caused Ronald to be the centre of her attention rather than achieved his desire to discredit Patrick.

Alice's ten-minute rest was up. She sauntered about with her long swing among the tables and the trailing ivy of the Oriflamme taking orders for coffee. Matthew and Ronald stayed for a while and she returned as often as she could to their table, once pausing with her tray, on the way to serve a customer, to say to Ronald what was still on her mind.

'The case may not come off. Have you any idea if the case will be brought?'

'No. It has nothing to do with me.'

'It would be easy to frame up a case against Patrick, with that letter.'

'Nothing will be framed up,' Ronald said. 'Please forget about the letter.'

Matthew said, 'Can I meet you after the shop's closed and take you home?'

'Yes,' she said, and she nodded. 'Yes.'

Matthew had not expected her assent.

'Are you sure?' he said, instantly afterwards feeling like a lout.

'Yes, yes, I'm sure.' She was looking at Ronald.

'I'll be back here at the Oriflamme at ten to twelve,' Matthew said. She was looking at Ronald.

'Goodnight, Alice,' Ronald said.

'Can't you do something for Patrick?' she said to Ronald.

He said, 'You should not expect anything of Patrick Seton. Leave him.'

Matthew and Ronald walked along the Chelsea Embankment. Matthew said, 'I didn't expect her to let me fetch her tonight. I'd better phone my sister. She's expecting me to stay with her tonight because my brother-in-law's gone over to Dublin with my other uncle, and she doesn't like to be alone in the house with the children. I'd better phone and tell her I'll be late. Did you mind me telling Alice about that document you've got to inspect? Was it confidential?'

'It was confidential.'

'Oh, you should have made that clear when you told me. But I wanted Alice to know what she's got hold of in this Patrick Seton.'

'Yes, she seems to be in love with him.'

'Did you think so?'

'Yes.'

'Lovely girl, isn't she? And carrying a child inside her.'

'Very attractive.'

'D'you think I've a chance with her?'

'Chance of what?'

'Well, it would have to be marriage. She's expecting the child, moreover. It makes her more desirable; not many would think so, but I do.'

'I think you'll have a chance after Patrick Seton has served a few months of his prison sentence.'

'Don't you think she'd be the sort of girl who would wait for him?'

'Not after she had heard his previous convictions read out in court.'

'The age of him,' Matthew said, 'and the look of him! What does she see in him, a girl like that? You would never see such a match in Ireland except in rare cases where the man had a bit of money and the girl was homeless.'

'She is obviously a soul-lover,' Ronald said.

'She's in love with his spiritualism, that's what it is. He must know a few tricks.'

'I think he's a genuine medium, from what I've heard.'

'I hope he doesn't get his divorce. It might not come off. Then Alice –'

'From what I recall,' Ronald said, 'he isn't a married man at all. At least, it wasn't declared the last time he was in court.'

'He's supposed to have been married for twenty-five years; so Alice says.'

'Well, perhaps he lied to the court. But there's usually a question of maintenance orders. I distinctly recall his being described as a bachelor.'

'What a good memory you've got,' Matthew said.

'Thanks,' said Ronald, and smiled at himself in the glass window of a shop.

'Why should he talk about a divorce if he isn't married, though?' Matthew said. 'Do you think he intends to marry Alice at all?'

'I'll find out what I can from Martin Bowles. He's prosecuting counsel.'

Matthew stopped walking and was looking out over the full-flowing river at the lights on the opposite bank.

'Have you been eating lots of onions?' Ronald said.

'No, not since yesterday. Can you smell them in my breath?'

'Yes.'

'Come on, let's have a drink to take it away before I pick up Alice. They don't like the smell of onions in your breath. Do you really think Patrick Seton is a bachelor?'

They sat in the public house and debated the question of Patrick's being a bachelor, and if so, why he had told Alice the story of a divorce.

'Perhaps he's putting her off from day to day,' Matthew said. 'You could understand it; her wanting to be married for the child, and him not wanting to marry at all. He may be a bachelor like us in that respect.'

Ronald silently contemplated the no-betting notice on the wall.

'He has no intention of marrying her at all,' Matthew said, becoming fierily convinced of it. 'What do you expect of a spiritualist? His mind's attuned to the ghouls of the air all day long. How can he be expected to consider the moral obligations of the flesh? The man's a dualist. No sacramental sense. There have been famous heresies very like spiritualism – they –'

'Have another drink,' Ronald said, who was accustomed to long evenings of proof that Matthew had emerged from his Jesuit school well versed in the heresies.

'Take the Albigensians. Or take the Quietists even. The Zoroastrians. Everything spiritual. Down with the body. Against sex –'

'Against marriage,' Ronald said. 'All bachelors. Like us.'

'I think the spiritualists have sex.' Matthew looked broodily at his knees. 'I'm afraid we are heretics,' he said, 'or possessed by devils.' His curls shone under the lamp. 'It shows a dualistic attitude, not to marry if you aren't going to be a priest or a religious. You've got to affirm the oneness of reality in some form or another.'

'We're not in fact heretics,' Ronald said, 'under the correct meaning of the term.'

'Well, we've got an heretical attitude, in a way.'

'Not in fact. But does it worry you?'

'Yes.'

'Do you want to marry?'

'No.'

'Then you've got a problem,' Ronald observed and went to fetch more drinks.

'I suppose an heretical attitude is part of original sin,' Matthew said as soon as Ronald returned within hearing. 'You can't avoid it.'

Ronald said, 'The Christian economy seems to me to be so ordered that original sin is necessary to salvation. And so far as remaining single is concerned that applies to a lot of people.'

They walked to Battersea where their attention was caught by the sound as of a horse galloping. They looked up a side-street in the direction of the sound and found it to come from a man lying on his back outside a pub. His legs were kicking out and his heels clop-clopped on the pavement. A few people had gathered in the roadway and a young policeman circled round the man as if he were a tiger.

'Is he drunk?' Matthew said.

Ronald went over to the young policeman. 'Turn his head to one side,' he said, 'or he might damage his tongue.'

'Are you a doctor?' said the policeman.

'No, but I understand fits. The man's an epileptic.' Ronald took his own wedge of cork from his pocket and handed it to the policeman. 'Stick this between his teeth. Then kneel on his knees and try and get his boots off.'

'There's an ambulance coming,' said the policeman.

'He could bite his tongue in the meantime,' Ronald said. 'There could be a lot of damage. I'd shove in the wedge if I were you.'

The policeman knelt and grasped the man's head. He

tried to thrust the wedge into the frothing mouth, but the man's convulsions kept throwing the policeman off.

The policeman looked up at Ronald. 'Would you mind trying to get his boots off, then, sir?'

'I doubt if I can do it,' Ronald said. He was greatly agitated, for if there was one thing he did not like to see it was another epileptic. The thought of touching the man horrified him. 'Matthew!' he called out. 'Come and lend a hand.'

Matthew approached and, as Ronald instructed, threw himself upon the man's jerking knees. The policeman jammed the wedge between the teeth. Ronald felt for the shoes as one thrusting his hands into flames. He shut his eyes, and felt for the laces, loosened them, threw the shoes aside so violently that one of them nearly hit an onlooker, and sprang back from the kicking figure.

The man was still jerking when the ambulance arrived, and he was lifted up by two men in hospital uniform and taken away.

'Did it upset you?' Matthew said as they went down to look at the river.

'Yes,' Ronald said.

'Will you be all right?'

'Oh yes, I'll be all right.'

Matthew went off to telephone to his sister and then to read a novel called *Marie Donadieu* in Lyons' Corner House until it should be time to go and meet Alice, while Ronald walked part of the way home, and then feeling unsafe, took a taxi the rest of the way. There, he resisted taking his phenobarbitone, shaky though he was, for on occasions of extra stress he rather cherished the feeling of being more alive and conscious than usual, he cherished his tension and liked to see how far he could stand it. This evening he got ready for bed without any intimations of an approaching fit, and although he had his little drugs ready to take, he did not take them, and managed to get a living troubled sleep instead of a dead and peaceful one.

7

'What is the size of the chalet?' Patrick breathed indifferently.

Dr Lyte said, 'Oh, large enough for two. There are four or five rooms, but as I say it is very difficult of access. You are only a kilometre and a half from the frontier on the one hand and only three from the bus stop on the other, but that's as the crow flies. If you aren't a fairly good climber you would have to be a crow.' He laughed. Patrick did not. 'I wouldn't recommend it, really I wouldn't,' said Dr Lyte.

'No, it sounds just our sort of thing,' Patrick whispered. 'Isolated. Mountains. We'll take it on for three weeks as soon as this wretched case is either squashed or over.'

Dr Lyte reached across his desk, lifted the silver lid of his inkpot, and let it drop again. He looked at his short white hands. He lifted his card-index box and placed it down again a quarter of an inch from its previous position. He fidgeted with his blotting paper. He said to Patrick, 'Suppose the case does come off?'

'Alice and I will go abroad immediately after the case.'

'But if . . .'

Patrick's blue eyes looked out at the sky above the roof. So blue, he thought, so calm. A muscle in his small chin twitched. 'I'm quite confident of being acquitted,' he said in his murmur. 'I may not be sent for trial, even. The police keep asking for time. No evidence. I've been remanded twice.'

Dr Lyte said, 'I don't know, really, why you haven't skipped away in the meantime. Why don't you go abroad?'

Patrick coughed. 'I feel I must stay and see this unfortunate occurrence through.' His shoulders moved resentfully. 'Do you think I'm afraid to – to – how shall I put it? – to stand trial?'

'No,' said Dr Lyte.

'We'll take over your chalet then,' Patrick said. 'Alice and I. One way or another, that will be before the end of the year.'

'I don't recommend it in November or December,' said Lyte.

'Alice likes the cold weather. Alice doesn't like tourist seasons. Alice likes the snow. Will it be snowing?'

'You'll be cut off. Supposing Alice were to take ill, in her condition? Really, you must wait till the spring. March would be all right, perhaps. April, certainly. But November, December. Have you ever been to a lonely part of Austria in November?'

'We shall be taking your chalet for a month.' Patrick smiled a little at Dr Lyte's protests; and the doctor, who did not like to be smiled at in this way, said, 'I've a good mind to refuse you.'

'Have you now?' Patrick said. 'Have you?'

Dr Lyte thought of his practice and his wife and his house at Wembley Park, his daughter at Cambridge and his married daughter; he thought, also, inconsequentially, of the field attached to a Kentish Georgian rectory which he had recently acquired; he thought of his professional friends, his cottage in France and his chalet in Austria. There was nothing he could think of that he wanted to lose, and he regretted the evening he ever set foot in Marlene's Sanctuary of Light. ('One hopes it will become a Sanctuary of Lyte in every sense,' some man had remarked on hearing his name on that one occasion, but the remark had shocked Marlene.) To say this doctor thought of all he could lose is perhaps to put too blunt a point on it, for he felt these things deeply, and all in a second or two while Patrick smiled a little with melancholy.

'You know,' said Dr Lyte, 'that Alice can't stand up to anything strenuous. Ober-Bleilach will be strenuous. The climbing –'

'I'll see she doesn't do too much. I'll see she takes her injection every day.'

'You'll have to take a supply of insulin with you,' Lyte said.

'Yes.'

'A good supply,' he said. 'You can't depend on local supplies. It's a remote place.'

'Yes. She knows how to look after herself.'

'Are you sure?'

'Yes.'

'You were saying the other day,' said the doctor, 'that you thought Alice might be negligent about her insulin.'

'No, I don't think so now. At least, I'll see that she isn't. If she's going to take too much of the stuff or too little she'll do it whether we go away or not.'

So she will, thought Dr Lyte, and he actively dispersed an uneasy idea that had begun to form in his mind.

'We'll take that chalet,' Patrick said as if his mind were on something else.

'Let's discuss the details, then, after the trial. You know, Patrick, I've got a roomful of patients waiting to see me.'

Patrick discerned a touch of defiance. He was aware that Dr Lyte possessed, in relationship to himself, a mixture of emotions, including various shades of fear, and so, to encourage them, Patrick said, 'I keep on getting through to that control who is so familiar with the unfortunate

occurrence in your past life. I can't help it. I keep on getting –
or rather he keeps on getting through to me. He keeps on
reminding me –'

'Are you short of ready cash?' said Lyte, and already he
had risen from his chair and was walking over to a cupboard
in which he kept a black tin cash-box.

'The Chief hasn't decided,' Inspector Fergusson said. 'It
depends on a number of factors to do with our evidence.'

'But when do you think this unfortunate occurrence will
be settled, Mr Fergusson?' Patrick trailed on.

'A month or two.'

'I have some little news for you,' Patrick said.

'Now, Patrick, I must warn you, we'll do our best but this
time we can't guarantee your protection. The Chief told me
to tell you. So news or no news . . .'

'I've been helpful to you,' Patrick said, shuffling his feet
bashfully and looking down at them. 'And I could go on
being helpful, Mr Fergusson.'

'What's the news, then?' Fergusson said.

'Well – after what you've just said, Mr Fergusson, I don't
really feel inclined –'

'I'm surprised at you, Patrick!' said Mr Fergusson. 'I
really am surprised.'

Patrick swallowed and looked frail and ashamed. His
knees closed in together and he grasped the seat of his chair
like a schoolboy.

Inspector Fergusson offered Patrick a cigarette. Patrick
took one; his hand was shaking.

'Well, Patrick,' said big strong Mr Fergusson, 'you hav-
en't ever let me down yet.'

'No,' Patrick said. 'I thought you were going to bear that
in mind with reference to Mrs Flower, the unfortunate . . .'

'I'm being straight with you,' said Fergusson, his square good shoulders blocking the lower half of the window-light, 'and I'm telling you that we can't promise to protect you this time. I can't promise anything. You've always had a square deal for any information you've passed on.'

'There's a lot that goes on in Spiritualism,' Patrick observed with timid sociability. 'From your point of view,' he said.

'Tell me, Patrick,' said big Mr Fergusson, 'did you never think of getting married? It might have made a man of you. It might have kept you straight.'

'I've always believed in free love. I've never believed in marriage,' Patrick murmured. 'Why should man-made laws . . .'

Fergusson tilted back his chair and heard him out: man-made laws, suppression of the individual, relics of the Victorian era . . . Patrick's thin voice died out '. . . and all repression of freedom of expression and self-fulfilment . . .' It sounded good-class reading-stuff.

'You've certainly got ideas of your own,' stated Fergusson, standing up. 'I'm a married man myself,' he stated. 'Well, Patrick, I've got work here in front of me to do. Keep in touch.'

Patrick stroked his hair. He stood up, opened his mouth to speak, and sat down again.

'I'd like to be as helpful as possib . . .' Patrick said.

'Well, tell me the tale and get it off your chest.' Inspector Fergusson drew a notepad towards him and poised his pen.

'There isn't actually a tale. Only a name. There was an unfortunate occurrence the other night –'

'What name?'

'Dr Mike Garland.'

'What about him?'

'He poses as a clairvoyant.'

'A fraud.'

'Oh, yes. He attempted to question me while I was under the other night. He's very friendly at the moment with Mrs Freda Flower.'

'Where does he live?'

'I'll find out, Mr Fergusson.'

'What does he do for a living?'

'I'll find out if you're interested, Mr Ferg . . .'

'Only for the records,' said the Inspector. 'What does he do for a living?'

'I'll find out, Mr Fergusson. I thought his name might be helpful,' Patrick said.

'Thanks.' Fergusson was scribbling his notes. 'Brief description, Patrick, please. You know what we want.'

Patrick cast his pale eyes to the ceiling. 'Nearly six foot, fairly stout, age about fifty, greying hair, fresh complexion, round face, blue eyes.'

'Right,' said Fergusson. 'What does he do for a living?'

'He goes about with a Father Socket.'

'Who's he – a clergyman?'

'I don't know, Mr Fergusson. I haven't met Father Socket.'

'Are you sure?' said Mr Fergusson.

'Yes, Mr Fergusson,' Patrick said. 'But I'll find out about him for you.'

'Right. What does Garland do for a living?'

'Mr Fergusson, I hope you can do something for me with regard to the unfortunate –'

'It's in the Chief's hands, Patrick. Defrauding a widow of her savings is a serious crime on the face of it.'

'I was tempted and fell,' Patrick said.

'So you said in your statement,' said Mr Fergusson, tapping the heap of files on his desk.

Patrick looked yearningly at the files as if wishing to retrieve the statement that lay in one of them.

'Mrs Flower still isn't prepared to give evidence, though?' Patrick said.

'She'll have to give evidence.'

'Satisfactory evidence?'

'We aren't sure of that, as yet.'

Dr Lyte sat in his consulting-room after the last of the evening surgery had departed and his receptionist had locked up and gone home. He was in a panic, and this caused him to lose his head so far as he was writing the letter at all; but it was the panic which, at the same time, prompted the lucidity of what he wrote.

Dear Patrick,

Please do not think I don't want you to borrow my chalet in Austria for your forthcoming holiday with Alice, but I feel bound to repeat that I think that it inadvisable, from the medical point of view, that Alice should be exposed to the certain inconvenience of this inaccessible place.

I just want to put a few of the drawbacks on record. In fact, I feel bound to do so.

You said previously that Alice was probably careless about her insulin injections. Although you told me today that your suspicions in this respect were unfounded, I feel bound to say that any carelessness in the administration of the injections (too much or too little) while Alice is in a condition of pregnancy, might prove fatal.

In fact, I should feel bound to obtain an undertaking from Alice on the whole question of her injections, before permitting the use of my chalet.

I should also wish to make certain that you took with you sufficient supplies of insulin, because the nearest town has no druggist.

Alice, I believe, would certainly die within a few days or even sooner, if deprived of her insulin. You know she has two sorts which she administers just before breakfast.

(a) Insulin soluble for immediate effect.

(b) Protamine zinc for more prolonged coverage throughout the evening and the following night. She needs 80 units.

But Alice understands all this. I understand she tests her urine for sugar and acetone first thing in the morning, and she can adjust the dosage accordingly. You must see that this is done.

The last time I saw Alice she told me she was still visiting the diabetic clinic every six months for routine assessment of progress.

If Alice were to take *too much* insulin and then, say, went for a hearty climb or long walk, she might easily die on the mountainside. Most . . .

Dr Lyte stopped writing. What am I saying, what am I doing? he thought. It came clearly to him, then, that he suspected Patrick of an intention to kill the woman, if you could call it an intention when a man could wander into a crime as if blown like a winged leaf.

What evidence have I got? Lyte thought. None at all. He wrote on, nevertheless.

. . . diabetics carry glucose or even lump sugar in their pockets to be taken at the first onset of the symptoms of hypoglycaemia – a dangerously low blood sugar-content, which the patient can check from the urine-test . . .

Dr Lyte put down his pen. If Patrick were to add a little sugar to her urine specimen so that she would take a hefty dose of insulin, and then to make her take a good walk without her little tin of glucose – Patrick might say to Alice 'Oh, you don't need your handbag' – she would probably pass out on the mountainside. Or suppose he substituted his own urine in the test-tube so that she would take an underdose? Or suppose he himself gave her the injections? Insulin was used in the concentration camps as a method of execution. Insulin, said Dr Lyte to himself, is a favoured mode of suicide amongst doctors and psychiatrists, it is rapid in effect. He looked round the room which he had furnished so carefully to match the red carpet and to be suitable to himself, and it seemed, in retrospect, that when he had chosen the furnishings of this consulting-room, he must have been pretending all the time that the world is not a miserable place. It was sometimes not easy to establish death by insulin. He wrote on:

Therefore I feel bound to warn you of the dangers . . .

Then he stopped. I feel bound. I feel bound to warn you. In what position, he thought, am I to issue warnings to Patrick Seton? It is he who comes with his unspoken warnings to me.

Dr Lyte read through his letter. Clearly if he had any suspicions of Patrick's intentions towards the girl, this letter betrayed it. Such a letter might – it certainly would – provoke a man like Patrick. One never knew where one was with a man like Patrick Seton. Patrick knew a lot about his early career. Patrick was dangerous.

And then, what evidence was there for his suspicions? Patrick had said, 'How long would it be before she died if she neglected to take insulin?' That was no ground for suspicion.

Lyte tore the letter up into little bits, placed the little bits, a few at a time, in his ash-tray and set fire to them with his cigarette lighter until they were all burned up.

Then he recalled that Patrick had said, 'She won't let me give her the injections. She won't let me see her taking the injections.'

Then he recalled quite clearly that Alice had told him, 'Patrick does the injection for me every day. Patrick is so good at it, I don't feel a thing.'

And then the whole problem was too much. The doctor was indignant at being subjected to it. The one incident in his career which he needed to hush up, Patrick had somehow got hold of. This one mistake had occurred twenty-seven years ago when he was still a single man, a different person altogether. You change when you marry and establish yourself, everything that happened previously had nothing to do with you any more. But Patrick sitting in his so-called trance had said plainly that night at the séance, 'There is a new visitor to our Circle, a man of the medical profession. Gloria wishes to tell him that she is watching over him, and remembers every detail of the incident in nineteen thirty-two about which there was a certain amount of mystery at the time. Gloria sends this message to the visitor in our midst who is a member of the medical profession: he should become a spiritualist and attend séances weekly. She is exhausted, now, and has no more to say for the present. Gloria wishes to say she is exhausted. The effort of speaking from the other side is exhausting. Gloria is tired. She feels weak. She is exhausted . . .'

Gloria had died as the result of an illegal operation in the summer of 1932. There had been inquiries. Nothing came of them. Cyril Lyte, newly qualified, was not even questioned, he was abroad during the questioning. He had been one of many lovers during the previous winter. 'I'm tired. I'm exhausted,' Gloria had said when the hasty operation was over. He had left her with the two middle-aged women, neither of whom knew his name. The two middle-aged women were lifting Gloria's feet and shoving pillows, cushions, blankets under them, for he had said she must not lose too much blood; be careful, keep her feet up, *up*. 'I'm exhausted': Gloria had died next day. He was abroad during the questioning. He became a Communist for a space, by way of atonement. Within a year he had mostly forgotten the incident and when he remembered it, assured himself he had done his best for her, and what proof had he that the child was his?

Patrick's message, twenty-seven years later in the dark séance room, nearly led him to a nervous breakdown. Whichever way he looked at it, whether Patrick had spoken in innocence or from hard knowledge, the message was frightening. 'Gloria sends this message . . . remembers every detail . . . is exhausted, is tired, is exhausted.' It sounds like hard knowledge, Lyte thought.

In the end, Cyril Lyte found it less frightening to believe that Patrick was a common blackmailer, and no medium between this world and the other. Patrick had called at the surgery the day after the séance. When the doctor had tormented himself for a week he gave way and challenged Patrick on the subject. At first he found Patrick vague as to the details of the message, but very soon asserting his power, and this comforted Dr Lyte. Patrick was no medium, he told himself. There was no danger from the dim spirit of Gloria, the only danger to be reckoned with was Patrick who was tangible and who must have known the truth all through the years that had passed since he himself had been a single man and so different. As he had sometimes, waking at nights in the weeks following Gloria's death, dreaded, he was convinced, now, she must have written a letter before she died, or told someone. Patrick had recognised him at the séance. And so Dr Lyte settled down to supply Patrick with cash, and sometimes to supply Patrick with drugs which assisted him in his trances – 'You're certainly a great medium!' Dr Lyte would permit himself to remark as he handed the drugs into Patrick's meek hands. He had heard somewhere that even genuine mediums used drugs; but the doctor strengthened his will against the idea and was determined not to believe it. 'You're certainly a great medium!' – and Patrick would sometimes wink with his eyelid which in any case drooped. Dr Lyte supplied cash and drugs. If he should seem to falter or keep Patrick too long in the waiting-room, Patrick would say, 'When are you coming to another séance? I may have another message for you.'

Cash, drugs, and now professional advice. How long would it take for Alice to die if she were deprived of insulin? How long if she took too much? She may be careless with her injections. She won't let me give them to her, she won't let me see her taking them.

'Patrick,' Alice had said, 'always gives me the injections himself, he's so good.'

'Your chalet in Austria,' Patrick had said. 'We shall be wanting it for a holiday after the unfortunate court case is settled. And I doubt if it will come to court, and if so it will only last half an hour; I'm certain of acquittal. How big is the chalet? How high up in the mountain? How far from the nearest town?'

Dr Lyte looked round his consulting-room and saw there was no escape. He tore a page from *The Times* and folded it into the shape of a cone. He scooped the black frail ash of the burnt letter into the cone, rolled it up tight. He decided to go to his club for a drink before going home, and as he left his surgery he dumped the paper containing the ashes of his letter to Patrick in the dustbin among the stained cotton wool and empty sample medicine packages of the day. He went to his club and was warmed by the immediate greetings of two of his oldest, most likeable friends.

The cheerful thought occurred to him that Patrick Seton might even be convicted of fraud if it came to a trial.

8

Ronald was changing to go to Isobel Billows's cocktail party when the housekeeper from the ground-floor flat came up and rang his bell.

'I let in your secretary this afternoon,' said the housekeeper. 'Just thought I'd let you know. I suppose it was all right.'

'What secretary?' Ronald said.

'The girl. The girl that came for your papers.'

'What girl?' Ronald said.

When the housekeeper, resentful and dispirited, had gone, Ronald looked mournfully and in vain in the drawer of his desk where he had left the letter which Patrick Seton was suspected of forging in the name of Mrs Freda Flower.

'She was, I should say, about twenty-eight, late twenties,' the housekeeper had said. 'A fair young woman, well, I should say near to fair-coloured hair, very pale. How was I to know? She said she was your secretary, and you wanted the papers in a hurry and you forgot to give her the key. I said, I suppose it's all right and I had my niece downstairs so I said, just let yourself out, you know the way. She looked all right. Remember there was that gentleman that came that morning when I was doing your cleaning, that came for your brief-case. Remember you sent him. How was I to know this wasn't another person that came to save you the trouble, on account of your difficulty?'

'I can't think who she can be,' Ronald said.

'Well, I don't take responsibility.'

'Well, no,' said Ronald, 'of course. Don't worry,' and as soon as she was gone he had opened the drawer, knowing the letter would not be there. He opened all the other drawers and looked through the tidy heaps of papers, but simply as a desperate act of diligence.

Ronald was filled with a great melancholy boredom from which he suffered periodically. It was not merely this affair which seemed to suffocate him, but the whole of life – people, small-time criminals, outraged housekeepers, and all his acquaintance from the beginning of time. When this overtook him Ronald was apt to refuse himself comfortable thoughts: on the contrary he used to tell himself: this sensation, this boredom and disgust, may later seem, in retrospect, to have been one of the happier moods of my life, so appalling may be the experiences to come. It is better, he thought, to be a pessimist in life, it makes life endurable. The slightest optimism invites disappointment.

Isobel Billows's house was in a newly smartened street at World's End which lies at that other end of Chelsea. The walls and ceiling of her drawing-room were papered in a dull red and black design. She was giving a cocktail party. Isobel had been three years divorced from her husband and always said to her new friends, 'I was the innocent party,' which they did not doubt, and the very statement of which proved, to some of her friends, that she was so in a sense.

Marlene Cooper's ear-rings swung with animation as she spoke seriously about spiritualism to Francis Eccles who had now got a job on the British Council. Tim, like a bright young manservant of good appearance, sinuously slid among the guests with a silver dish of shrimps; these shrimps were curled up as if in sleep on the top of small biscuits. Isobel Billows herself, large, soft-featured, middle-aged and handsome, had given up trying to introduce everyone and was surveying the standing crowd from a corner while Ewart Thornton talked to her, he having had three Martinis, in the course of which he had told Isobel that he had mounds of homework, that a grammar-school master had no status these days, that spiritualism was the meeting-ground between science and religion, and that he always bought his shirts and flannel trousers from Marks & Spencer's. It was at the point of his fourth Martini that Ewart's deepest pride emerged, to enchant Isobel and make her feel she was really in the swing by having him at her party. She listened to him wonderingly as he told her of the real miner's cottage of his birth in Carmarthenshire where his father still lived, and the real crofter's cottage in Perthshire where his grandparents had lived till late. 'Latham Street Council School; Traherne Grammar School; Sheffield Red Brick – only the brick isn't red,' boasted Ewart. 'Three shillings and sixpence a week pocket money all the while I was a student. From the age of ten to the age of thirteen I was employed by a fishmonger to deliver fish after school hours and on Saturday mornings. My earnings were four shillings a week which, with the similar earnings of my brothers went into the family funds. I was given a pair of stout boots every year at Easter. Most of my clothes were home made. We had outdoor sanitation which we shared with two other families –'

'Were you ever in trouble with the police?' Isobel said, looking round in the hope that someone was listening.

Ewart looked gravely at a vase of flowers, as if searching his memory, but obviously he had lost ground. At last he said, 'No, to be quite honest, no. But I recall being chased by a policeman. With some boys in some rough game. Yes, definitely chased down a back-street.' He took out his snuff-box and looked vexed. 'I was definitely underprivileged by birth,' he said, 'though not delinquent.'

Isobel said encouragingly, 'What was your accent like?'

'Southern Welsh. You can still hear the trace of it, mind you.'

'So you can,' said Isobel, who could not.

She loved the hairy tweed suit and his middle-aged large-ness, his drooping jowl. She wondered why he had never married. She thought, next, that in some way she ought to feel more grateful for her acquaintance with him than she was, and she wondered why this was so, and found the reason in his being now only a grammar-school master after such likely beginnings; a really dramatic rise in life would have been preferable. But still, he was the real thing, and a great asset to a party.

Ewart took a pinch of snuff and said, 'My father was a real miner, a real one. Half the men that claim to have come from mining stock, when you look into it, turn out to be the sons of mine-managers or clerks in the coal offices.'

Tim came round with his tray of shrimps.

'Have a shrimp,' he said.

Isobel said, 'Tim, stay and talk to Ewart. I must have a word with your aunt over there.'

Tim took her place with his dish beside Ewart and started eating the shrimps off the tops of the biscuits.

'I daresay,' Ewart Thornton said, in a definite man-to-man way, as to a senior prefect, 'your aunt has told you that she is trying to get together a number of people willing to give evidence as to the bona fides of Patrick Seton, in case he is brought to court by that absurd widow.'

'No, Marlene hasn't said anything,' Tim said, eating shrimps.

'She will no doubt be after you,' said Ewart. 'She will want you to give evidence in court for Patrick Seton. I advise you to do no such thing. I advise you rather to come forward as a witness for Mrs Freda Flower. Not that I care for Mrs Flower, a silly woman, but I feel Patrick Seton is an undesirable character who does no credit to the Circle. Of course he's a good medium but –'

'Have a shrimp,' Tim said, 'before I eat the lot.'

'No, thanks. He's a competent medium but there are many brilliant mediums by whom he could be replaced. He is not irreplaceable. Your aunt, I'm afraid, is not inclined to listen to reason. I feel we should all do our best to support Mrs Flower and –'

'Have a drink,' Tim said, lifting a small glass of liqueur off a tray as the caterers' man passed them by with his tray.

'Thanks. We should all support Mrs Flower and not Patrick Seton.'

'I shan't support either,' Tim said, cheerfully. 'I don't know a thing about either of them.'

'Oh, come!' Ewart said. 'You've attended the séances when both have been present.'

'Only as a novice,' Tim said. 'Really, I'd rather not be involved.'

'Be reasonable, my boy,' Ewart said.

Tim ate a shrimp. 'Am being reasonable,' he said, and licked his finger tips.

'It's a matter of principle,' Ewart said. 'Surely you've got principles.'

'None whatsoever when you actually look into it,' Tim said.

'I thought as much,' Ewart said. 'You fellows that have had every advantage in life –'

'Was brought up rough, me,' said Tim, eating two of the biscuits which were now deprived of shrimps.

'Tim!' shrieked Marlene from not very far away. 'Come over here a minute, I've been wanting to speak to you all evening.'

'Must see my aunt,' Tim said, and putting down the dish, took off his glasses, wiped them, put them on, took up a bowl of olives, and joined Marlene.

A serving table had been set up for the caterers in front of the window; it was spread with a white cloth and was laid out with bottles and glittering glasses. Ronald Bridges and Martin Bowles stood out of the way between a corner of this table and the wall.

'I could go to Switzerland for Christmas,' Martin said, 'if I could get in one small fraction of the money that's owing to me. Dozens of briefs but no pay. Solicitors are crooks, they won't part with money.'

'What do you look like in your wig?' Ronald said.

'Quite nice.'

Ronald thought this probably true, for Martin was going bald and the impression of an increasingly high forehead had, over the past five years, thrown his good features out of balance.

Martin said, 'I've been invited to Switzerland for Christmas with a party. All married couples except for me, if I go. It makes one feel young being with married couples.'

'Or insignificant,' Ronald said.

'Yes, or insignificant. I always feel a bit *less* than a married man. Why is that, do you think? Is it because they've got more money than us?'

'No, married men mostly have less. Obviously.'

'Well, they seem to have more money, in a queer sort of way, to be economically stronger than single chaps.'

'It's an illusion. The truth is, a married man is psychologically stronger.'

'Yes, it's psychological. They make one feel young, even men one was at school with. How are you getting on with that forged letter in the Seton case?'

'It's a question of responsibility, I think – if they have kids,' Ronald said, to keep Martin off the subject of the letter.

But, 'How's the forgery work?' Martin said.

'The letter has been stolen from my flat,' Ronald said, 'I'm sorry to say.'

'Come along,' said Isobel Billows, 'you bachelors in a huddle, over there.' She slid her white arm through Martin's and pressed him into a group which included Marlene with her swinging ear-rings, Tim with his bowl of olives, a girl wearing a pink dress, and Francis Eccles, who, in the confidence of his new job on the British Council, was exuberantly philosophising to the girl and Marlene.

'You see,' he was saying, 'we are all fundamentally looking at each other and talking across the street from windows of different buildings which look similar from the outside. You don't know what my building is like inside and I don't know what yours is like. You probably think my house is comfortably furnished with its music-room and libraries, like yours. But it isn't. My house is a laboratory with test-tubes, capillaries, and – what do you call them? – bunsen burners. My house contains a hospital ward, my house –'

'Do you live in a very splendid house?' Martin said to the girl, for his ears had selected from Eccie's speech only the bit about the music-room and libraries.

The girl was mightily irritated. 'Eccie is talking in metaphor,' she said. 'I live in a bedsitter.'

'I live in a basement flat,' said Eccie, still dazed from his elaboration. He looked from one to the other.

'Oh, I see,' Martin said. 'Well, you see, I've only got a crude legal mind. I –'

'Carry on,' said the girl to Eccie.

Isobel slid her white plump arm through the dark blue of Eccie's sleeve. 'Eccie, I want you,' she said, and bore him off somewhere else.

Martin said to the girl, 'I'm afraid I interrupted . . .' but he was now looking for Ronald, anxious to know whether Ronald could possibly have been serious when he said the letter had been stolen, and if so, to tell Ronald how furious he was.

He smiled formally to the girl and withdrew, first backward a few steps, then sideways, then right about, so that he could join Ronald where he was standing with Marlene Cooper and Tim.

'– must do something to justify your existence,' Marlene was saying to Tim, 'and now is the chance to show your mettle.'

'Never did have any mettle,' Tim said. 'Want an olive, Ronald?'

Ronald looked into his glass at the tiny drop of cocktail left at the bottom of it.

'Have an olive, Martin,' Tim said.

'What we want to do,' Marlene said, 'is to present a body of witnesses to the court. We can all testify in our own words. You, Tim, you've seen Patrick and you've heard him. You know he's a real medium, that's all you've got to say. There's no commitment attached. But we must give Patrick a character. He's being positively framed by Freda Flower and that vile lover of hers. There may be no case, but as I say, on the other hand, there may be a case.'

Tim said, 'Martin Bowles here is the prosecuting counsel in the case, Marlene.'

Marlene tilted her face to Martin's. 'Are you?' she said, 'Oh, are you?'

'Look,' said Martin, 'I really can't discuss –'

'I should think you couldn't,' Marlene said. 'You wouldn't have a leg to stand on. Nor will you have if it comes to court, let me tell you that. We are all behind Patrick. I'm behind him. Tim's behind –'

'I'd rather not be involved,' Tim said.

'But you are involved,' said his aunt.

'How did it happen?' Martin said as he drove Ronald home.

'A woman came to the house this morning and pretended to be my secretary. The housekeeper let her in. The letter was gone when I looked for it. I think I know who's got it.'

'Who?'

'Patrick Seton's girl-friend. It wasn't she who actually came to the flat, but I think Matthew Finch knows the girl.'

'Who? Which girl?' Martin inquired in his legal voice. 'You don't make it clear which is which.'

'I'll try and get the letter back.'

'We'd better have the police informed right away,' Martin said.

'All right,' Ronald said.

'Well, I know it won't do your reputation much good,' Martin said, 'losing an important document like that. But I don't suppose you depend much on your forgery detection work, do you?'

'I like it,' Ronald said.

'Do you think you *can* get it back?'

'I don't know,' Ronald said, deliberately, as one refusing to be a mouse even while the claws were upon him.

'I'm not trying to make things difficult,' Martin said, 'but . . .'

'But what?'

'Well, you say you can't work from the photostats. I daresay the photostats would be taken as some sort of evidence. But you can't give any evidence of forgery from a photostat, can you?'

'Not really. I've got to test the ink and study the writing on the folds in the paper. That sort of thing.'

'You've got us in a pickle,' Martin said.

'Matthew Finch knows the girl. I'll see if he can do something about it.'

'He was at the party tonight, wasn't he?'

'Yes.'

'Did you speak to him about this?'

'Yes.'

'You told him what had happened?'

'Yes. I made the mistake of telling him about the letter in the first place. Then he informed the girl. He thinks the girl who got into my rooms must be the girl he knows who works with Patrick Seton's girl in a coffee-bar. This girl is the friend of the other girl, and –'

'Who? Which girl is which? What are their names?'

'Alice and Elsie,' Ronald said. 'I think we'd better get the police to handle it, as you suggested.'

Martin had stopped for the traffic of South Kensington. He sat back from the wheel and pondered. Then, as he started up the car again, he said, 'Let's leave it that you get the letter back by tomorrow night or we'll get the police to find it. If it hasn't been destroyed by then.'

'It has probably been destroyed by now,' Ronald said in a louder voice than usual. 'And actually I think we must inform the police in any case.'

'They might ask you awkward questions,' Martin said.

'How do you mean?'

'Well, it's obvious you've been careless.'

'That can't be helped now.'

His melancholy and boredom returned with such force when he was alone again in his flat that he recited to himself as an exercise against it, a passage from the Epistle to the Philippians, which was at present meaningless to his numb mind, in the sense that a coat of paint is meaningless to a window-frame, and yet both colours and preserves it: 'All that rings true, all that commands reverence, and all that makes for right; all that is pure, all that is lovely, all that is gracious in the telling; virtue and merit, wherever virtue and merit are found – let this be the argument of your thoughts.'

For Ronald was suddenly obsessed by the party, and by the figures who had moved under Isobel's chandelier, and who, in Ronald's present mind, seemed to gesticulate like automatic animals; they had made sociable noises which struck him as hysterical. Isobel's party stormed upon him like a play in which the actors had begun to jump off the stage, so that he was no longer simply the witness of a comfortable satire, but was suddenly surrounded by a company of ridiculous demons.

This passage from Philippians was a mental, not a spiritual exercise; a mere charm to ward off the disgust, despair, and brain-burning.

This was the beginning of November. It is the month, Ronald told himself in passing, when the dead rise up and come piling upon you to warm themselves. One is affected as if by a depressive drug, one shivers. It is only the time of year, that's the trouble.

With desperate method he began to abstract his acquaintance, in his mind's eye, from the party, and examined them deliberately to see the worst he could find in them. One must define, he thought: that is essential.

Isobel Billows, with her hungry lusts, her generosity wherever she thought generosity was a good investment, smiled up at him in the glaring eye of his mind.

'What's wrong with me?' she said.

'Nothing,' he said, 'but yourself.'

'Oh, Ronald, you always see the worst side of everything, there's a diabolical side to your nature.'

'What do you mean, diabolical?'

'Well, possessed by a devil, that's the reason for your epilepsy.'

'Adulterous bitch.'

'Oh, Ronald, you don't know how basely men treat me. Men have always treated me very badly.'

'A woman of your class shouldn't talk like that.'

'But they come and sponge on me, Ronald, and then they go away and say, "Oh, her. You don't want to have anything to do with her. Don't listen to her."'

Martin Bowles was her lover, and was also her financial adviser, and, in his legal capacity, handled her property. '. . . and you see,' Martin said – he was sitting at his desk in chambers, in the bright eye of Ronald's imagination, leaning one hand on his high bald forehead – 'I haven't much freedom, what with my old ma and the housekeeper, and then there's Isobel, I'm fairly tied to Isobel.'

'Will you marry Isobel?'

'No, oh no. It's a question of business interests.'

'Have you misappropriated Isobel's money?'

'No, oh no. I'm on the right side of the law.'

'Yes, the right side of the law.'

'Don't be vulgar, Ronald.'

'It was you who employed the phrase.'

'Isobel's very well off although she pretends to be poor. She doesn't live up to her money, you know.'

'Fraudulent conversion, it's revolting.'

'Not at all. There's nothing fraudulent about it, I'm perfectly safe in the law. There's a large sum involved, Ronald, but I'm perfectly safe.'

'Forty thousand?'

'How do you come to know all this, Ronald?'

'From piecing together what I hear and see in one direction and another.'

'My old ma's a tyrant, quite a drag upon my life.'

'You shouldn't be living with your mother, at your age. It makes a mess of a man. It makes for a mean spirit, living with mama after the age of thirty.'

'You know, Ronald, you should have been more careful with that letter.'

'Yes.'

'And now you've gone and lost it. Shall we inform the police? Shall we ruin your little reputation as a reliable expert? You shouldn't have talked.'

'Please yourself. I don't particularly want to get the letter back. Why should I hound Patrick Seton? He has offended in the same way as you, on a smaller scale than you, but less cleverly than you.'

'This is rather absurd,' said Martin Bowles in the mind's ear of Ronald. 'I won't have it.'

'I won't have it,' Marlene Cooper said, brushing her earrings past Ronald's mouth as if he were not there. 'I won't have Tim remaining on friendly terms with that revolting bald barrister.'

'I like Martin Bowles,' Tim said.

'If Patrick's case comes to court your friend will be prosecuting counsel.'

'Someone's got to be prosecuting counsel,' Tim said.

'Well, you must give up your association with him.'

'I haven't got any particular association with him. Martin is just a friend,' Tim said.

'But, Tim, dear, I saw you with him at Isobel's party, laughing away as if nothing had happened. Do you realise that when you give evidence for Patrick, the man is sure to cross-examine you?'

'I don't want to be involved,' Tim said. 'I'm not giving any evidence. We treat your conspiracy as a joke.'

'You are weak,' Marlene said, 'like your father and his father before him.'

And so he is, Ronald thought, viciously, for he was especially fond of Tim. He doesn't want to be involved at all; except, of course, with Hildegarde.

'I did everything for Ronald that a woman possibly could do,' Hildegarde said. 'I washed his shirts, mended his clothes, I bought the theatre tickets, and I set the alarm clock for him. I made every possible allowance for his disability. I even helped him in his job. I made a study of handwriting and even ancient manuscripts. What more could I have done?'

'Nothing at all,' said Tim in the bemused ear of Ronald's imagination, as he sat there in his flat in the small hours of the morning. 'Nothing at all,' said Tim. 'Move over, darling, and don't kick.'

'It makes me kick,' Hildegarde said, 'to think of Ronald. If only he had given me some excuse when he broke with me . . .'

'Shut up about Ronald,' Tim said. 'It's jolly off-putting.'

'Does he know about us?' Hildegarde said.

'No, of course not.'

'He mustn't know about us,' she said. 'It would upset him and he would never forgive you. I don't want to break up your friendship with Ronald.'

'You're sweet,' Tim said, snuggling down. 'Lovely to think tomorrow's Sunday,' he said, 'and a long lie in.'

'Let me put your pillow straight, sweet boy,' said Hildegarde. 'You are all crumpled up.'

Matthew had told Ronald: 'I saw Hildegarde Krall the other evening in the Pandaemonium Club at Hampstead. She was wearing jeans, looked very nice.'

'Was she alone?'

'Yes, alone.'

'Did you speak to her?'

'Only briefly. She left early. Walter Prett was with me. She left when he started making a nuisance of himself and insulted Francis Eccles.'

Tim, Hildegarde, Matthew Finch, Francis Eccles, Walter Prett. Ronald got through the list by half past three in the morning. Who are they, he thought, in any case, to me? Why be oppressed by a great disgust? 'We must go to court,' Ewart Thornton says, 'we must oppose Patrick Seton at all costs. Let us give evidence for a Mrs Freda Flower, about whose wrongs none of us cares.' But why does he induce in me a condition near to madness?

Because one is formed in that way, and at times of utter disenchantment no distraction whatsoever avails, even the small advertisements in the newspapers are vile, in the same way that I, in my epilepsy, am repulsive. He recited over to himself the passage from Philippians: '. . . all that is gracious in the telling; virtue and merit, wherever virtue and merit are found – let this be the argument of your thoughts.' By a violent wrench of the mind Ronald was capable of applying this exhortation in a feelingless way, to the company of demons which had been passing through his thoughts. He forced upon their characters what attributes of vulnerable grace he could bring to mind. He felt sick. Isobel is brave simply to go on breathing; another woman might have committed suicide ten years ago; she knows how to decorate her house and how to dress. Marlene is handsome, Tim is lovable, Ewart Thornton is intelligent, has gone far in the world, considering his initial disadvantages, and moreover he is a schoolmaster, and, moreover, one who respects his career and so finds difficulty in the practice of it. Martin Bowles is considerate to his mother. Matthew Finch is afflicted by sex and is blessed with a simple love of the old laws. Walter Prett is beset by neglect and foolish fantasies and he loves art and is honest in his profession. Hildegarde has a tremendous character. Eccie has a job on the British Council . . .

By four o'clock he was in bed. At five o'clock he rose and vomited. Next morning he had an epileptic seizure lasting half an hour; it was a type of fit in which his drugs were useless. This often happened to Ronald after he had made some effort of will towards graciousness, as if a devil in his body was taking its revenge.

He resolved to go to Confession, less to rid himself of the past night's thoughts – since his priest made a distinction between sins of thought and these convulsive dances and dialogues of the mind – than to receive, in absolution, a friendly gesture of recognition from the maker of heaven and earth, vigilant manipulator of the Falling Sickness.

9

'I can't help feeling sorry for little Patrick Seton,' said Matthew Finch. 'That widow and her friends seem to be ganging up on him in a most unpleasant way.'

'I'm sorry for him too, in a way,' Ronald said.

'He's half Irish,' said Matthew.

'The thing is: about this letter.'

'It sounds like Alice's friend, Elsie,' Matthew said. 'I'll see Elsie this afternoon.'

'It may be destroyed by now.'

'I doubt that,' Matthew said. 'Alice is a sentimental girl.'

'It's hardly a sentimental letter.'

'What does it say?'

'Get the letter back and you'll find out.'

'I know I'm to blame for this, I shouldn't have told Alice you had it,' Matthew said. 'I'm a foolish fellow, you know.'

'Where will you see Elsie?'

'I'll go round to the coffee-bar. She's always on duty on Saturday afternoons. I've got to see my cousin later, but –'

Ronald's telephone rang. Martin Bowles said, 'I say, Ronald. I thought it best to have Fergusson told that the letter had been stolen. I hope you –'

'Who's Fergusson?' Ronald said.

'The detective-inspector who keeps his eye on Patrick Seton. He says he'll be seeing Seton about it and doesn't seem to be worried about getting it back, that is, if Seton has it. I hope you agree that was the best course. If it comes out in court –'

'Yes, it was quite the most sensible thing to do,' Ronald said. 'I'm much relieved.'

'Sure you don't mind? If it comes out in court that you –'

'No, I don't mind a bit. In fact I'm glad. I ought to have done something of the kind straight away. The police should be informed of a theft of this kind. Only, in these particular circumstances, I doubt if Seton actually has the letter. His girl's got it, we think.'

'Who's *we?*'

'I've just been discussing it with Matthew Finch. As you know, he's a friend of the two girls in question.'

'*Which* two girls?'

'Seton's girl and the other girl, her friend, the one we think stole the letter for Seton's girl.'

'I really can't make out who these girls are, Ronald. What has Matthew Finch to do with this?'

'Well, you know I was indiscreet enough in the first place to tell him I was working on the letter. And he was indiscreet enough to tell Elsie, and –'

'Who's Elsie?'

'She's the other girl who's a friend of Seton's girl. I told you –'

'Yes, but I didn't make notes. Look, Ronald, you can't conduct a case like this.'

'I'm not conducting the case.'

'If it comes out in court that you've committed these indiscretions, you won't blame me, will you?'

'No,' Ronald said.

'I expect Fergusson will want to see you,' Martin said. 'A nice chap. Straight with you if you're straight with him.'

'What the hell are you talking about?'

'Now, Ronald, don't be –'

Ronald hung up. 'Some detective-inspector is going to find the letter,' he said. 'So let's forget it.'

'I've got you into trouble,' Matthew said. 'My sister thought probably this would happen when I told her about the letter –'

'Where are you lunching? I haven't done my shopping yet, what with one thing and another.'

'I've got you into trouble with my talk,' Matthew said. 'Would you like me to see Elsie in any case? It wouldn't do any harm, would it?'

'You'd better see Elsie,' Ronald said. 'Because I doubt if the detective-inspector will find the letter.'

'You said just now he was going to find it.'

'I know I did,' said Ronald. 'And I'll end up in the bin, I daresay. Come on, let's go out.'

The telephone rang again just as they were leaving. Ronald returned to answer it.

'Oh, Ronald,' said Martin.

'Yes.'

'Are you all right?'

'Yes.'

'Look, Ronald, I don't want you to misunderstand me. It's just that I'm bound by certain rules, you know. One has to observe certain –'

'Of course,' Ronald said. 'Obviously.'

'You'll help Fergusson all you can? I've told him you will.'

'Of course. But look, I don't really think Patrick Seton has the letter. I think it's something the girls have cooked up.'

'Which girls?'

'Polly and Molly,' Ronald said.

'Who?'

'Cassandra and Clytemnestra,' Ronald said.

'Look, Ronald. This is awkward for me. You know me, you like me, don't you?'

Here it comes, Ronald thought.

'Of course,' he said.

'Well, put yourself in my place. I've got my old ma on my hands. She's going blind. Can't see the television. The housekeeper's going blind. They fight like cat and dog, they were pulling each other's hair the other day. Can't get a new housekeeper, and anyway my old ma won't have anyone new. The housekeeper –'

'Hold on a minute,' Ronald said, and placing his hand over the receiver, murmured to Matthew, who was hovering at the door, to make himself comfortable on the sofa for at least five minutes. Have a drink. Cigarette – 'Yes, hallo,' he said, returning to Martin on the telephone.

'The housekeeper,' Martin said, 'was my old nurse and my old ma won't get rid of her, she's got nowhere to go and we can't afford a pension. Then I do the shopping for the weekend. Not on weekdays, I draw the line there. Then Isobel's affairs take a bit of looking after, you know. I give her my professional services, she doesn't realise what I save her. Still, Isobel's a good sort, as you know, and very attractive. I say, Ronald, would you say Isobel was an attractive woman?'

'Oh yes,' Ronald said.

'Doesn't show her years,' Martin said. 'Of course she's got the money and the leisure. She depends on me a lot, you know. She's had a lot of bad luck with men, and I think she appreciates me in a way. Wouldn't you think so?'

'Oh, I think she does.'

'Look, Ronald, come along to my club for lunch. You see –'

'Sorry, I'm not free.'

'You see, there's a personal problem I'd like to consult you about. Could you make it 1.30?'

'Sorry, really I'm not free.'

'I can't make it tomorrow,' Martin said, 'because the housekeeper goes off in the afternoon and I've promised to read *Jane Eyre* to my old ma. She says she was forbidden *Jane Eyre* as a girl. I don't see why, do you? You see, she can't see well and the television isn't much use to her. Then tomorrow night I've simply got to collect Isobel off a train. When can we meet?'

'I'll come and see you in your chambers one day next week. I've got to go now, Martin.'

'I'll ring you on Monday, then. Sure you're not worried about Fergusson looking into this theft?'

'No, but I doubt –'

'It's breaking and entering, and stealing, to be precise. They'll be sending a couple of fellows round to ask questions.'

'I see.'

'You should have been more careful, Ronald. You can't conduct a case . . .'

When they were seated in the pub Ronald said, 'You can tell Elsie that the cops will be looking for her.'

'Now, she's a nice poor girl,' Matthew said.

'Well, give the poor girl a fright. Tell her the cops will be after her finger-prints or something.'

Elsie Forrest climbed the stairs to an attic flat in Shepherd's Bush, and pressed the bell on a door marked 'The Rev. Father T.W. Socket, M.A.' The door was opened by Mike Garland, wearing a green-and-white-striped dressing-gown over his suit, and looking, with his pink cheeks, like a lump of sticky bright confectionery. He blocked the door.

'Father Socket is expecting me,' Elsie said, 'to do some typing.'

'Oh, I don't know whether it's convenient, now. But come in.'

'I like that!' Elsie said as she walked into the large front sitting-room. 'I've taken the afternoon off from the coffee-bar especially to help Father Socket. So I should hope it is convenient.'

'I daresay it will be,' Mike Garland said. 'Take a seat.'

Elsie was irritated when he said 'Take a seat', for on all the chairs in the room were cushions that she herself had made for Father Socket, and this obviously gave her rights which rose above formalities. She had not expected to see this strange man with his peculiar garb in Father Socket's flat. She usually walked straight into the kitchen and put the kettle on the gas.

Elsie heard voices from Father Socket's bedroom. She wondered if the Master was ill, but did not like to investigate in the presence of the stranger.

The room was hung with Chinese scrolls which reached to the low bookcases. These contained the books of which Elsie had made a list, and for each of which, under the Master's instructions, she had made an index card. The Master was learned. He was a real priest, he told her, ordained by no man-made bishop but by Fire and the Holy Ghost; and a range of brightly woven vestments was hung in a cupboard in his bedroom to prove it.

Elsie had never before been to Father Socket's on a Saturday afternoon. Thursday afternoon was her usual time, and it was then she typed his manuscripts, over and over again – for he was always revising them, never satisfied, like the true Master of writing that he was.

'He ought to pay you for all that work,' Alice had said.

But to Elsie it was a labour of love typing out his papers on the subjects of the Cabbala, Theosophy, Witchcraft, Spiritualism, and Bacon wrote Shakespeare, besides many other topics.

'It's a labour of love,' Elsie said to Alice. After all, Alice had Patrick; and it was nice for a girl to have someone on the spiritual side of life. Men like Father Socket lifted one up whereas young men so often pulled one down.

'You've got queer tastes,' Alice had said the day before, sitting in the window with Elsie, at dusk.

'There isn't any sex between Father Socket and me,' Elsie said.

'That's a detail,' Alice said.

'He smells of a perfume, like musk or incense,' Elsie said.

'You always smell things,' Alice said.

'Patrick smells of goat, like a real bachelor.'

'Go on with you. Patrick's a man of the world. He's been married.'

'That boy Matthew Finch who'd been eating onions that time. . . . It's terrible, the smell of onions. Because I used to sleep beside my uncle, we were all in the one room, in Sheffield where I was born. My uncle was the only one of them that didn't drink, drink, drink. So I went with Matthew and yet afterwards I didn't like myself for it. It's all explained in psychology.'

'Disgusting,' Alice whispered. 'Onions.'

They laughed as they sat in the darkening room, in a down-scale trill, one following the other.

'It wasn't funny at the time,' Elsie whispered. 'He didn't go right on to the end in case I got a baby, I suppose. That's what makes me really upset; when they go so far and no farther.'

'You don't want a baby without a man to marry you,' Alice said.

'It makes you feel there's not much of a man in them when they only go so far.'

'If Patrick wasn't the man he is,' Alice said, 'he wouldn't be much of a *man*.'

'I always said he wasn't much of a man to look at. Thin about the thighs. You can't disguise it.'

'But he's so different to other men. Patrick treats you with a difference.'

'Oh yes, he's all talk. Still, talk makes a difference. Father Socket talks beautifully. That's what gets me, Alice. The boys are after one thing and one thing only, but a man who's a bit older and can talk, and if he's got a beautiful voice . . .'

They sat hand-in-hand on the window seat and looked down on the lights of long Ebury Street.

'Yes,' Alice said, 'I suppose the main thing about Patrick is the talk.'

'Do you think he's going to marry you?'

'Of course. As soon as the divorce comes through.'

'I can't believe in that divorce, you know.'

'What d'you mean?'

'Are you sure he's got a wife?'

'He says so.'

'You don't look well, Alice.'

'No, it's difficult for a diabetic in pregnancy. I've got a craving for parsnips, too. I'd like a whole plate of parsnips.'

'Aren't you afraid of Patrick?'

'Afraid? What is there to be afraid of?'

'Well, nothing that you know about. It's all those things you don't know about him. They say, about his forgeries –'

'Yes,' said Alice's voice in the dark, 'I'm afraid of the things I don't know. I don't want to know.'

'I feel the same,' Elsie said as she sat, almost invisible, 'about the Master.'

'You're not tied to him,' Alice said, 'like I am to Patrick.'

'But there's a bond between the Master and me.'

'He's got a hold on you,' Alice said. 'Shall we put the light on?'

'Not yet,' Elsie said. 'I go on Thursdays and I do a bit of typing and then I stop. And he talks and reads poetry. Then I do a bit more typing. Then he reads me a bit of what he's just written of his spiritual autobiography.'

'Patrick recites poetry,' Alice said.

'Father Socket's voice is beautiful. He was brought up in a big rectory and he broke away from the Church of England. It's true you don't have to go to church to believe in God. I agree with that. Father Socket knows psychology.'

'Put on the light,' Alice said, and, when Elsie had switched on the light she jumped from her seat, and now they spoke aloud.

'He ought to pay you for all that work. We're both of us far too soft,' Alice said.

'It's a labour of love,' Elsie said. 'I'm going to his flat tomorrow afternoon. He asked me specially to come, so I've put off the coffee-bar.'

'That's money down the drain,' Alice said. 'At least Patrick gives me a bit of money.'

'So he ought, in your condition. But where does he get the money?'

'I don't know,' Alice said.

'He's hiding something from you,' Elsie said.

'There's always something hidden,' Alice said, in such a way that Elsie was startled, uncertain whether Alice knew about the letter concealed in her handbag. She looked at Alice, to make sure, but Alice was holding her stomach and pulling her face with indigestion.

The gilt sunlight which sometimes happens in November poured through the window of Father Socket's flat on Saturday afternoon. Elsie waited, withering, in the sitting-room, listening to the voices coming now from the spare bedroom where apparently the stranger was lodged. Father Socket must have put him up for the night, and here he was staying on to the afternoon and keeping him back from his work.

Then she knew, of course, with a kind of exasperation, that the stranger was one of the Master's friends, and that they were all perverts, and she had really known it all along.

The voices rose to the pitch of a quarrel of which Elsie could not make out all the words. She went and stood by the door, the better to hear. '. . . where to draw the line, Mike . . . appearance's sake . . . the girl is . . .' and then a door closed, muting the voices to a querulous rise and fall. This filled her with irritation and impatience. She was inclined to leave the flat with a banging of doors, or at least to bang one door as a token. But then she thought of the letter in her handbag, and what palpitations she had gone through to obtain it, what risks taken. She had looked forward all the previous day and part of the night to her triumphant casual opening of her handbag and the producing of the letter before the aston-ished eyes of the Master.

Last week he had said, 'Do you know the man well?'

'I've seen him in the coffee-bar. He's quite nice. He works in a handwriting museum.'

'Ah yes,' said Father Socket, 'in the City.'

'He isn't very strong. He takes fits. He's quite nice-look-ing, but a bit odd, you know, fussy in his ways. You can tell from the way they put their sugar in the coffee, and stir it, and place the spoon back in the saucer. And his paper neatly folded with his umbrella and all that. A confirmed bachelor. Not that I mean anything by that. He's a friend of a friend of mine, an Irish fellow called Matthew Finch.'

'And this man's name?'

'Ronald somebody. Well, Matthew was in the Oriflamme with him the other night, and talking to Alice. He was talking about this letter that Patrick Seton wrote. Ronald is to test it for forgery. The police gave it to him and –'

'Not the police, surely. It would be in the hands of the police solicitor. Unless the case is in abeyance, in which case, possibly the police . . .'

'One or the other. So Ronald's got this letter that Patrick forged. Alice was upset and I saw her next day. She wants to try to get the letter back through Matthew. Matthew is keen on Alice.'

Father Socket had thought this unwise. So, when she came to talk it over with him, had Elsie.

'Alice may even go a long way with Matthew,' she said, 'to get that letter.'

'Do you know where this Ronald lives?' Father Socket had said.

'I could find out.'

'I should like to have a look at that letter myself,' he said.

'Would you?' she said.

Here, then, she was with the letter in her handbag, and Father Socket quarrelling in the spare bedroom with the big man in the green-and-white-striped dressing-gown, and she sitting waiting like a fool, having lost an afternoon's work at the coffee-bar.

She opened the door of the sitting-room and bumped into Father Socket just as he was about to enter. His small face looked puffy and red. He looked suspicious at finding her so near to the door and seemed convinced she had been listening to the quarrel.

'I've been waiting a long time, Father,' she said.

'Oh, poor creature! Oh, poor creature! I am so very sorry. Come and sit down.'

He wore his best cassock and his broad hips swung under it as he put to rights a deep pink chrysanthemum which had fallen from its vase.

He turned and jerked his thumb over his shoulder to indicate the stranger in the other room. The gesture startled Elsie, for she had never seen the Master anything but utterly dignified. He mouthed and breathed a message to her, contorting his face as if she were a lip-reader. 'My – friend's – up – set. Won't – remove – dressing-gown.'

'Who is he, Father?' Elsie said in a normal voice.

He hunched his shoulders and flapped his hands to hush her.

She whispered, 'Who is he?'

The Master jerked his thumb once more over his shoulder and was about to convey a reply when Mike Garland walked in. He still wore his bright dressing-gown.

'Ah, Mike,' said Father Socket, pulling himself straight, 'come and meet my amanuensis Miss Elsie Forrest. Dr Garland, Miss Forrest.'

'We've already met, at the door,' Elsie said.

'How do you do,' Mike said. He sat down defiantly.

'Something unforeseen has arisen,' Father Socket said to Elsie, 'and so I'm afraid I've brought you here on a wild-goose chase, my dear, this afternoon. However, I will make some tea and I must read you my new translation of Horace. Where did I put it?'

'I'll make tea,' Elsie said.

'I shall prepare some tea,' Mike said. Elsie noticed as he left the room that he wore lipstick.

'Have you received any information from young Matthew?' Father Socket said to her softly when Mike had left the room.

'Matthew?'

'Or young Ronald? – The letter I mean. I don't of course want Mike to know anything about this. – But you haven't had time to investigate the possibility of obtaining it . . .'

Elsie clutched her handbag, indignant and very put out, especially by Mike's lipstick. 'No, I haven't any news,' she said. 'I expect the letter is locked away somewhere safely.'

Father Socket sighed and looked at the carpet.

'Poor Patrick Seton!' he said. 'He does need taking care of. I feel if I could get matters in hand I could do something for Patrick.'

'He isn't any good to Alice. I don't mind if he gets sent for trial!'

'Hush,' said Father Socket, looking at the door.

'I'd like to see Alice rid of him,' she said, sitting down in a hard high chair, 'good medium though he is, he's –'

'Ah,' said Father Socket, 'Patrick has many enemies.' Again he jerked his thumb over his shoulder and mouthed, 'He's – one of – them.' He pulled his spine straight in his chair and said, 'But I am not an enemy. What Patrick needs is *control*. Someone ought to control him. Find out about that letter, my dear, find out. If once we know where it is – where young Ronald keeps it, I daresay we should be able to obtain it. I am thinking in dear Patrick's best interests. I have no wish to impede the course of the law of the kingdom, but the laws of the spirit come first, we ought to serve God rather than man, we must – Ah – tea!' He rose to admit the tinkling tea-tray with Mike rosily proceeding behind it.

During tea, Elsie ate a slice of walnut cake very quickly because she was so very upset inside at the sight of Mike in his highly sexual attire. She clutched her handbag all the closer, and was damned if she would part with the letter now that Father Socket had let her down so badly. Be damned to his paternal solicitude for dear Patrick. She should have known before, indeed she had really, inside, known all along that the Master was homosexual as Alice had said. She could have put up with it, even preferred it, if he had no sex at all, was above sex, but if there was one thing she detested . . .

Father Socket, meanwhile, said, 'Let me read you my little translation of the much-translated Horace, one, nine. Mine pays special attention to alliterative quantities . . .'

The impudence of it, Elsie thought, talking round me all these months, and reading his poetry, and there I've been typing out his papers, page after page, Thursday after Thursday . . .

'Mount Soracte's dazzling snow,' boomed Father Socket in his reading voice, 'piling upon the branches . . .'

'Stroking my hair and saying, "There, my child," week after week, and putting on,' thought Elsie, 'the holiness and spiritual life and all that.'

'So, Thaliarch . . .' said Father Socket.

Elsie swallowed the last of her cake and washed it down with the last of her tea. She gathered together her gloves and clutched her handbag. Father Socket, without interrupting his reading, moved one hand to bid her sit still. In her distress she had swallowed a whole walnut off the top of the cake, and it went down in a lump, causing her face to go red. Mike Garland looked at her and smiled with one half of his mouth.

Father Socket read on,

> 'All else trust to the gods by whose command
>   Contending winds and seething seas desist,
>   Until the sacred cypress-tree
>   And ancient ash no longer quake.'

Father Socket interrupted himself to tap the paper with his forefinger. 'Now the cypress tree *was* sacred,' he said, 'and although Horace . . .'

Elsie rose and sped to the door.

'*El*sie!' said Father Socket, in a kind of wail, letting his paper drop.

'Elsie!' he called after her as she opened the outside door and ran down the stairs. 'What's wrong with the girl? – Elsie, this is quite a proper decent poem, I assure you. It is Horace, it is merely –'

'I've got the letter that Patrick Seton forged,' Elsie shouted up at him. 'But I intend keeping it. It's here in my bag, but I'm keeping it.'

Matthew sat at a table in the Oriflamme watching Alice who had told him, 'Elsie won't be here this afternoon.'

'I thought she always worked on Saturday afternoons.'

'Well, she's not coming today, I don't think.'

'Any idea where she is?'

'No idea. She may come in later, of course.'

'I'll wait,' Matthew said. 'I'm on duty tonight from six, but I'll wait till five.'

'You're very keen,' said Alice.

'No I'm not,' he said. 'I like sitting here watching you.'

'While waiting for Elsie.'

'I've got to see Elsie on some business. Can you guess what it is?'

'No,' Alice said, 'and I wouldn't care to try.'

135

'She's a very nice girl, of course. A beautiful girl,' Matthew said.

'Oh, is she beautiful? – Not that I'm saying –'

'Well, now,' Matthew said, 'I believe in original sin, and that all the utterances of man are inevitably deep in error. Therefore I speak so as to err on the happy side.'

'She has a beautiful nature, Elsie has, I'll say that,' said Alice anxiously. 'I'm sorry she's not here for you. But I'll give her a message for you. You can't sit here drinking coffee all afternoon.'

'I'll take a cup of tea,' Matthew said. 'Do you serve teas?'

'No.' Alice hung around him, as if waiting for more information. It was early yet for the afternoon trade and only two other tables were occupied. 'Elsie may not come,' she said.

'Sit down a minute,' Matthew said, 'and rest yourself.' Her small stomach showed a slight pear-shaped swelling which appealed considerably to Matthew.

She sat down, resting her wrists on the table and drooping her long neck. Her shoulder-blades curved gracefully.

'Has Elsie got the letter?' Matthew said.

'What letter?' Alice said.

'Has she mentioned anything to you about the letter in Patrick's case? The one he forged –'

'The widow wrote it. Patrick did not forge it. That's a lie. It will be proved when –'

'Has Elsie seen the letter?'

'Elsie? Why should Elsie see the letter? Ask your posh friend Ronald with his rolled umbrella about the letter. He's working on it, isn't he? I bet he's being paid to say it's a forgery. He hasn't got anything to do with Elsie if that's what's in your mind.'

'Ronald's all right.'

'Well, so's Patrick.'

'He isn't, you know.'

'A lot of people are jealous of Patrick. It's the price he has to pay. Why are you waiting for Elsie?'

'You're jealous of Elsie,' he said.

She jumped up and went to the bar where she ordered coffee for him. When it was ready she brought it over to his table and placed it before him with a gesture which was as near to throwing it at him as was compatible with not spilling a single drop of the coffee. Meanwhile, he admired her pear-shaped stomach.

'I said tea,' Matthew said. 'However, this will do, Alice, my dear.'

'I said we don't do teas. Patrick is a poet beneath the skin,' she said.

'I'm a poet in the marrow of my bones,' he said.

She stroked her head, drawing her hand up and over the high piled hair and, looking up at the blue and starry ceiling, disappeared into the back quarters.

Matthew wrote a secret poem to Alice to while away the afternoon. As he wrote she served him with three more cups of coffee and a slice of walnut cake.

There was still no sign of Elsie at half past five, so he paid his bill and left the secret poem on the table where she later found it.

To Alice, Carrying her Tray

> O punk me a mims my joyble prime
> > And never be blay to me.
> The wist may reeve and the bly go dim
> > But I'll gim flate by thee.

And all agone and all to come,
　The sumper limm beware.
I'll meet thee ever away away
　At Wanhope-by-the-Pear.

IO

Next day, Sunday morning, Sunday afternoon and the long jaded evening – the very clocks seeming to yawn – occurred all over London and especially in Kensington, Chelsea, and Hampstead, where there were newspapers, bells, talk, sleep, fate.

Some bachelors went to church. Some kept open bed all morning and padded to and from it, with trays of eggs and coffee; these men wriggled their toes when they had got back to bed and, however hard they tried, could not prevent some irritating crumbs of toast from falling on the sheets; they smoked a cigarette, slept, then rose at twelve.

Those who were conducting love affairs in service flatlets found it convenient that the maids did not come in with their vacuum cleaners on Sundays. They made coffee and toast on the little grill in the alcove behind the curtain.

Tim Raymond had a large front furnished room on the first floor of a house in Gloucester Road, Kensington. The carpet was green, the walls a paler green, the sofa and easy chairs were covered with deep brown plush. He had hung on the walls of this furnished room some sea-scape water-colours executed by a deceased uncle; he had placed on the lower shelves of a book-case, behind the glass, three pieces of Georgian silver – a coffee pot, a fruit dish and a salt, relics of a great-aunt; on the upper shelves were some fat light-brown calf-bound racing calendars dating from 1909, which Tim rightly thought looked nice.

There was a divan bed, in which Hildegarde Krall still lay half-asleep, and in the opposite wall an alcove containing a small electric grill and a wash-basin where Tim was brushing his teeth.

Hildegarde's head was turned away from Tim, and at this angle of profile he thought she looked masculine. She turned round and propped up on her elbow to watch him. She said, 'It's twenty to eleven.'

Tim brushed his teeth at her, turning his head towards her.

She said, 'Is it raining?'

The telephone rang. Tim spat out his tooth-water into the basin and went to answer it. 'I suppose it's my Aunt Marlene,' he said.

'Hallo,' he said. 'Yes, Marlene. No, I've been up for hours. Yes. No, I'm afraid not today. No, not, I'm afraid. I'm afraid not. All day today, no. Well, yes, I do see, Marlene, but I don't want to be involved, really. One doesn't want . . . Well, Aunt Marlene, I hardly ever really saw him in action, I mean. I mean, I know he's a good medium, but really don't you think the law should take its course? Yes, the law, but I mean it should take – They cross-examine all witnesses, you know. I can't possibly manage today, Marlene. Tomorrow, yes, at six.' Tim tucked the receiver under his chin and wiped his glasses on a handkerchief. 'At six, yes. Yes,' he said, 'tomorrow. Oh, I'm lovely, how are you? Goodbye, darling. Yes, ye – six.'

He flopped into the brown plush chair and lit a cigarette. 'I'm too young for all this,' he said. The telephone rang again.

'Hallo – Marlene! No, not at all. Yes, Marlene – Well, can't we discuss it tomorrow? Yes, of course, do tell me now – Yes. Yes. Oh, but Ronald's probably away. Away for the weekend.

In fact, I'm sure he is, I think so. I haven't got his number, Marlene, isn't he in the book? He wouldn't discuss it with you, anyway, he's awfully strict about confidential – Oh, no, I'm sure he couldn't have lost anything. He never loses – No, you've been misinformed, really. No, I'm sorry, I haven't got Ronald's number. I'll ring him at his office in the morning. Yes, don't worry. The morning. I'll ring – No, not at all. I say, I must go, I'll be late for – Yes. Bye-bye.'

'What has Ronald lost?' said Hildegarde.

'A letter connected with a criminal investigation.'

'Ronald has lost it? He needs someone to look after him. I used to do everything for him. I used to –'

'Yes, you told me.'

'Well, so I did. What does your aunt want with Ronald?'

'I don't know. I don't want to be involved, quite frankly.'

'I used to mend all Ronald's clothes. I used to buy the theatre tickets. I used to rush to his flat after my work and –'

'I know,' said Tim, 'you told me.' And he plugged in his electric razor, the noise of which drowned her voice.

Ronald came out of church after the eleven o'clock Mass and noticed that the youngest priest was standing in the porch saying appropriate things to the home-going faithful. Ronald did not like seeing this very young priest, not because he disliked the priest but because the priest was young, and of a physical type similar to himself, and reminded Ronald of his own blighted vocation. This very young priest prided himself on knowing the majority of the Parish by name.

'Well, Eileen,' he said, as they emerged. 'Well, Patsy. Well, Mrs Mills. Well, John, and what can I do you for?'

'Oh, good *morning*, Father.' . . . 'How's yourself, Father.' . . . 'Oh, Father, when are you coming to see us?' . . .

'The bingo drive was nice, Father.' '. . . delightful sermon, Father.'

'Well, Tom,' said the priest. 'Well, Mary, and how's your mother?'

'A bit better, thank you, Father.'

'Well, Ronald,' said this very young priest as Ronald came out.

'Well, Sonny,' Ronald said.

The young priest stared after Ronald as he rapidly walked his way, then remembered Ronald Bridges was an epileptic, and turned to the next comer.

'Well, Matthew,' he said, 'and how's life with you?'

'All right, thank you, Father,' said Matthew Finch. 'Father, if you'll excuse me I can't stop. I've got to catch up with Ronald Bridges, Father, before he gets on the bus. But I'll be seeing you, Father.'

Matthew caught up with Ronald at the bus stop.

'I managed to see Elsie early this morning,' he said. 'She's got the letter but she won't part with it unless I sleep with her again.'

Ronald said, 'Tell me later,' for a number of the church people in the bus queue had turned to take note of this talk.

'I told her she'd be arrested,' Matthew rattled on, 'for entering your flat on false pretences and for robbery. I told her –'

'Come back with me and then tell me all,' Ronald said.

'Well, she wants me to sleep with her again, and I'm not going to. She's a pervert, I can tell you that much, and I don't like perverted girls. If she isn't a pervert she's a nymphomaniac, it's just the same.'

The bus drew up. Ronald and Matthew followed the queue on to it. Those who had formed the most interested audience for Matthew followed them upstairs. Two girls sat behind them, giggling.

'Don't say any more now,' Ronald murmured. 'People can hear you.'

'Two to South Kensington, please. I don't want,' Matthew said, 'to sleep with Elsie, I want to sleep with Alice. If I was to sleep with Elsie again I'd have to pretend it was Alice. And anyway, I'm not sleeping with girls any more, it's a mortal sin and you can't deny it,' and he took his change from the conductor. 'Elsie,' he said, 'is –'

'Shut up.'

'Elsie,' Matthew whispered, 'is a bit jealous of Alice and her beauty. She hasn't a man of her own, and she was after some spiritualist clergyman but she found out he was homosexual, and she couldn't stand for it. Homosexuals send her raving mad. She was going to give him the letter yesterday, and didn't she find out yesterday –'

'What did this clergyman want with the letter?'

'He's in the spiritualist group. They all want to plot against Patrick Seton or plot for him, there's a great schism going on in the Circle just now.'

They got off at South Kensington and walked to Ronald's flat.

'Elsie is going to use that letter to get a man and it isn't going to be me,' Matthew said. 'She's got some passionate ways in sex. Not that I'm narrow-minded, only she's not beautiful like Alice, and you can't allow for funny passions in a girl that isn't beautiful.'

In the flat, Ronald said, 'I'd better see Elsie. Will she be at the Oriflamme today?'

'Yes, at six tonight.'

'What's her address?'

'Ten Vesey Street near Victoria, first-floor flat.'

Ronald wrote it down. Matthew said, 'But don't go there. She's a dangerous woman. She –'

The telephone rang. 'Marlene Cooper here,' said the voice. 'Ronald, you'll remember coming to lunch with me. I'm Tim's aunt.' She articulated the vowels as if addressing a mental defective.

'Yes, how are you?' Ronald said.

'Listen carefully,' she said. 'You have lost a document, haven't you?'

'A document?' Ronald said.

'I'm sorry if you're going to take up that attitude,' she said.

'Attitude?' Ronald said.

'Yes, because there might be a chance of my helping you.'

'Helping me?'

'Yes, helping you. I think I might be able to give you the name of the person who holds the document, and this would save you a lot of embarrassment, if only –'

'Embarrassment?'

'It is not a forgery,' Marlene said. 'And if you would come along here and discuss the matter, I think you would find it to your advantage. Can you manage six o'clock? It isn't a forgery, that must be made plain. Patrick Seton must be cleared of this slander. I will explain everything. Sherry at six o'clock or six-thirty and stay for supper, Ronald –'

'Forgery?' Ronald said.

'It is not a forgery,' Marlene said. 'On that I insist. And if you will agree simply to say so to your superiors I can give you the name and address of a certain young woman.'

'Thanks,' Ronald said, 'but really I don't like young women.'

'Can you manage today, six o'clock?' Marlene said.

'I'm afraid not. I've got to see a young woman.'

He said to Matthew after he had hung up, 'Tim's auntie is a woman of few scruples when she's after something.'

'Would you come across the road for a drink?' Matthew said. 'All women under the sun are unscrupulous if there's something they want.'

'She was prepared to sell me Elsie's name and address,' Ronald said. 'But as I've got it from you for free, I'll purchase a drink for you.'

'But isn't it a great mistake to be bitter about the female sex!' Matthew said. 'We owe them everything.'

On Sunday afternoon Isobel Billows stoked up the fire and sent Martin Bowles to fetch in some more coal. He put the brief he was reading down on the floor beside his chair and went to do her bidding. As he could not hear the front-door bell from the back of the house where he was filling the scuttle with coal, he was surprised, on his return, to find Walter Prett, the art-critic, plumply occupying his chair. Walter had one foot on Martin's brief.

'You are trampling on my brief,' Martin said, bending to extricate it from under Walter's heel. He smoothed out the squashed manilla cover of the file which held his brief. 'There's a hundred and eighty pounds' worth of business in here,' Martin said fretfully.

'Don't be vulgar,' said Walter.

'Now, bachelors,' said Isobel, 'don't quarrel.'

'I deny there's anything particularly vulgar about money,' Martin said.

'Did you put on the kettle as you came through the kitchen?' Isobel said.

'No, you didn't ask me to,' said Martin.

'Well, go and do it now,' Walter said.

'Walter!' said Isobel, and she pushed the Sunday papers

off her lap and got up, setting her fair hair straight. 'We'll have some tea,' she said and departed.

Walter said, 'I wonder if you'd let me have –'

'No,' said Martin.

'Vulgar little fellow,' Walter said, tossing his snow-white locks. His dark face turned a shade more towards purple. He took a cigarette from a packet which was lying on the arm of his chair. They were Martin's cigarettes. Martin lifted the deprived packet and put it in his pocket.

Walter tore a strip of newspaper and lit his cigarette from the fire.

'I didn't see you here at the party,' Martin said.

'Which party?'

'Oh, sorry. I suppose you weren't invited.'

'I believe Isobel *did* mention something,' Walter said. 'But I was busy.'

Martin began reading his brief.

'Too busy,' said Walter, 'to mix with those common little people that hang round Isobel at her parties. Pimps and tarts and Jews.'

Martin read on.

'Spongers and soaks. Third-rate lower-middle-class . . .'

Isobel pushed open the door with her tray.

'Walter is describing the people who come to your parties,' Martin said, 'Isobel dear.'

'What people?' said Isobel, settling the tray.

'The sort of people who were at your cocktail party the other night.'

'Oh, Walter,' Isobel said. 'My party – I tried to get you on the phone, but you were always out. And I meant to send you a card but completely forgot, hoping to get you on the phone, you see –'

'I wouldn't have come,' Walter shouted. 'A vulgar third-rate set. Journalists. British Council lecturers. Schoolmasters.

A typical divorcée's salon.' And so saying he rose, lifted the tray of tea things, smashed it down into the fireplace, wormed his bulk into the ancient camel-hair coat which he had thrown on a chair, and left, banging both doors.

'You must have upset him,' Isobel said to Martin.

'A good thing too. He only came here to sponge on you. He tried to touch me – you weren't five seconds out of the room.'

'Oh, what a creature! And he can be so interesting when he likes. It's my favourite china . . . ' She started to cry.

'Send him a bill.'

'Don't be silly.'

'You must be protected,' Martin said, with his arm around her, 'from spongers.'

He was hoping the fuss would not now make it difficult for him to get away after tea, for he had promised his old mother to be home for Sunday supper.

'I am not a possessive woman,' his mother always said to him. 'You are perfectly free. Just use the house as a lodging and come and go as you please. Or take a flat, live elsewhere, do anything you like. Don't think of me, I've *had* my life. I am not a possessive woman.'

'She is not a possessive woman,' he told his friends. 'My old ma says, "Take a flat if you like, go and live somewhere else, I don't want you tied to my apron-strings." She isn't a possessive mother. But,' Martin told his friends, 'I've got to stay with her. You can't let your old widowed mother stew in Kensington when she's got arthritis. All her cronies have got arthritis. And she fights with Carrie, she literally fights with Carrie. Literally, they pull each other's hair.'

Carrie was Martin's old nurse, now, by courtesy, the housekeeper. When Martin was first called to the bar, and was short of money, old Carrie would wander off to the post office and draw out three pounds at a time of her savings; these three pounds she would privately slip to Martin. Several times Martin told his mother of this, intending it as a rebuke to her for her meanness. Mrs Bowles then wrote a cheque for Martin and, when he was out of the way, went and had a row with Carrie.

These latter days Carrie lived with Mrs Bowles as an equal. Sometimes they quarrelled and had a real fight, pulling each other's hair and, with feeble veined hands, pushing each other's faces, pushing spectacles awry and knocking at each other's jaws with their helpless knuckles. Carrie had left all her life's savings to Martin, and she had saved since she was a girl of fourteen. Mrs Bowles suspected that Carrie's fortune now surpassed her own dwindling funds, and therefore Carrie was a real rival.

'I'm not a possessive woman,' said Mrs Bowles.

'You should of pushed him out the nest long ago,' said Carrie. 'You should take a lesson off the birds. You got to push them out. When my brother was a boy thirteen my mother said to him, "There's five shillings, now go." That's pushing them out the nest. My brother had a good position in a club before he died.'

'This is a different case. A barrister has a struggle. I'm not a possessive woman. Let him marry, let him go.'

'You got to *put* them out,' Carrie said.

'Are you telling me to turn my own son out of doors?' said his mother, and her eyes, which bulged naturally, shone with a bevelled light.

'Yes,' said Carrie. 'It would make a man of him.'

'Then why do you give him money?'

'Me give him money? – Catch me.'

'Martin told me. Last week you gave him money. Twice the week before that. Last month you –'

'Well, you keep him short, don't you?'

So Martin could never bring himself to leave Carrie and his mother, even although he no longer needed Carrie's little offerings. He lost his hair. He worried about his old mother if he went away to the country with Isobel for the weekend. He tried to entertain them and to be a good son. They bored him, but when they went away from home he missed the boredom, and the feud between them which sometimes broke into it.

'Carrie will have to go away to a home,' said his old mother, 'if her arthritis gets bad.'

'No,' said Martin. 'Carrie stays here.'

'You're after that money of hers. You may be disappointed,' his mother said. He hated her fiercely for her continual robbing him of any better motive.

'I'm fond of Carrie,' he said. But now his mother had left him wondering if he really meant it.

'Your mother will be bedridden before long,' Carrie said. 'What's to happen then?'

'We'll get a daily nurse,' Martin said. 'We'll manage.'

'They won't stop,' Carrie said. 'Not with your mother. Look at Millie.'

'Oh, nurses are different from maids. Maids always come and go.'

'Millie was a good girl. She would of stopped if your mother hadn't made her life a misery.'

He took them both to the country to his mother's younger sister on occasions. Then he went shopping for small supplies of groceries, pined for the boredom, and cooked whatever meals he did not have with Isobel. He missed the two old women pottering about and blaming each other.

'I've lost a vest, Carrie.'

'I haven't got your vest.'

'I have not said you've taken my vest. I think Millie must have taken it.'

'What would Millie of wanted with a vest down to her knees?' said Carrie.

'It was a good warm vest,' said Mrs Bowles.

'You've put it away in the wrong place,' said Carrie, 'that's what you've done. Look among the table linen.'

This was what Martin missed when they went away to the country, and then, even on his comfortable weekends with Isobel, he thought of the empty house and the time when he was due to drive down to fetch them home and plonk them in their chairs in front of the television.

'It isn't clear.'

'Be quiet, Carrie.'

'I'm going to turn it up.'

'Sit still, Carrie.'

Carrie's niece had once offered to take her off their hands.

'Let her go,' said Mrs Bowles, and in her anger strained a muscle in her shoulder while heaving Carrie's trunk from the box-room out on to the landing.

Carrie surveyed the box. 'I'll go when it suits me,' she said, 'and it won't be to my relations I'll go. I could make myself a home tomorrow if it suited me.'

Martin had heaved the trunk back into its old place, for it had left a clear oblong shape on the dusty floor. Martin brushed his trousers and washed his hands.

'Fetch me the liniment for my shoulder,' said his mother, 'there's a good boy.'

He had bought them the television, and now, comforting Isobel for her broken china, he was wondering how he could get home in time for supper, as he had promised them he would.

He picked up the broken pieces and said, 'You mustn't allow Walter Prett into the house again.'

'He's never done this before,' she said.

'Does he come often?' Martin stood up in his alarm, with half the sugar basin in his hand, so that a little shower of sugar fell to the carpet.

'No, Martin,' she said.

He was suspicious because of the 'No, Martin,' instead of merely 'No.'

'He's disreputable,' Martin said. 'A sponger and a drunk.'

'Yes, Martin, I know.'

He was frantic with curiosity. 'What could any woman see in him?'

'He can be interesting when –'

'When he's not drunk.'

'Well, he's got something about him, he's different from anybody else.'

She got down and picked up all the china. 'Pour me a drink,' she said.

Martin looked at his watch and at her plump behind as she knelt over the broken pieces, and wanted to kick it. For he felt suddenly that he was to her only the man who handled her property and shares, and that she slept with him only to ensure his loyalty and save herself the trouble of investigating the property deals.

'I can't stay very long. My old ma's expecting me for supper,' he said.

'Let's have a drink.' She sniffed away the last of her tears and carried off the tray of broken china.

He had poured their drinks when she returned with new make-up on her face. He had often felt the only safe course would be to marry her, and he felt this now, with fear, because she did not always attract him, and he was not sure she would accept him. At the times when she stood out for her rights, not crudely, but with all the implicit assumptions, he thought her face too fat and found her thick neck and shoulders repulsive. At this moment, when she leaned against the mantelpiece with her drink in her hand, finding himself without the right to question her about the frequency of Walter Prett's visits, he thought her jaw was too square and masculine. He saw it would be safer to marry her. Often, when she had said, 'Martin, what should I do without you? I should never be able to manage my affairs without you,' he had recognised her strong-boned beauty and thought how a sculptor might do something about it. Even at these moments, when he had found the idea of marrying Isobel a soothing one, the panic returned that she might refuse. The thought was not to be borne. He recalled the two old women and thought, after all, it would not be the decent thing to leave them alone.

'Carrie, you have wiped the oven with the floor cloth.'

'How could I of wiped the oven with the floor cloth, when the floor cloth's looking you in the face over there . . . ?'

He left at seven, and on the way home pulled up at a telephone kiosk. He wanted to talk secretly to Ronald Bridges and tell Ronald a little bit about Walter Prett's offensive behaviour, and to put himself right with Ronald, feeling now as if Ronald's eye had been invisibly upon him all the afternoon. He was never comfortable when he did not feel all right with Ronald.

But there was no answer from Ronald's number. Soon Martin was eating cold lamb and beetroot opposite Carrie and next to his mother.

He laid his bald head on his hands and said, 'Oh, stop nagging each other, you two women.' And they stopped their quarrel for a little space.

*

Towards half past seven on Sunday evening, Ewart Thornton was seated in Marlene Cooper's flat in Bayswater. He said, 'I've got a pile of homework to do. Maths papers.'

'Never mind that now,' she said. 'Come and have supper.'

He had been smoking a pipe. He tapped it out and worked himself stiffly and hugely out of the deep upholstered chair.

'Maths papers,' he said. 'Preliminary tests.'

'Ewart,' she said at supper, 'the Interior Spiral will be meeting on Tuesday at eight-thirty to discuss our evidence with regard to Patrick Seton. We must present a united front if it comes to a court case as I suspect it will. Now, whom can we trust?'

'Well, you can trust me, for one,' said Ewart, 'but I must say I won't be able to give any evidence in court.'

'What!' said Marlene, holding the cold peas in the serving-spoon suspended.

'I can't come to court.'

She tipped the peas on to his plate and still stared at him. 'You must,' she said. 'I'm counting on you.'

'It will be too near the end of term,' he said.

'Why,' she said, 'have we got to quarrel every time we meet, Ewart?' She started to eat.

'There is no quarrel,' he said, sprinkling pepper on his salad.

'You can't let me down,' she said, 'after all this preparation. Patrick's future may depend upon it.'

'I'm not convinced of Patrick's innocence. As you know, I'm a man of principle. I'm not sure that Mrs Flower isn't in the right.'

'But all you need to say is that Patrick is a genuine medium, and that Freda Flower ran after him unmercifully, as you know she did. As you know.'

'Marlene,' he said, 'I advise you to keep out of the case altogether. You are talking wildly. No one would be interested in my evidence.'

'Well, this is sudden,' she said.

'I have told you my views. I've advised –'

'Yes, but I thought, as a member of the Interior Spiral, when it came to the point, Ewart, you would stand by me and . . .' She was crying, and it satisfied him to see her cry and to think that he had brought about this drooping of her stately neck, the leaning of her head on her hand, the tremor of her jade ear-rings, the resigned dabbing of her eyes with her handkerchief, and the final offended sniff.

He introduced his fork into his mouth judiciously and chewed like a wise man until she should be delivered of her distress.

'I don't see why you are so surprised. I've told you all along that I consider it absurd to go into the witness box on Patrick Seton's behalf. It would do him far more harm than –'

'Oh, Ewart,' she said. 'No, you were never definite. I can't believe it.'

It was true he had never been quite definite on the subject before tonight, but he had said enough, from time to time, to allow him now to extricate himself from any charge of sudden betrayal. He recalled that some time previous he had said to Marlene, 'I can see Mrs Flower's point of view. Of course, she was foolish to hand him over the money, even allowing it was a gift –'

'Oh, it was a gift. Patrick says so. He can prove it. There's a letter.'

'It's a large sum for her to give.'

On another occasion he had said, 'My sympathies are not entirely with Patrick. He may be a good medium, but as a citizen –'

'It is time spiritualism was recognised as a mark of good citizenship,' Marlene said.

More recently, at a meeting of the Interior Spiral – the secret group within the Group – Ewart Thornton had said, 'There is bound to be a certain amount of prejudice against spiritualists if the case is brought up. My advice is to keep out of it and let the law take its course. Mud sticks.'

'We must fight prejudice,' Marlene had said. 'And we all intend to support Patrick in every way. We must decide what we are going to say. We can't carry on the Group without Patrick.' On that occasion Patrick had arrived, frail as a sapling birch with rain on its silver head. 'We are just discussing,' Marlene said, 'our combined witness on your behalf, in the event of its being called for.'

'Ah-ah,' Patrick sighed, hunching his shoulders together, 'the unfortunate occurrence.'

'And what is more,' Marlene said, 'we want your assistance in settling what we are to say about Freda Flower. You will have to give us the relevant dates so that –'

'We do not all know Mrs Flower,' Ewart had said.

'Oh, don't we?' said Marlene.

Ewart had thus feebly worked towards this moment on Sunday evening when, sitting at Marlene's supper table, he said, 'I've told you all along that I consider it absurd to go into the witness box.'

'Oh, Ewart. No, you were never definite. I can't believe it.'

'Think back,' he said. 'I've told you all along what my position is.'

He leaned both arms confidently on the table, and felt a great awkwardness inside him, and looked at Marlene with an overpowering stare until he perceived her submission: she thought him altogether sure of his rectitude.

Then he experienced a sense of this rectitude, and was satisfied. He would have liked to have disappointed her more than this, because he was greatly attracted by her and greatly disapproved of her. He disapproved of, and was attracted by what she took for granted in life – by her freedom to indulge her spirit, and buy the acquiescence of her followers, and run up debts without worry, and cultivate spiritualists and mediums, and have no need of lovers. He was attracted by and disapproved of the departed Harry who had bought ear-rings to dangle against this tall lady's neck, and who had died and been buried and dug up again by her, and cremated, and who was now being trafficked with beyond the grave. He had feasted on anecdotes of her past life, and wanted more, and was avid, in an old woman's way, for her downfall.

'I have counted on you,' Marlene was saying, 'to witness for Patrick because it would be such good publicity for the Infinity. People would know we are not cranks. No one would take you for a crank, Ewart.'

This did not move him. He liked very much to see Marlene with her private means trying to win him over; and he knew already he was not a crank. He set his face squarely at her, and felt glad he had conferred with Freda Flower and had canvassed witnesses for Freda.

'Ronald Bridges,' she said, 'has also let me down rather badly today.'

'He isn't one of us, surely?'

'Oh, he's not a spiritualist. But he has let me down, all the same. One thing about Patrick,' she said, 'he has never let me down.'

He was anxious to go, for he wanted to telephone to Freda Flower from the cosy seclusion of his own study at Campden Hill. He loved a gossip with a homely woman like Freda Flower, and it had been most pleasant, recently, to settle in to telling her how things were going in the Wider Infinity group, and what was being said. For, like a Christian convert of the jungle who secretly returns by night to the fetish tree, or like one who openly supports a political party and then, at last, marks his vote for the opposite party, he felt justified in Freda Flower to the extent of these telephone conversations even although she was an unsuitable person to meet.

'Freda, I was at a party last night at Isobel Billows's. You won't know her – she's not a member of the Circle. But a lot of us were there. I did my very best, Freda, to persuade members to come forward in your favour. After all, where did all the money go? The members know that Patrick has had far too much handling of the funds, in any case. I tried to impress it on young Tim Raymond, but I'm afraid he is too young and irresponsible. And, my dear, I'm not saying anything against Marlene, but she . . .'

'Patrick Seton could look you in the eyes,' she would say, 'and tell a lie so that you would believe you were telling the lie, not him.'

'I can well believe you, my dear,' he would say time and again, into the telephone receiver, lolling back largely in his chair and pulling his waistcoat over his stomach. 'And I can't think why you hesitate to give your evidence in full force.'

Marlene was piling the supper things on to a tray. She looked at Ewart several times as she did so, to see if he appeared as if he could still be persuaded. He stood up like a righteous husband, and contemptuously added the pepper pot to the tray.

'I won't keep you, then, Ewart, if you are in a hurry to get back to your work,' she said.

But he was anxious to help Marlene wash the dishes before returning to gossip with Freda Flower. He liked putting an apron around his large body and he liked holding the cloth in his hands to dry the dishes one by one. Sometimes at the end of term, after the examinations, he invited three of his best boys to dinner on Saturday at his rooms, and he liked that very much – planning the menu, buying in the food, preparing it, cooking it for them, fussing over the stove for them, seeing they had enough to eat, like a solicitous mother.

He wiped Marlene's dishes and put them away carefully and proudly. He was encouraged by her dejection and satisfied, now, he had taken the only course.

His hips were wide for a man. He smoothed the apron while waiting, cloth in hand, for the next plate. Marlene did a vexed scouring of a saucepan. Ewart made neat the bow which tied the apron strings behind him.

'Is that the lot?' he said.

'Will you be here tomorrow night?' she said, 'for the Interior Spiral.'

'I'm afraid not, my dear.' He was prepared to be charming.

'I can't understand you,' she said. She took off her apron. He untied his and held it out to her. She cast the aprons, with graceful carelessness, over the back of a chair.

He touched her arm consolingly as a man of integrity to a woman who could not be expected to understand integrity.

'You will come to the séance on Wednesday?'

He looked reproachful. 'Oh, yes,' he said. Marlene must be made to understand that simply because he refused to support her favourite he was not therefore a lapsed spiritualist.

'Good,' she said sadly, 'I'm glad, Ewart. I'm grateful for that.'

She went over to that serving-aperture in the wall which divided the kitchen from the séance room and flicked a straying fold in the short curtain.

'Patrick will take the chair on Wednesday,' she said.

'It may be his last appearance,' Ewart said.

'Not if I know it,' she said and moved past him out of the kitchen.

He put on his hat, scarf, and coat in the hall.

'Thank you for a pleasant evening,' he said.

'I am disappointed, Ewart.'

'You will be grateful one day, Marlene.'

He kissed her on both cheeks and departed to his rooms at Campden Hill where, from the depths of his leather arm-chair, he telephoned to Freda Flower.

'I have definitely made a stand, Freda, as regards Patrick Seton. It had to come, Freda. Now, Freda, don't be silly. That is sheer superstition. Patrick can do you no further harm. I believe you've still got a weak spot for Patrick, Freda, but believe me . . . And if I were you, my dear, I'd keep away from Mike Garland. Yes, keep him away from you. Yes, keep away from . . . We'll clean up the whole organisation between us, you and I together. And Marlene will come to heel . . .'

His hips expanded in the chair, and his chin went into extra folds as his face sank into the skull. A smile of comfortable womanliness spread far into his cheeks as he spoke and his eyes were avid, as if they had never moved dispassionately over an examination paper. 'Yes, Freda my dear, I made no bones about it and I just said to her, I said . . .'

Meanwhile the Rev. T.W. Socket said to Mike Garland who had at that moment arrived at his flat, 'Mrs Flower is resolved to go ahead with the case.'

'She has no alternative. It's in the hands of the police.'

'But will she be a willing witness? That's what they need.'

'I've done my best with her,' said Mike Garland.

'I hope you didn't have to de-Flower her,' said the Reverend Socket who then closed his eyes and shook with mirth.

Mike Garland smiled unpleasantly.

'I don't trust Mrs Flower,' he said. 'I don't know for certain, but I think she may have been discussing me with the police. A plain-clothes man called last night. Somebody's been talking to the police.'

'What did he want? What did he ask?'

'About my clairvoyant activities. Where did I operate? What did I charge for a horoscope? I told him. I showed him the card index. All postal commissions, I said.'

'I'm glad I suggested that card index,' said Socket. 'There is nothing like having a card index in the house. You can always produce a card index. It puts them off their stroke.'

'I invited the man to look through it, but he didn't trouble.'

'Who has tipped them off, I wonder?'

'He mentioned Freda Flower.'

'Really, in what connection?'

'He asked me if I knew her. I said yes, she was a friend.'

'How many girls have you got staying with Freda Flower at the moment?'

'Only three.'

'Transfer them to Ramsgate right away,' said Father Socket. 'I blame Marlene Cooper for this. You made an enemy of her the other night, I'm afraid. It was ill-considered of you to challenge Patrick Seton at an open séance.'

'I can't transfer the girls to Ramsgate right away.'

'Why not?'

'Because Freda Flower will be suspicious if they all leave at once. She thinks they work in the all-night kitchen at Lyons' Corner House. I can't trust Freda Flower.'

'Whom can we trust?' said Father Socket.

'Someone has tipped the police,' said Mike Garland.

'Could it be Elsie? Surely it couldn't be Elsie.'

'She stole that letter – she's capable of anything.'

'I told you, didn't I?' said Father Socket, 'that you should have been more discreet when Elsie called yesterday.'

'Having stolen a letter which was Crown property I doubt if she would go to the police. Besides, what could she say? That I was wearing my green-striped dressing-gown?' Mike Garland smiled with full lips pressed together.

'This is grave,' said Father Socket. He was inserting a roll of tape into a recording machine. He switched it on. It was his own voice rendering Shelley's *Ode to the West Wind*. He stood listening to it, with critical attention, while Mike leant back with eyes closed.

When it was finished Father Socket said, 'I should have taken "Drive my dead thoughts . . ." more slowly. They are all monosyllabic words, each word should be spoken with equal stress. Drive – my – dead – thoughts . . . like that.'

'It gives one a *frisson*,' said Mike.

'All troubles are passing,' said Father Socket. 'My son, the fever of life will soon be over and gone. We will take this police inquiry in our stride. Do not be disturbed, Mike. Patrick Seton will be brought to trial, the Wider Infinity will be brought to disrepute, the Temple will be cleansed, and we shall then take over the affairs of the Circle ourselves.'

'We'll take over the whole shooting-match,' said Mike. 'How you soothe me, Father.'

'Some will have to go,' said the Rev. Socket. 'Marlene, of course, will no longer be in control. We shall not meet at Marlene's flat, we shall meet here. Ewart Thornton will have to go. Freda Flower – she is suspect, and to say the least, has been a trouble-maker – she will have to go. It makes one's eyes narrow. We may retain Tim Raymond, a biddable youth. We shall –'

'But I didn't like that plain-clothes policeman calling on me last night,' Mike whispered. 'I didn't like it at all.'

'Do nothing for two weeks,' said Father Socket. 'My son, go nowhere, do nothing.'

'But the girls –'

'I shall myself convey the girls to Ramsgate,' said Father Socket, 'one by one.'

Mike Garland took comfort from his elder partner whom he had revered for eight years, since that summer evening at Ramsgate when he had just heard Father Socket preach. This was in a private house, before the séance had commenced. Mike, newly released from Maidstone prison, where he had served a sentence for soliciting, was deeply moved when he heard Father Socket say, 'There are those amongst us who are not of the human race, but are aliens, and nevertheless must walk in the midst of mankind disguised as members of the human race. He who hath ears let him hear.' Mike told Father Socket after the séance, 'I was deeply moved by what you said tonight.' Father Socket adopted him. Mike was then forty. He had a job as a waiter in a huge hotel. For the winter he had intended to return to London and take up private service as a manservant, for he had made a good butler in his time, with many profitable sidelines. Father Socket had changed all that. He had bestowed larger thoughts on Mike, who began to experience a late flowering in his soul. Father Socket cited the classics and André Gide, and although Mike did not actually read them, he understood, for the first time in his life, that the world contained scriptures to support his homosexuality which, till now, had been shifty and creedless. Mike gave up his job as a waiter and went into training as a clairvoyant. His appearance assisted him, he flowered. Father Socket instructed him in the theory and practice of clairvoyance, and Mike's late overflowing of the soul actually did evoke pronounced psychic talents. Father Socket's villa at Ramsgate was filled twice weekly with residential widows and retired military men – for it was widows and retired colonels who were the chief clients – come to receive clairvoyance from Mike.

'There are certain aids to perception which it is unwise – nay, lacking in humility – for the clairvoyant to ignore,' Father Socket told Mike, and he taught him how to observe his subjects and how, in the daylight hours, to gain useful information as to their private lives. Mike's previous career in the catering and domestic worlds assisted him, for he knew his way about the back stairs of hotels and boarding houses, he knew a friendly waiter when he saw one.

'But we must not neglect the little things of life,' said Father Socket. 'The gas bill must be paid.' Mike knew a street photographer. He knew which wealthy men were taking the air on the front with their friends during illicit weekends. The couples were photographed, the man handed a ticket, and the ticket was thrown away. Mike acquired these photographs at a higher price than the nominal three for seven-and-sixpence. But he did not lose on the deal and, even though certain members of hotel staffs had to be paid out of his earnings, still Father Socket's gas bills were paid.

'Never touch a woman,' said Father Socket, 'for a woman cannot enter the Kingdom. Have dealings with a woman and the virtue departs from you. You should read the Ancients on the subject.'

Mike felt secure with Father Socket in all his summer and all his winter activities. He was no longer an aimless chancer sliding in and out of illegal avenues, feeling resentful all the while. Mike now was at rights with the world, he was somebody. He had a religion and a Way of Life, set forth by Father Socket. Mike, tall, straight, with his pink-and-white cheeks, did not appear to be an adoring type; nevertheless he adored Father Socket and was jealous of any other potential acolytes who might put in a tentative appearance, and would not stand for them.

Now, after eight prosperous years, Mike could not believe that a mere visit from a plain-clothes policeman could shake the benign rock which translated Horace, recited Shelley, knew the writings of the Early Fathers, and studied the Cabbala. This winter's venture, a continuation of last summer's venture, was a private cinema show lasting half an hour. It comprised two films, entitled, respectively, *The Truth about Nudism* and *Nature's Way*. The three girls, who appeared on the stage in person afterwards, were more or less thrown in with the price of the ticket. Mike had thought the employment of these girls unnecessary. 'Suppose the place is raided, it is easier to destroy the film than to conceal the girls.'

'The show would lose its attraction,' said Father Socket, 'without a peppering of real flesh and blood. I prefer, myself, the more artistic exclusiveness of the film, but we must allow for the cruder tastes of the Many.'

They lodged the girls with unsuspecting Freda Flower, who was known to Father Socket as a spiritualist and a widow and who touchingly gave him fifty cigarettes every Christmas and a spray of carnations on the birthday of the late Sir Oliver Lodge.

'Freda will take the girls,' said Father Socket. 'Now that Patrick Seton has let her down so badly over her savings, the good woman will need the money.'

Mike had not been happy about Freda taking the girls to lodge. 'Never have to do with a woman . . . they draw the virtue out of you.'

A slight disturbance in Mike's mind had recently occurred to make him wonder if perhaps Father Socket was not more interested in women as such than he claimed to be. There was a certain Elsie, who did his typing. He was furiously jealous of Elsie. And these girls. But Mike, shivering as from a flash of clairvoyance, cast the thought from him.

But when Father Socket said, 'I shall myself convey the girls to Ramsgate. One by one. You must lie low. I confess I don't like the sound of this policeman who visited you. Are you sure he was a policeman? Did you ask for his credentials? You should always demand their credentials.' – When Father Socket spoke like this, Mike recalled his first hesitation in dealing with Freda Flower, he remembered his flash of doubt, whether Father Socket was reaching an age – sixty-two – when he might become weak. In a fever of clairvoyance and apprehension he looked at his patron and everlasting lean-upon, and said, 'Never have dealings with women, Father. They are denied the Kingdom. They suck the virtue –'

'Well, my son,' said Father Socket, 'don't be fearful.' He patted Mike's shoulder. 'After all, you are now forty-eight and you must endure whatever may betide.'

'Things look unlucky,' said Mike, rising tall above Father Socket. 'We had bad luck with Elsie Forrest yesterday, and that was a start. We should have got that letter out of her. Perhaps our good luck is turning.'

'I told you not to put in an appearance in that dressing-gown with that stuff on your face,' Father Socket said. 'I told you she was not a true spirit. Whatever must the girl have thought?'

*

Alice Dawes sat up in bed combing her long black hair on that Sunday evening. A syringe lay on the table beside her.

'Some time next week, I imagine,' said Patrick, in his murmur.

'And the divorce – now how about the divorce case?'

'Oh yes, I meant to tell you. The divorce has been held up. Something technical – but never mind that, I've got our honeymoon all arranged.'

'Held up? How can we have a honeymoon if we can't get married?'

'A holiday, dear. We shall be married eventually.'

'I wish you'd tell me more about your divorce.'

'You trust me,' said Patrick softly, 'don't you?' He put out his hand and stroked her arm.

'Of course,' she said, and after a space she said, 'Are you sure the case will come up next month?'

'The divorce will –'

'No, not the divorce. The case, the charge of fraud.'

'It may not come to anything after all. The police may decide they haven't good enough evidence.'

'I should like to give that Freda Flower a piece of my mind. Saying you forged the letter. Have you seen anything of Elsie?'

'No, I wish she hadn't touched the letter. It puts me in an awkward position. The police think I'm behind the theft.' He placed his head on one side with pathos.

'Do they know? Who told them?'

'The man who lost it, I suppose.'

'That's Ronald Bridges,' Alice said. 'He takes fits. What's in the letter?'

'Not very much. It came with the cheque Freda sent me and it says "Please use this money to further your psychic and spiritualistic work. I leave it entirely in your hands" –

something like that. An unprincipled woman. I should never have taken the money.'

Alice moved in a desperate access of temper against Freda Flower and her own doubts; she sat up violently and began to throw back the covers and reach for her clothes at the same time. 'I'll go and see that woman right away. I'll frighten the wits out of her –'

'No, no,' Patrick said.

'I'll tell her it won't be you who's going to gaol, it will be her that's going to Holloway if she stands up before the magistrate and says you forged that letter. I'll tell her, and she can see for herself, that I'm pregnant, and I'll say, "What right have you," I'll say, "to come between me and the man I love with a court case? You should have thought it over," I'll say, "before you sent him that cheque –"'

'No, no, keep calm,' Patrick said.

'I'll say, "You should have thought it over, and no doubt you thought he would marry you when he got his divorce, you ridiculous old bag," I'll say, "now he's devoted the money to a cause and distributed it among the spiritualist students, now you say you didn't give it to him," I'll say. And I'll say, "Mrs Flower," I'll say, "you know the police are prejudiced and everyone's prejudiced against spiritualism, and they will swear it's a forgery and pay their men to swear to it. Now, Mrs Flower," I'll say, "where will that get you, Mrs Flower? It will get you to Holloway, that's where. You think you're going to come between Patrick and me? No, Mrs Flower," I'll say. "Oh no, Mrs Flower."' Alice curled up and wept noisily.

Patrick sat in his calm, watching her, and he experienced that murmuring of his mind which was his memory. He could not recall where he had seen a similar sight before, but he felt he had. His memory was impressionistic, formed of a few distinguishable sensations among a mass of cloudy matter generally forming his past. He remembered most of all his childhood, and could possibly have brought to mind the latent image of being taken with his class round an art gallery by his art teacher, a woman. She is endeavouring to explain impressionist art by bidding them look at the palm of their hands for a moment, and nowhere else. 'All round your hand you are aware of objects – you see them, but not distinctly. What you see round the palm of your hand is an *impression*.' Patrick's memory had become this type of impression and if he focused his attention for long upon the things of the past it was mainly of his childhood that he thought, a happy childhood, and his lifelong justification for all his subsequent actions. It had bewildered him when the prison psychoanalysts had put it to him as a matter of course that something had been wrong with his childhood. That is not the case at all: something has been wrong, from time to time, ever since. Life has been full of unfortunate occurrences, and the dream of childhood still remains in his mind as that from which everything else deviates. He is a dreamy child: a dreamer of dreams, they say with pride, as he wanders back from walks in the botanical gardens, or looks up from his book. *Mary Rose* by J.M. Barrie is Patrick's favourite, and he is taken to the theatre to see it acted, and is sharply shocked by the sight of the real actresses and actors with painted faces performing outwardly on the open platform this tender romance about the girl who was stolen by the fairies on a Hebridean island. As a young man he memorises the early poems of W.B. Yeats and will never forget them. Now, on his first enchanted visit to the Western Isles he first encounters an unfortunate occurrence, having sat up reciting to an American lady far into the night and the next morning being accused of having taken money from her purse. He is thinking of her, in his poetic innocence, as a kindred soul to whom money does not matter, but now she carries on as if money mattered. A little while, and he learns from a man that the early Christians shared all their worldly possessions one with the other, and Patrick memorises this lesson and repeats it to all. Another little while, and he has sex relations with a woman, and is upset by all the disgusting details and is eventually carried away into transports. There is a lot of nasty stuff in life which comes breaking up our ecstasy, our inheritance. I think, said Patrick, people should read more poetry and dream their dreams, and I do not recognise man-made laws and dogmas. There is always a fuss about some petty cash, or punctuality. 'Tread softly,' he recites to the young girls he meets, 'because you tread on my dreams.' The girls are usually enchanted. 'I have spread my dreams under your feet,' he says, 'tread softly . . .' Even older ladies are enchanted. His wispy father fully accepts the position of Patrick, and dies. The widowed mother cannot understand how he is not getting on in life, with such fine stuff in him. She protests, at last, that she is penniless, and when she dies, and turns out not to have been quite penniless, Patrick is amazed. He had not thought her to be a materialist at heart. There is a girl at the time going to have a baby, and that is her business. He removes to London, then, away from these unfortunate occurrences and finds his feet as a spiritualist and becomes a remarkable medium, which he always was, without knowing it, all along. There are ups and downs and he always does his best to help Mr Fergusson with information. Patrick trembles with fear and relief when he thinks of Mr Fergusson who first put him on a charge; and that was the first meeting.

Patrick has tried to explain how let down he always feels by people who trust him and enter into an agreement to trust him, as it were against their better judgement blinding themselves, and then suddenly no longer trust him, and turn upon him. Mr Fergusson perhaps understands this.

There is another charge, and the unfortunate sentence, but afterwards Mr Fergusson, with his strong-looking chest and reliable uniform, is still sitting at the police station, and they make another arrangement about information so that Patrick feels much better and feels he has a real friend in Mr Fergusson with his few words, even though Mr Fergusson cannot help putting him on a charge sometimes; and he is afraid of Mr Fergusson.

Patrick contemplates Alice curled up in distress. It is so much easier to get away from a girl in any other part of the country than in London. In the provinces one only has to go to London and disappear. But once you have a girl in your life in London she knows all your associates, you have established yourself, she knows some of your affairs; she knows where to find you; and it is impossible to disappear from Alice without disappearing from the centre of things, the spiritualist movement – Marlene – his Circle – 'My bread and butter.' Patrick is indignant. He has loved Alice.

He has not taken any money from her. He has given her money, has supported her for nearly a year. She has agreed to trust him, it is a pact. She is mine, he is thinking. The others were not mine but this one is mine. I have loved her, I still love her. I don't take anything from Alice. I give. And I will release her spirit from this gross body. He looks with justification at the syringe by her bedside, and is perfectly convinced about how things will go in Austria (all being well), since a man has to protect his bread and butter, and Alice has agreed to die, though not in so many words.

Patrick watched her calmly and reflected that he had been weak with Alice. She had talked and talked about marriage, as if he were a materialist with a belief in empty forms. He had told her frequently he was not a person of conventions: 'I live by the life of the spirit.' She had only replied, 'I'm not conventional, either.' And when she had conceived this disgusting baby she had been frantic for marriage. It was absurd that she refused to have the baby done away with and was frantic for marriage.

It was her love for him and his spiritual values that made her so like the other women, crumpled up on the bed after their fury. A little dread entered in among his bones: it was about the chances of the Flower case coming up, and the possibility of a conviction. He absented himself from this idea and gave himself up to spiritual reflection again. Before Alice had recovered herself, he, watching from his chair, was surprised by a sensation which he had never experienced before. This was an acute throb of anticipatory pleasure at the mental vision of Alice, crumpled up – in the same position as she now was on the bed – on the mountainside in Austria. She is mine, I haven't taken a penny from this one, I have given to this one. I can do what pleases me. I love this one. She has agreed to trust. Crumpled up on the mountainside in Austria, Alice, overloaded with insulin, far from help, beyond the reach of a doctor, beyond help – far from the intrusive knowledge of his friends and enemies in London, outside the scope of his bread and butter, free from her heavy body, beyond good and evil. She has agreed to it, not in so many words, but . . .

She looked up from the bed, and was startled. But the fear left her face. There is a pact, he thought. She has agreed to believe in me.

It was still Sunday night and Ronald had gone up the stairs to Elsie Forrest's room at 10 Vesey Street near Victoria and had sat on the stairs awaiting her return at half past eleven, when, as she approached her door, he stood up.

'Christ!' she said when she saw him.

'I hope I didn't give you a fright.'

'What d'you want?'

'To come inside and talk to you,' Ronald said.

'You threaten me, I'll wake up the house.'

Ronald sat down on the top stair. 'I'm not threatening you. I'm only asking if I may talk to you. If you don't want me to talk to you, would you mind talking to me?'

She opened the door. 'Come on in,' she said, and stood and looked at him as he walked into her bed-sitting-room.

'I've got nothing in the place to drink,' she said.

'Not even tea?' said Ronald.

She said, 'Take your things off and sit down.'

She took off her own coat and hung it in the cupboard, from which she brought a coat-hanger and carefully set Ronald's coat upon it and set it up on a hook behind the door. Ronald sat on the divan and stretched out his legs.

As she put the kettle on the little electric grill stove behind a curtain she said, 'What was it you wanted to talk about?' She looked at him from the sides of her eyes as she set out the tea-cups.

'Anything you like.'

She was looking at him, not to size up what he had come to talk about, but in an evaluating way which made Ronald feel like something in the sales.

'You're Ronald Bridges,' she said.

'You're Elsie Forrest,' he said.

'You want the letter,' she said. She went over to the window and drew the limp short makeshift curtains.

He said, 'Have the police been to see you?'

'No,' she said. 'And you know they haven't. You wouldn't be fool enough to tell the cops until you had tried to get it back yourself. It would tell against your reputation, losing a confidential document, wouldn't it? Why didn't you keep it confidential if it was confidential?'

'I don't know,' he said.

'You wouldn't be foolish enough to tell the cops,' she said.

'No,' he said. 'But a friend of mine has done so.'

'I don't believe it,' she said. 'No detectives have called here.'

'I've told them to leave it to me for the time being.'

'I don't believe it,' she said.

'All right,' he said. 'The kettle's boiling over,' he said.

She made the tea, and Ronald watched her. She looked very neurotic, moving in a jerky way, her body giving little twitches of habitual umbrage. Her blonde greasy hair hung over her face as she poured out the tea.

'Your friend Matthew Finch came to see me,' she said.

'Yes, I know,' Ronald said.

'He was after the letter.'

'Yes, I know.'

'He didn't get it,' she said.

'I know.'

'And that's why you've come after it.'

'I didn't need to come after it,' he said.

'All right,' she said, 'send the police. I'll face all that.' She sat down beside him on the sofa and, folding her hands in her lap, looked straight ahead of her. 'I've faced it already,' she said with tragic intensity, such as Alice employed when talking to a man and the stress of the occasion demanded it.

All at once, Ronald quite liked her.

'I have died,' she said, 'many deaths.'

'Tell me,' he said, 'how that has happened.'

She pushed back her hair from her bumpy forehead. She had a warped young face.

'I have loved too much and trusted too much,' she said, perceiving the success of her style, 'I have given and I haven't received.'

'Have you had a lot of sex relations?' Ronald said.

'I have had sex without any relationships. I don't know why I'm telling you this in the first five minutes.'

'You've met the wrong chaps,' Ronald said.

'All the chaps are wrong ones. If they aren't married they are queer; if they aren't queer they are hard; if they aren't hard they are soft. I can't get anywhere with men, somehow. Why am I telling you all this?'

'I'm the uncle type,' Ronald said.

'Why d'you say that? Are you interested in psychology? – I'm very interested in psychology. Why are you the uncle type?'

'Because everyone tells me their troubles,' Ronald said.

'And don't you tell people your troubles?'

'No,' Ronald said, 'my troubles are largely self-evident and I'm not the filial type. To be able to tell people your troubles you have to be a born son. Or daughter, as the case may be.'

'I must be a born daughter,' Elsie said, 'according to psychology.'

'At the moment you're being a niece if I'm being an uncle. Let's keep our terms of reference in order.'

'Well, I know a Father Socket,' Elsie said. 'He's just let me down badly. I looked on him as a father, and now I've found out he's a homosexual.'

'You can overlook that,' Ronald said, 'if you think of him as second cousin.'

'I can't overlook it. I hate queers. I want to conceive a child.'

'Fond of babies?'

'Not particularly. It's not a question of having a child so much as conceiving a child by a man I love.'

'You'd better get a husband,' Ronald said. 'That would be the obvious course.'

'There aren't any husbands that I know of. My own brother's unfaithful to his wife; it makes me sick. And he expects me to encourage him. "Lend us your room for the afternoon, Elsie," he says. And when I won't lend the room he says, "You're not much of a sister." I said, "I object to the type of woman you pick up with." So I do. I couldn't have them coming here. That's what my brother's like. I always knew he would make a rotten husband.'

'You'd better find a husband that isn't like your brother.'

'There aren't any husbands so far as I've met. All the men I know want to lean on me or take it out on me. I did all Father Socket's typing. That friend of yours, Matthew Finch, he only wanted to commit a sin with me and he ate a lot of onions and breathed on my face so I shouldn't enjoy it. If he's your friend, I can only say –'

'Oh, if he's my friend, we might leave him out of the discussion.'

'Now, there's another thing – the way you men stick together against us.'

'Haven't you any friends?'

'Well, there's Alice.'

'We'll leave her out of the discussion, then.'

'No we won't. Alice is a case. She's mad in love with that little weed Patrick Seton. I'll admit he's a brilliant medium. But what else is there to him? Now she's getting a child by him. And what's he done about it? Wanted her to have it taken away. She thinks he's going to marry her, and she's mistaken. I've told her. I've told Alice. I've told her he'll never marry her. He says he's getting a divorce, and the divorce never happens. And she believes him. Any awkwardness, and he recites poetry to her to explain everything away. I'll bet he hasn't got a wife. He was never the husband type from the start. He won't marry Alice. She refuses to see that.'

'Then why are you defending him, like a sister?'

'I'm not defending him at all, I'm –'

'You're concealing the evidence of his forgery.'

'Oh, the letter – I'm hanging on to that. I know that's what you've come for. But I'm keeping it and I'll take the consequences. I've already faced the consequences. So you can go.'

Ronald got up and went to take his coat off the hanger.

'Stay the night,' she said, 'and I'll give you the letter in the morning.'

Ronald sat down again. 'No,' he said.

'Why? Don't you want to sleep with me?'

'No,' Ronald said.

'Why, tell me why? Is there something wrong with me?'

'Uncles don't sleep with nieces,' Ronald said.

'Isn't that carrying the idea a bit far?'

'Yes,' Ronald said, 'it is. I'm not an uncle, I'm a stranger. That's why I can't sleep with you.'

'Am I a stranger?'

'Yes,' Ronald said.

'You're only playing for time,' she said. 'I'm well aware you're trying to handle me. It's the letter you're after. Take all and give nothing.'

'I thought we were having an interesting conversation, mutually appreciated as between strangers,' Ronald said.

'Yes, and when you go away you'll feel "Well, I haven't got the letter but at least I cheered up the poor girl for an hour."

And what d'you suppose *I'll* feel? It's much better for men not to come at all if they're always going to go away and leave me alone. I'm not lonely before they come. I'm only lonely when they go away.'

'There's a whole philosophy attached to that,' Ronald said. 'It turns on the question whether it's best not to be born in the first place.'

'That's a silly question,' she said, 'because if you weren't born you couldn't ask it.'

'Yes, it is silly. But, since one has been born, it's one of the mad questions one has been born to ask.'

'I think it's better to be born. At least you know where you are,' Elsie said.

'Aren't you contradicting yourself?' Ronald said.

'I don't care if I am. There's a big difference between feeling lonely after a man's gone away and not being born at all. Being born is basic. You don't need to have company in the same way as you need to be born.'

'There's a lot in what you say,' Ronald said.

'I say it's a mistake to have company, I wish I could stop it.'

'You only need stick a note on your door saying "Away for a few weeks" and leave it there.'

'I haven't the guts,' she said. 'And I don't get much companionship out of the men I know. All they want is sex, and perhaps we have an evening out with sex in view, but they're anxious to get back to their mums and aunties or their wives.'

'You should make them entertain you without sex,' Ronald said, '– an intelligent girl like you.'

'They don't want intelligence. They don't come if there's no sex. I'm a sexy type, I get excited about it. And that's what they like. But it only leaves me lonely.'

'Don't you enjoy it at the time?'

'No. But I can't do without it, and these men know it. They fumble about with their french letters or they tear open their horrible little packets of contraceptives like kids with sweets, or they expect me to have a rubber stop-gap all ready fitted. All the time I want to be in love with the man and conceive his child, but I keep thinking of the birth-control and something inside me turns in its grave. You can't enjoy sex in that frame of mind.'

'I know the feeling,' Ronald said, 'it's like contemplating suicide.'

'Have you thought of committing suicide?'

'Yes,' he said, 'but something inside me turns in its grave.'

'I've thought of suicide, but in the end I always decide to wait in case another possibility turns up. I might meet a man that wants to live with me and not keep slamming the door in my face with birth-control. There were plenty wanted to live with Alice before she took up with Patrick Seton. And now *she's* in for a let-down, though she won't admit it. But at least she's had her sex with a baby coming up.'

'You can't have babies all over the place,' Ronald said. 'It isn't practical.'

'I know,' she said.

'Will you give me back the letter?' Ronald said.

'Why should I?'

'Because you took it,' Ronald said.

'It's the first time I've taken anything worth having off a man. And I want to keep it.'

'What for?'

'It may come in useful. It may help Alice. If Patrick gets convicted she'll be in the cart. I'd like to see him in gaol, but still he's Alice's man, and I don't see why I shouldn't destroy the evidence against him. I'm quite sure it's a forgery.'

'You won't destroy the letter,' Ronald said.

'How do you know?'

'It has too many possibilities of exploitation. You could form a blood-brotherhood with several persons out of that letter. You have already offered to give it to me if I slept with you.'

'Well, how do you know I would have given it to you in the end?'

'You're mistaken if you think it's going to make any difference to the evidence against Patrick whether you keep it or not,' Ronald said. 'There are photo-copies which will be accepted in court together with evidence of the loss of the original.'

'Why do you want it, then?'

'To save my own reputation. I get jobs from the police in the detection of forgeries. I shouldn't have told anyone about this document – that was my mistake. And it's obviously my responsibility that it was stolen. But if I can produce the letter after all, the matter will be forgotten.'

'If I give you the letter will you promise to come and talk to me again?'

'No,' Ronald said.

'I don't see why I should give you the letter. You've been talking as a friend and getting round me, and all you want is the letter.'

'I'm not a friend, I'm a stranger,' Ronald said. 'I've quite liked talking to you.'

'Well, I'm a stranger too. And I'm keeping the letter. There's a price on it.'

'Give it to me for love.'

'What love do I get out of it?'

'That's not the point.'

'Well, you've got a nerve, I'll say that. But you all come for what you can get.'

'Give it to me for love,' Ronald said. 'The best type of love to give is sacrificial. It's an embarrassing type of love to receive, if that's any consolation to you. The best type of love you can receive is to be taken for granted as a dependable person and otherwise ignored – that's more comfortable.'

'It's all talk,' she said. 'I'm tired. I've been doing a late shift at the Oriflamme.'

'Well, think about it in the morning.' He took down his coat and shouldered his way into it.

'If I give you the letter now,' she said, 'will you come back again some time?'

'It's unlikely,' he said. 'You go to bed. Thank you for talking.'

'If I don't give you the letter what will you do?'

'I'll come back and try again.'

'Christ!' she said, 'you're driving me mad.' She went over to the window and, thrusting her arm far into the deep makeshift hem, drew out a four-folded paper. 'Take it and run quickly,' she said. 'Run now before I change my mind.' She came and pushed it into the pocket of Ronald's coat. 'Go away,' she said, 'get out of my sight.'

He sat down in his coat and smoothed out the paper. 'You've crumpled it but let's hear what it sounds like,' he said and read aloud,

'Dear Patrick,

I would like you to accept the enclosed cheque for two thousand pounds. Please use the money to further your psychic and spiritualistic work. I leave the details of its disposal entirely to you.

May I say how greatly I admire and have been inspired by your great Work. I shall never be able to thank you enough.

                                    Yours sincerely,
                                    Freda Flower'

'You've crumpled it,' Ronald said, 'but at least you haven't folded it. In forgery detection you have to watch out for the folds.'

'Why's that?'

'Sometimes a line has been inked over after the fold has been made. The forger very often has second thoughts about the job after the paper has been folded, and to make everything perfect he unfolds the paper again and he touches something up; let's say the stroke of an "f". It's possible to see under the microscope if that sort of thing has been done.'

'Is that what Patrick's done, do you think?' She peered over at the letter. 'It looks like a woman's writing to me.'

'So it does to me. He's a clever forger. He's done it before. He's been convicted, served a sentence.'

'Well, Alice doesn't know that. Well, she does know it in a way, but she won't face it. The baby makes her believe in Patrick.'

'She'll know sooner or later.'

'Will he be sent to prison?'

'Oh, one can't guess,' Ronald said, 'it's not such an easy thing to prove. This may be a difficult document. Experts often disagree. Seton's side would have their own expert. And then, everything depends largely on the witnesses. If Mrs Flower's evidence should break down, for instance –'

'But if they know he's a forger from the past, surely –'

'The court isn't told till after the verdict.'

'Alice thinks the case won't come off.'

'No, perhaps it won't come off. Perhaps he won't be sent for trial.'

'Is it confidential that Patrick has been to prison?'

'No, it's common property.' He was examining the letter upside-down.

'Perhaps I won't tell Alice. She thinks they're going to get married, some hope. Anyway, he's taking her away to Austria as soon as the charge is settled one way or another.'

Ronald folded the letter and put it far away into his inner pocket. 'I must go,' he said.

'Will you come again, Ronald?'

'It's unlikely,' he said.

'You've got your letter,' she said.

'Thank you,' he said.

'You need someone to look after you,' she said.

'I was once engaged to a girl who wanted to be a mother to me. It didn't work.'

'You think I'm not good enough for you,' she said. 'Not your class.'

'I'm an epileptic,' he said. 'It rather puts one out of the reach of class.'

'I know you're an epileptic,' she said. 'I was told.'

'Well, goodnight, Elsie.' He went down the stairs and out into the dark streets of Monday morning.

I I

'It's treachery,' Alice said, quite loud in the empty café.

'Now look, Alice,' Elsie said, 'I've never signed any blood-pact with you. We're friends. And being friends doesn't mean being blood-sisters. For goodness' sake let's keep our relationships straight. Treachery is not the word.'

'Where did you get all this kind of talk?' Alice said.

'Now don't you turn cat, Alice. You need a friend just at this moment.'

'To think that you actually handed over that letter without even letting me see it,' Alice said, 'and now the case is coming up and the letter will be used against Patrick.'

'To begin with,' said Elsie, 'I didn't know whether he was going to go for trial or not when I gave him the letter. Secondly, it wouldn't have made any difference to the case because they photo'd the letter and that would have been good enough. Third, I gave it to Ronald for his own sake and I'd do it again –'

'What you wouldn't do for a night with a man . . .'

'He didn't so much as shake hands with me. Fourthly, it was more his letter than mine, and –'

'It's Patrick's letter,' Alice said, 'by law.'

'No, it's Crown property, excuse me. But it's his forgery, all right. Five, if you don't believe Patrick forged the letter I don't see what you're worried about. They can't prove a forgery if there isn't a forgery. It goes by folds in the paper and pauses in the writing. They see it under the microscope. Ronald –'

'Oh, shut up,' said Alice, 'with your one, two, three, four, five. You're such a clever cookie since you saw that man, a pity you don't stop to think he's in the pay of the police.'

'Well, it's his job.'

'Yes, to fake up the evidence. He'll say whatever they want him to say.'

'You don't know Ronald,' said Elsie.

'Now he's got the letter, you won't be seeing *him* again,' Alice said. 'You wait and see.'

'I know,' Elsie said.

'God,' said Alice, 'it's kicking again. I feel faint when it does that.'

Elsie leaned over the café table and looked at Alice's stomach as she clutched it. 'Take your hand away,' Elsie said, 'and let me see.'

Alice took her hand away.

'I can't see anything,' Elsie said.

'Don't stare like that. Someone might come in the shop.'

'No one will come in, it's too early. I can't see it move.'

'You have to look close. It only looks like a butterfly, but it feels like a footballer inside me.'

Elsie slid round to the seat beside Alice and put her hand on Alice's round stomach. 'I can feel it!' she said. 'Kick, kick. I can feel it.'

'It makes me giddy,' Alice said.

'I'll go and draw you another espresso.'

'All right,' Alice said.

'I wish I had something alive and kicking inside me,' Elsie said.

*

Tim Raymond sat in his club, looking as lonely as possible in the hope that someone married would take him home to supper, but prepared, if not, to dine alone at eight o'clock. Hildegarde had just written from Gloucestershire, after a long silence, to say she was entering a convent. On hearing this news Tim had telephoned to Ronald. 'Have you heard from Hildegarde?'

'That's the second girl you've driven to religion,' Ronald said.

'*I've* driven?'

'Well, yes, in a way.'

'Hildegarde told you about our affair?'

'Well, not directly. Anyway, of course I knew about it and now that's the second girl –'

'I know,' Tim said. Two years ago his first real girl-friend had entered an Anglican Sisterhood.

'What about that other one you were thinking of marrying?' Ronald said.

'Oh, that's all off. *She* hasn't taken to religion.'

'Well, two's plenty.'

'I wonder why they take to religion.'

'There must be something wrong with you,' Ronald said.

'So there must. Do you know, I always felt Hildegarde was still keen on you, Ronald.'

'Well, she must have got over it. What Order has she entered?'

'Some Canoness affair. I feel rather shattered. Not that I felt all that strongly about Hildegarde, it's just that a loss is a loss. And I didn't know she was R.C. When did she go Roman?'

'Two years ago,' Ronald said, 'and two months. I forget the odd days.'

'What a good memory you've got. Did she join under your influence?'

'Yes. I rather regretted it later.'

'Why?'

'Because she lapsed.'

'Well, she's gone back. There's definitely something odd about Hildegarde. She was a spiritualist for a time, not long ago.'

'Under your influence?'

'Well, it gave us something to talk about. One has to have something to talk about. Hildegarde was a difficult girl to find something to talk about with. Anyway she gave up spiritualism when I got out of it and she must have gone bang back to Rome. Funny going from spiritualism back to Catholicism, don't you think, all prejudices apart? A bit extreme. There are other religions she could have tried if she had to have a religion.'

'There are only two religions, the spiritualist and the Catholic,' Ronald said.

'I say, that's going a bit far. There's the Greek Orthodox and the Quakers and of course the C. of E. and some people are Buddhists, and –'

'You must take it in a figurative sense,' Ronald said, 'or leave it, because I need a drink.'

'Well, that's the news. I thought I'd let you know. Come and drink with me.'

'I'm going out. I'm late, actually,' Ronald said.

'I've got nothing to do tonight,' Tim said. 'What would you do?'

'See a film.'

'Don't want to, somehow.'

'Sit in your club and look as lonely and miserable as possible. Someone will turn up and take you home.'

Tim was doing this when the porter came to announce that his Aunt Marlene was inquiring for him downstairs.

'I'm not here,' Tim said, and moved to another chair. The chair he had been occupying was placed in the window and the curtains had been left undrawn. He suspected that Marlene had seen him from the street. He took off his glasses, polished them with his handkerchief, and put them on again.

An almost telepathic communication from the entrance hall – for nothing could be heard from that direction – told him that an argument was going on between Marlene and the porter at the desk. Tim tip-toed attentively to the door, tripping over the legs of someone whose face was hidden by a newspaper, so that Tim's hand came to rest on the man's lap.

'Oh,' Tim said, 'it's you, Eccie.' He straightened up, by which time the porter had appeared again.

'The lady said she is convinced you are in the building. I've told her I would have another look.'

'I'm going along to the bar,' Tim said. 'Tell her you've had another look.'

'I'm not sure,' said Eccie, 'that the British Council is going to suit me. Their notions of art –'

'Come along to the bar,' Tim said, urgently. 'My aunt's downstairs.'

'Well, she won't come up here.'

'Oh, won't she?' said Tim.

Eccie puckered his face in puzzlement and followed Tim, who, looking over the banister, perceived a corner of his aunt in the hall as she argued with the porter.

They slipped into the bar.

'I have a series of twelve lectures,' Eccie declared over his drink. 'They have gone down well for twelve years. They are old and tried and have stood the test of time at the old Institute. They cover the Renaissance to Kandinsky. They were the nucleus of the Art course at the Institute. Thousands of people passed through our hands south of the Humber. I travelled the length and breadth, to W.V.S. centres, National Service units, prisons, summer schools – all over the place. And everywhere I went those lectures got a tremendous reception. They were highly appreciated. From the Renaissance to Kandinsky, with a set of colour reproductions, tested and tried. And now, when I'm all fixed for my injections for Malta, the chap at the British Council says – and mind you it's we who pay them, it's the taxpayer, you and I, whose money goes into their pockets – he calls me in and he says –'

'Tim, oh, there you are!'

Marlene stood by the other door leading from the back stairs.

Tim put down his drink and disappeared out of the opposite door. Marlene did not pursue him, as he expected, through the bar. She retreated down the back stairs to the first landing, walked along a passage, and came out on to the big oak-panelled first-floor landing where she again encountered Tim.

She said, 'The trial is on, and it is settled that you are to be a witness. We have decided, on Patrick's own advice, not to give evidence for his character as he prefers his character to speak for itself. But there is a question of a statement that Patrick made to the police under duress, while still in a state of trance after a séance. We must testify about this séance. I have the date and the time. Eleven-thirty on the morning of August the twelfth. Patrick made his statement at twelve noon. He was not properly out of his trance. You are to give evidence that you saw him in a trance at eleven-thirty, but we must decide exactly what you are to say because you are inclined to be hesitant and vague. I am calling a meeting –'

'Marlene, you shouldn't be here.'

'Get your coat immediately,' she said, 'and come with me.'

'I'm just going to the lavatory,' Tim said and disappeared with his long legs up the main staircase like an anxious spider. He did not, however, go into the lavatory, but into the library where an aged member and a young man were bending over an architectural-looking plan spread out on the table. They looked up at Tim. The aged member said 'Who?' and they both looked down again at their plan. Tim wandered over to the window and there slipped behind the curtains. Marlene waited outside the lavatory. A man emerged with eyebrows which were by nature fixed in slight astonishment, and which, when he saw Marlene, seemed to try to rise. 'Is my nephew in there?' Marlene said.

The man moved off, assuming her to be one of the maids gone mad in her private life.

Marlene waited. In ten minutes' time she knocked loudly on the door.

'Tim,' she said.

'Tim!' she said.

'Listen, Tim,' she said. 'I will take you across to Prunier's. We can discuss everything there. You *know* you like Prunier's.'

'Timothy!' she said.

A very young man came round the corner. 'Oh!' he said at Marlene's back.

'Would you mind going in there and telling my nephew, Tim Raymond, that he's wanted urgently? A matter of life and death. Hurry.'

The young man went in as one accustomed to military training, leaving the door open. Marlene stood in the doorway and watched while he politely looked round.

'There's nobody here,' said the young man.

The aged member from the library approached the door, followed by his young companion.

Marlene was saying, 'Nonsense. He is hiding from me. Have a good look.'

'Who?' said the aged member behind her.

'Let *me* look,' said Marlene, entering this tiled enclosure.

'Who?' said the old man.

He was ushered away by his fellows.

Marlene continued her simple but fruitless search. When she came out she caught sight of the porter as he came up the stairs with the look of one who had been sent.

Marlene tripped along the passage and into the library. The room appeared to be unoccupied. A thin and feeble little cloud of cigarette smoke proceeded from the join of the window curtains. Marlene observed the bulge where Tim had pulled a chair behind the curtain to console his vigil, and made straight for it.

'Tim, you are wasting my time.'

Footsteps approached outside and the door-handle was turned. Marlene got behind the curtain with Tim just before the porter put his head round the door. As soon as he had withdrawn Tim moved out to the far side of the big table.

'It is a matter of life and death,' Marlene said.

'I've got to go to the lavatory,' Tim said. This was genuine, and he departed.

Marlene found a place of concealment at the end of the passage. Tim came out of the lavatory and, looking to right and left, darted upstairs. Marlene followed, in time to catch him as he attempted to close a door behind him. She pushed her way in against him and confronted him in a bleak vacant bedroom. She locked the door.

'Now, Tim,' she said, 'what's all this fuss about?'

'I don't want to give evidence in Seton's case,' he said. 'It's got nothing to do with me, Marlene.'

'It isn't a matter of what you want. It's a question of what is necessary.'

'No,' said Tim, 'really.'

'What?' she said.

'Nothing doing,' Tim said.

'You are out of your mind,' she said.

Tim made a dash for the door, unlocked it, fled downstairs, grabbed his coat and dashed into the street where he turned several corners, and then caught a taxi.

Marlene walked solemnly downstairs and demanded some scrap paper from the hall porter.

'Mr Raymond has left, Madam.'

'I wish to leave a note.'

She folded it in four when she had written it and wrote Tim's name on the outside. She gave it to the porter who, when she had gone, read the message: 'I shall see my solicitor tomorrow with a view to altering the legacy arrangements. Marlene Cooper.'

Ewart Thornton sat with his elbow resting on the arm of his wide chair, and in his hand the telephone receiver.

'There is a meeting tonight. Of course I shall not be present. Freda my dear, there is something you should know about the Wider Infinity. There is a group within the Group. A secret group within the Group. Now you didn't know that, Freda dear, did you? Doesn't it surprise you?'

Freda Flower sat in her chair by the telephone, looking up at a cobweb in the corner of the ceiling which she dared not sweep away for fear of bad luck, and spoke into the telephone.

'You amaze me, Ewart,' she said.

'I thought that would surprise you,' he said. 'My dear, this secret group within the Group is called the Interior Spiral.'

'That's a make of mattress, isn't it?' she said.

'It may be, it may be. I say, my dear Freda, you are taking this seriously, aren't you?'

'I think it's a very serious matter indeed, Ewart. After all, it was my money that was –'

'Yes, quite. Well, as I was saying, there is this secret group, and I admit I was a member. There was some good in it, Freda, we did a lot of good. But an evil spirit got abroad amongst us. I have resigned. There is a conspiracy amongst them to support Patrick Seton at the trial. Of course, this is illegal and they won't have a leg to stand on, but –'

'Oh, Ewart, oh, Ewart. I do wish I had never gone to the police about that money. They will make me say more things against Patrick, and with him standing there in the dock, with his eyes on me. I don't know how I managed the other day in the Magistrate's Court. I came home to bed, and –'

'You only have to speak the truth, Freda. It is the truth, isn't it? You did give him that money to buy bonds?'

'Oh yes, but –'

'And he used it for his own purposes?'

'Yes, but –'

'And forged a letter to cover himself?'

'Yes, it's true, but . . . Oh, Ewart, I somehow knew all the time he was deceiving me and I let it go. It makes –'

'You knew?'

'Well, I knew and I didn't know. I wouldn't admit it to myself. And now to get up in the criminal court with his eyes on me again and stick to the facts as Mr Fergusson says, it will be such a sort of let-down, a betrayal, and poor little Patrick, he's so thin.'

'Tell me, Freda dear – I'm a man of the world – was there any – were there any *relations* between you and Patrick Seton? In confidence, my dear?'

'Well, Ewart, I don't want to talk about it, naturally I've got my pride. But he got round me, you know, Ewart, and I let myself go. He –'

'My dear, if this is mentioned in court, deny it. Simply flatly deny it. It is irrelevant to the case. I doubt very much if Patrick would bring it up in court – it would go against him, if anything. You were foolish, Freda my dear.'

'I know I'm a foolish woman. It's not just the disgrace of it coming up that's worrying me. But it was terrible the other day to stand up in front of Patrick and denounce him to the magistrate after being together like that. He looked at me. It –'

'That's just his trick, my dear. Don't you see? He counts on women being weak. He –'

'Oh, I do believe he meant everything in his heart at the time when we were together, really. And he can see through everything, Ewart. You don't know how psychic he is. He's in touch with my poor husband. He's in touch with the Beyond. He –'

'Are you afraid of him?' Ewart said.

'Yes.'

'What are you afraid of?'

'His looking at me. He used to recite "Season of mists and mellow fruitfulness", it was a deepening experience, Ewart.'

'You must definitely speak to Father Socket, Freda. If you feel an evil eye upon you, Father Socket will exorcise it for you –'

'Father Socket has gone away. Dr Garland can't find him anywhere. He isn't at Ramsgate and he's left the flat. Dr Garland's upset. Dr Garland's sent those girls away – and between you and me, good riddance. You don't tell *me* they were waitresses. No fear.'

'There must have been a break between Socket and Mike Garland,' Ewart said. 'My dear. Tell me more.'

'Oh, definitely a break. I don't know what about.'

'Have you seen Mike Garland recently?'

'No. There's rent owing for the girls.'

'Freda my dear, you simply must keep clear of these cranks.'

'Ewart, I feel I can count on you. If only I didn't have to go to court and stand up. The case might go on for a whole day or more. Will you be at the trial?'

'Oh no. Exams.'

'I should like to see you. Won't you come over?'

'Sorry. Loads of homework.' The comfort went out of his face at the notion of his telephone-relationship getting out of hand.

'Suppose Patrick gets off?' she said.

'He won't get off if you stick to the facts.'

'But this Interior Spiral. They might get up and say anything. Suppose Patrick gets off? – He'll do me damage, Ewart, and I'll only have myself to blame.'

'The Interior Spiral, as I was about to tell you, Freda my dear, is dwindling fast. Marlene will find herself with very few friends when it comes to a court case.'

'Suppose Patrick *doesn't* get off? – He'll do me damage.'

Ewart Thornton suddenly desired to ring off. The act of gossiping with her over the telephone was a need, but the need was fulfilled in the act. He did not like it when the conversation seemed to be getting somewhere. 'Patrick will do me harm.' She upset him by going on like this. What if Patrick did her harm? Ewart felt uneasy about Patrick. He might well do harm. It was best to keep out of Patrick's reach. Patrick was definitely in touch with things out there in the Unseen.

'Patrick,' said Freda, 'has the *power* to do –'

'Freda my dear, I must go. Mounds of homework.'

He sulked for a moment after he had put down the receiver, then he rose fatly, and presently stood up tall so that his hips lost their broadness. He tidied his room for the night. He put this away and that in its place, and sighed for his superannuation.

Marlene sat in her indignation, awaiting the meeting of the Interior Spiral. Everyone was late. It was a quarter to nine and the meeting had been called for half past eight. The six coffee-cups and the plate of biscuits stood on the tray like messages of regret for inability to attend. Ewart Thornton had said he would not come. Still, one had hoped . . . Tim, to whom had been offered this unique opportunity of becoming acquainted with the Interior Spiral, was *out*. Out – she had seen her solicitor that morning and Tim was out of her Will. Five others had promised, were expected, might still come, would surely . . . Patrick himself, why was he late? The two retired spinsters, the Cottons from round the corner, where were they? Disloyally attending those life classes they had recently taken up, Marlene had no doubt. She had told them of the urgency. Billy Raines, the photographer? Osbert Jacob? Jacynthe – The door bell rang.

It was Patrick.

'I'm sorry to be late,' he uttered in his half-voice, 'but Alice, I've had trouble with Alice. Keeps talking of suicide . . . one day . . . suicide. It's sure to happen.'

'That girl should be in a home,' Marlene said. 'You are too good to her, Patrick. She is only after what she can get. You are too good.'

She placed her arm round his shoulders and he rested his head upon her bosom of bones.

'Well,' she said, 'take your coat off, Patrick. It is nine o'clock and no one has come. I fear we are deserted, but we are not a sinking ship. Not yet. I told everyone of the urgency, and what was to be discussed. After all I have done for the Infinity. My own nephew, my own flesh and blood, has –'
The door bell rang.

At first she thought it was the Rector of Dees coming up the stairs. She had not expected the Rector of Dees, since he was getting on in years and the trains were so irregular. But she had written to him. And now he had come. 'In my hour of need,' she called down the stairs. 'Dear Rector.'

He looked up from his wide-brimmed hat. It was not the Rector of Dees, it was Father Socket of the enemy faction, protector of Dr Garland so-called.

'Well,' said Marlene, blocking the doorway.

Father Socket removed his hat and looked humble. 'May I come and break bread with you?' he said.

'Come this way,' Marlene said.

She took him into her sitting-room where Patrick stood by the fire. Father Socket held out his hand to Patrick.

'I have come to make my peace,' he said.

Patrick placed his effortless hand in the strong white-hairy one of Father Socket. White hairs bristled on Father Socket's face. He had not shaved.

'Dear lady,' he said to Marlene. 'I have been through the deep waters.'

'Did you say you were hungry?' said she, perceiving he had come as an ally.

'It was a manner of speaking,' he said. 'I have come to ask you to accept what assistance I can offer in your courageous efforts to –'

'You want to witness for Patrick at the trial?'

'I do. I have been greatly deceived in my clairvoyant protégé, Dr Garland. The serpent's –'

'He is no clairvoyant,' said Marlene, 'and he is no doctor.'

'You are right,' said Father Socket. 'And would that I had known it earlier. He is tonight under arrest for activities the nature of which I will not sully my lips by describing. I myself have just come from the police station where I was given to understand that attempts had been made to implicate myself in these activities. Fortunately –'

'What were the activities?'

'Young women were involved. I say no more,' said Father Socket. 'Fortunately there is no shred of evidence against me. I have been away for some days, and I find on my return this afternoon that my flat has been searched in my absence. Needless to say, nothing of the least incriminating nature was found. My name is clear. I have come straight to you to offer my services in atonement for the harm done to Mr Seton by Dr Garland.'

'Doctor so-called,' said Marlene.

'A very wise move,' Patrick said meekly to Father Socket.

Father Socket looked at him, opened his mouth and closed it again.

'We must have our refreshments,' said Marlene. 'The Interior Spiral goes on!' She went to heat the coffee.

'A very wise move,' Patrick said to Father Socket.

'The police have no evidence against me,' Socket said.

'Not unless I lay it before them,' Patrick said meekly, 'because I have proof of the facts.'

'I have come to offer my services, my son,' said Socket. 'I cannot do more. Under the influence of my cloth, my evidence –'

'Come now,' Marlene said, bearing in the coffee pot, 'we

shall refresh ourselves while we discuss the details. How glad I am, after all, that the members of our little Interior have defected! They were not worth their salt. All things work together for good. Do you take sugar, Father?'

'No, nor coffee at this hour, if I may be excused.'

'Details,' said Marlene. 'Now, it is a question, before we see Patrick's counsel, of what you were doing on the morning of the twelfth of August. You were at Patrick's rooms on that morning, receiving a private séance. Patrick was in a trance . . . You saw a police car pull up outside just as you were leaving the premises . . . his statement . . . in a trance.'

By midnight they were rehearsed.

'Before you leave,' Marlene said, 'shall we go into the Sanctuary for a few moments' spiritual repose?'

In the Sanctuary a dim green light was burning. Patrick automatically took the carved oak séance chair while Marlene and Socket sat facing him.

They breathed deeply. Suddenly Patrick's head jerked backwards. Marlene whispered to Socket, 'Take my hand. He is going into a trance. He may prophesy.'

Patrick gurgled. His eyes rolled upward. Water began to run from the sides of his mouth which at last he opened wide. In a voice not his, he pronounced, 'I creep.'

Marlene's arms went rigid. Socket tried to release his hand but could not.

Patrick's mouth was foaming. His head dropped and his eyes closed. He breathed loudly. His fingers twitched on the end of the chair-arm. Presently he lifted up his head again and his eyes opened into slits.

Marlene said, 'He's coming round.'

They left the Sanctuary of Light, Marlene assisting Patrick.

'Did I give utterance?' Patrick said. 'What did I say?'

*

Walter Prett leaned his bulk over the bar of the wine club in Hampstead. It had just opened and he was the first customer. He said to the barmaid, 'I say, Chloe, you know everyone, don't you?'

'Just about,' she said.

'Do you know Isobel Billows?'

'Now who is she?' Chloe said, concentrating her sharp young face on the subject.

'She was married to Carr Billows of Billows Flour.'

'Oh, Flourbags?'

'Yes, his first wife.'

'I don't know of her,' Chloe said. 'What about her?'

'She's got lots of money. I broke her china the other day.'

'Whatever do you mean, you naughty boy?'

'I'll have another,' Walter said.

'You broke her china?'

'Yes, all her china tea-cups. They were on a tray. I smashed the lot.'

'Why d'you do that?' Chloe said, polishing the glasses on the counter so that her time should not be not altogether wasted.

'Why? That's what I ask myself between opening times. I love that woman, Chloe. And yet I go and behave like a hog.'

'Just a minute,' said Chloe, drawing inspiration from the embossed cornice. 'Just a minute. Haven't I heard that she's got a barrister friend?'

'She has indeed. Martin Bowles. Do you know him?'

'No, I don't think –'

'No, you wouldn't know him. He's nobody. Only he hangs round Isobel for her money. He's the financial wizard, you see. And lines his own pocket on the right side of the law. A common little, vulgar little –'

'Now don't start that,' Chloe said, 'Walter, please. Not at this hour of the evening. Hallo, Eccie,' she said as Francis Eccles came in.

'And he's bald,' said Walter. 'At least I've got a good head of hair.' He shook his white mane.

'You could do with a trim,' said Chloe.

'I've resigned from the British Council,' said Eccie.

Walter hugged him like a bear and embraced him on both cheeks. He drew from his pocket three five-pound notes and gave one to Eccie. 'What's this for?' Eccie said.

'A congratulatory gift.'

'The return of a loan,' said Chloe. 'I remember the last time you were here –'

'Vulgar little lower-middle-class ideas you have, Chloe. I do not borrow and return. I take. I give.'

'You can give me sixteen and six and clear out,' Chloe said. 'I won't be talked to like that.'

Walter beamed at her.

'Yes, it's all right when you're in the right mood,' Chloe said, 'but you turn about like the weather.'

'My lectures,' said Eccie, 'were designed to reveal the essence of art from Botticelli to Kandinsky, with reference to the lives of the artists themselves, supported by coloured plates, excellent reproductions. Those lectures have stood the test –'

'I should leave out the lives of the artists,' Walter said. 'They don't bear looking into.'

'Oh, come, I wouldn't say that.'

'They break up ladies' china cups,' Walter said mournfully.

'Since when were you an artist?' Chloe said.

Walter looked dangerous.

'Walter, now, Walter,' said Eccie, 'don't *do* anything.'

'I have spent a long time not doing anything,' Walter said.

'The sins of the artist are sins of omission. You should do a lecture on that, Eccie, with reference to the lives of the art-critics.'

'Well, as I was saying,' Eccie said, 'this chap called me in, and he said . . .'

'I pray,' said Alice, 'day and night. I go into churches and pray if the doors are open, and I pray that Patrick will be saved from prison.'

'I wouldn't build on it,' Elsie said.

'I am building on it. I pray for Patrick, and that's the test. If Patrick doesn't get off, I don't believe in God.'

'Patrick hasn't much chance, with the statement he made to the police against him.'

'He was half in a trance when he made that statement. There's a police officer that's got an influence on Patrick, and he talked him into it. Patrick was just out of a trance.'

'The jury won't know what a trance is.'

'They'll learn.'

'There's a prejudice against spiritualism,' Elsie said.

'Oh, can't you look on the bright side, Elsie?'

'I don't know what's bright about you having Patrick wearing you down for the rest of your life.'

'Well, he's my choice, Elsie.'

'I know that. I'm afraid for you.'

'Don't be afraid for me. And you needn't be afraid for Patrick either, now that Father Socket's come forward to speak for him. There's no denying the impression Father Socket makes on people.'

'Father Socket?' Elsie said. 'He's against Patrick. He was in with Mike Garland. A couple of *those*.'

'There's been a rift. Garland is in trouble with the police and let Father Socket down. So Father Socket has come in with Patrick now. It's going to be all right, I feel it. Father Socket was with Patrick on the morning of the twelfth of August, and he saw Patrick in a trance just before the police came –'

'Twelfth of August was my birthday,' Elsie said.

'So it was. Well, that was the day that Patrick made the statement. But everything's all right now.'

'I don't see you need to pray for Patrick if you're so sure of that.'

'It's a test of God,' said Alice.

Elsie telephoned from Victoria Station to Ronald. 'I've got to see you. It's about the evidence for Patrick Seton. Father Socket is going to give false evidence. I've got to see you.'

'Father who?'

'That Father I told you about, that let me down.'

'Oh, yes.'

'Well, he's going to say that on the morning of twelfth of August – which was my birthday and I had the day off – he's going to swear –'

'Look,' said Ronald, 'I'm not the police.'

'Can't I tell you? I'd rather give you the story.'

'It's not my business. Go straight to the police station. Ask for Detective-Inspector Fergusson. Have you any evidence?'

'No, only my word.'

'Well, it's as good as Socket's. Go and see Mr Fergusson.'

'I'll ring and tell you what he says.'

'No need to,' Ronald said. 'It's not my business.'

'Then I don't know if I shall bother,' Elsie said. 'It's not my business either.'

*

Marlene was on the night train to Scotland.

'I'm very sorry, Patrick,' she had said, standing at the door of her flat, her baggage packed and visible in the hall behind her, keeping him out. 'Very sorry indeed. But on consideration I simply must safeguard my reputation for the sake of the Circle. Nothing has changed, my feelings are the same, but on consideration I can't give evidence. And as it happens I've been called away urgently. You have Father Socket. I am no loss.'

She thought, now, perhaps she had been hard on Tim. It had been well-meaning of him to telephone to her.

'I say, Marlene, do keep out of the Seton case. You'll be charged with suborning, Marlene dear. The police may be on the alert for suborners, Ronald Bridges gave me the tip.'

'What is suborning?'

'Conspiracy. Cooking up evidence in a law case before-hand.'

'There has been no cooking up on my part. There is no contrary proof whatsoever. There –'

'It's a criminal offence, Marlene dear, you might go to Holloway prison. I should hate –'

'You beastly little fellow. You snivelling . . .'

She had hung up the receiver in the middle of his pro-tests. All the same, on consideration . . .

The train to Dundee was a rocky one. She stood up in her bunk and tried to adjust the air-conditioning equipment of the sleeping compartment, but failed. She pressed the bell. No one came. She wondered if Patrick might have some spiritual power over her, even in Scotland. She could not sleep.

'The key,' said Dr Lyte miserably, handing Patrick the key.

'A month's supply of insulin,' he said, handing Patrick the prescription. 'When will you be going?'

'The day after the trial. Alice is upset, you know. Very depressed. She needs the holiday.'

'I'll be seeing you in court then tomorrow, Mr Fergusson.'

'Yes, Patrick. Be there at quarter past ten.'

'If I get off, Mr Fergusson, I may have some news for you.'

'Let's have your information now, then, Patrick.'

'I'd rather wait and see if I get off.'

'Your news wouldn't be about Socket, would it?'

'I'd rather not say, Mr Fergusson.'

'We need information about Socket. I don't mind admitting it,' said Fergusson.

'That statement I signed in August – you'll be using it in court?' Patrick said.

'Yes, Patrick. We can't let you get away with that, I'm afraid. You've been useful to us, but a statement's a statement. It's filed.'

'You got me in a weak moment when I gave you that statement,' Patrick whispered. 'I was upset, you remember, Mr Fergusson—' He looked at the broad shoulders and did not want ever to have to leave the chair in which he sat contemplating them, and go out into the streets again.

'I have no recollection,' said Fergusson, 'that you were upset.'

'Don't you remember, I was all shaken up that morning?'

'Yes, Patrick, I know that. But as far as the law is concerned I have no recollection.'

'There's the question of the letter,' Patrick said.

'It was foolish of you to go and forge that letter. Another couple of years on your sentence at least.'

'Our expert is convinced the letter's genuine,' Patrick mumbled.

'Our expert isn't,' said Fergusson.

Patrick wrenched himself away. But when he had plunged out into the street again, he felt better, and considering the chances, was confident of his release, so that he did not give thought to the matter again that day, but thought of Alice.

12

From time to time throughout the trial, Patrick Seton sat in the dock visualising, with fretful eagerness, Alice as she should lie on the mountainside, crumpled up, overdosed with insulin; the liberation of Alice's spirit was so imminent, it was like a sunny radiance to distract his understanding from the proceedings of the court.

When the time came for him to speak, he was lucid and calm and clear-voiced. Alice had never heard him speak so clearly, she was astonished.

'His voice has changed, hasn't it?' she whispered to Matthew, up in the public gallery.

'I don't know,' Matthew said. 'How should I know what his voice is like?'

'I think he must be making a special effort,' Alice whispered. 'He feels a strong clear voice is called for.'

'Don't talk. I want to listen,' Matthew said, 'to this bit.'

'He's doing well, isn't he?' said Alice. 'After the mess they made of the Prosecution case this morning –'

'Don't talk,' Matthew said, leaning over the rail of the gallery. 'I want to listen.'

'I do think,' Alice said, 'that Elsie might have come.'

Ronald walked through the late-night streets, recovering his strength. He had spent the day in court. He had been the third witness for the Prosecution.

'Have you ever in your life made a mistake?' said the Defence Counsel in his cross-examination.

'Yes,' said Ronald.

'This couldn't be one of them?'

'I have never, so far as I know, made a mistake in a case of forgery.'

'So far as you know. Thank you, Mr Bridges – Oh, oh . . .'

'Oh!' said the whole world at once, 'what's happened? He's falling, fainting.'

Ronald had put on his best dark suit for the occasion. He had arrived at the Criminal Court at ten minutes past ten. He had never before seen Martin Bowles in his wig and gown in court; it was an amazing sight. Martin had become instantly wise, unimpeachable. Once, at Isobel Billows's, she having found Martin's wig at the back of his car and brought it into the house, Ronald had seen her try it on and, watching herself in the rather dim gilt-framed looking-glass, recite,

'The quality of mercy is not strained . . .'

'They always say that,' said Martin. 'Women, when they try on a lawyer's wig, always do that.'

The case opened at half past ten. Hugh Farmer, Counsel for the Defence, lolled back against the bench, sometimes whispering to his pupil behind him while the indictment was read for the second time. He was thinking of his elder daughter, at the moment taking her most important examination in music.

'Fraudulent conversion . . . forgery . . . Mrs Freda Flower.'

Martin Bowles got up to open the case for the Prosecution. Hugh Farmer watched him respectfully as Martin gave small reasonable waves of his hand, with upturned palm, towards the jury.

'Detective-Inspector Fergusson will read you a statement made and signed by the accused . . .

'Mrs Freda Flower will tell you . . .

'I will call an expert in the detection of forgery who will give evidence on the count of . . .'

Now Fergusson was in the witness box, not in uniform. He took his oath. He read Patrick's statement: '. . . I was tempted, and fell. The cheque was for premium and defence bonds. Mrs Flower asked me to obtain them for her. She felt they were safer with me. I did not buy the bonds. I do not know where the money has gone. I have read this over . . .'

Hugh Farmer got up to cross-examine.

'Mr Fergusson, when you saw Mr Seton on the afternoon of twelfth August, the day on which you say he made this statement, did you notice anything peculiar about him?'

'Nothing whatsoever,' said Fergusson.

'Are you sure?'

'Absolutely certain,' said Fergusson.

'Nothing about the eyes? No slight foaming at the mouth?'

The judge said, 'Mr Farmer, what is the –'

'It is relevant, my lord. My client is a spiritualistic medium and I shall show that he was in a trance when he signed that statement at the police station.' He resumed his cross-examination.

'You said just now you were unaware, when you obtained this statement from Mr Seton, that he had received a letter from Mrs Flower asking him to use the money for his own purposes?'

'He said nothing about a letter on that occasion.'

'Then Mr Seton called on you the following week and

told you he had made his statement while in a dazed condition, and wished to withdraw it?'

'I have no recollection of that.'

'He told you he had in his possession a letter from Mrs Flower in which she made it plain that the cheque was freely given for his use in his profession?'

'I have no recollection of him saying that.'

'When you say you have no recollection you mean that in fact you do not remember whether he said it or whether he did not? He might in fact have stated his desire to withdraw his statement or to make a further statement, but it has slipped your recollection.'

'He didn't ask to withdraw his statement or make a further one. He said nothing about a letter on that occasion.'

'You have said you did not know about the existence of a letter from Mrs Flower until some weeks later.'

'That is correct . . .'

'You said . . .'

Alice whispered to Matthew, 'You can see the power he's got over Patrick. Just look at poor Patrick.'

Patrick was sitting in the dock between two policemen, looking at tall square Fergusson with his head slightly to one side and tears shining in his pale eyes.

Next came Freda Flower. She began to swear on the Bible, glanced towards Patrick, and ended on a faltering note.

'You are a widow?' said Martin Bowles. '. . . You let rooms for a living? . . . Do you know the accused? . . . How long have you known the accused? . . . Did he offer to do a little decorating and painting in your house? . . . When did you become interested in the spiritualist movement? . . . Did you attend séances with the accused?'

'Yes,' said Freda Flower. '. . . Yes . . . Yes . . . That's right . . . I started going to spiritualist meetings with Mr

Seton, that would be about three months after he came to my house.'

'He was in charge of these meetings?'

'Oh no, he was the medium.'

'Can you describe to the court in your own words what took place when Mr Seton acted as a medium?'

'Well, he went under and I must say he always gave every satisfaction as a medium, I must say that. He –'

'When you say he went under, Mrs Flower, what does that mean? He sat in a chair, did he not?'

'Yes, he was bound to the chair hands and feet.'

'And this was in the dark.'

'Well, there was always a small light burning in the Sanctuary.'

'There was a dim light in the séance room where the meetings were held – Am I right? . . .'

'Yes, that's right . . . bound hand and foot to a chair . . .'

'Could you describe the trance, please? You must remember that most people present in this court have not attended a spiritualist meeting.'

'He closed his eyes and went under.'

'He appeared to lose consciousness?' said Martin.

'No, because he spoke as a medium after that. The control took over, you see.'

'He appeared to be unaware of what was going on around him?'

'Oh, yes.'

'Will you describe his appearance?'

'Well, you see, he's a medium. His eyes rolled upward and he foamed a bit at the mouth and his legs and arms twitched as far as was possible because they were bound to the chair.'

'Did he obtain messages purporting to come from an invisible world?'

'Yes, he got through to the other side. He –'

'Were any of these messages directed specifically to you?'

'Yes, he got through to my late husband.' She looked at Patrick and looked away. Patrick was accusing her. 'His messages were often a great comfort,' she said.

'These messages from your late husband through the mediumship of Seton contained practical advice?'

'Yes, sometimes . . . Well, not exactly practical, but –'

'Will you give an example?'

'Well, only advice to keep happy and cheerful,' she said, on the verge of tears.

'Anything else?'

'Well, it's difficult . . .'

'On one occasion there was something about money?'

The Defence Counsel was allowed his objection.

Martin said, 'Were you advised as to your friends, the company you kept?'

'Yes,' said Freda, 'my late husband wanted me to be friends with Mr Seton.'

'Was this according to what the accused said while in his trance?'

'Yes.'

'Now,' said Martin, 'about this cheque for two thousand pounds . . .'

Up in the gallery Matthew said to Alice, 'She's giving very bad evidence.'

'What other sort of evidence could she give?' said Alice.

'Will you look at this cheque for two thousand pounds made out to Patrick Seton and say if that is your signature?' Martin was saying.

'Yes,' she said, 'it's mine.'

'Martin Bowles is a clot,' Matthew said.

'He hasn't got much of a case,' said Alice.

Martin was referring to Freda Flower's deposition.

'Yes,' she said. '. . . Yes, I told him to buy them for me.' . . . 'No, it was his suggestion.' . . . 'I thought he had bought the bonds . . . Well, I thought the bonds would be safer with him . . .'

'What do you mean by safer?' said the judge.

'I thought he would keep them safer than me,' she said.

Patrick looked up at Alice. She smiled at him. Her pregnancy, he thought, is hidden by the railings of the balcony. I'm winning. She won't live.

'I did in a way promise him a little help with his spiritual research. I said he should ask me for money.'

Some of the jury were making notes.

'And did he ask you?'

'No, he never asked . . .'

Martin read out the letter to the court. 'I should add,' he said, 'that the letter is undated.'

'Will you look at this letter,' he said, 'and tell the court whether you wrote it or not?'

'No, I never wrote it.'

'Is that handwriting similar to your own?'

'It looks very like my writing. But I couldn't have written it unless I was in a trance or something.'

'Have you ever been in a trance?' said the judge.

'I don't think so, my lord.'

'Don't you know? Have you ever foamed at the mouth and rolled up your eyes, and twitched?'

'No, my lord.'

Matthew said, as the cross-examination began, 'Now we're for it.'

'Serve her right,' Alice said. 'She's just showing herself up for what she is.'

'You have said that Mr Seton gave every satisfaction as a medium?' said Patrick's counsel.

'Yes, he was always a good medium.'

'You had every faith in his powers?'

'Yes.'

'And still have?'

'Oh, yes.'

'You had every reason to believe that he was genuine, whatever may be the opinions of others on spiritualism in general?'

'Oh, he was genuine, I admit.'

'And you say he brought you comfort, and did repairs and decorations to your house?'

'Oh, yes, he –'

'Did you pay him for those repairs and decorations?'

'Well, not exactly. I let the rent go. We were very friendly, you see, after I got to know him.'

'And, finding him trustworthy as a medium, you had confidence in his practical advice and judgement?'

'Yes, I told him everything.'

'His lordship has asked you whether you have ever been in a trance. I am going to repeat that question.'

'I don't think so, sir.'

'Think carefully. Because you said' – he consulted his notes – 'you told the court, when you looked at the letter, "It looks very like my writing. I couldn't have written it unless I was in a trance or something."' His voice rose with nasal emphasis on the words 'or something', and he repeated her words again: 'unless I was in a trance or something'. He put down his notes and breathed deeply. 'Now, Mrs Flower,' he said, 'I am going to put it to you that you have, in fact, had the experience of trances.'

'I couldn't say,' she said. 'It only looks funny that my

handwriting should be on the letter and I don't remember writing it.'

'And it may have been written while you were in a trance?'

The judge said, 'Has anyone ever seen you in a state of trance? Has anyone ever told you or suggested to you that you have been in a trance?'

'No, sir. But I could have been in a trance on my own.'

'Were you in anything like a trance last April when it is suggested that the letter was written?' said the judge.

'I couldn't really say. I was poorly in April.'

The Defence Counsel continued: 'You admit the possibility that one day when you were alone you wrote that letter while in a state of trance?'

'It *is* possible. If you'd seen as much as I have of spiritualism, you would know that the gift can descend on anyone, even an untrained person.'

'By "gift",' said the judge, 'do you mean a state of trance?'

'Yes, and then becoming a medium and getting in touch,' she said.

'Let us get this clear,' said the judge. 'A person in a state of trance as you call it, rolls up his or her eyes, foams at the mouth, and twitches. Then he or she begins to speak?'

'Sometimes they say nothing.'

'What happens,' said the judge, 'when they come out of their trance? Describe it.'

'They look very exhausted, sir, and don't know where they are for some minutes.'

'Have you ever experienced a sensation, while alone, of exhaustion and not knowing where you are, by which you could assume you had just come out of a trance?'

'Sometimes I've dropped off and felt a bit strange, my lord, for a few minutes.'

'Have there been any other signs of a trance such as saliva from foaming at the mouth?'

'Oh no, sir.'

'Do you yourself think you have been in a state of unconsciousness,' said the judge, very slow and clear, 'and at the same time able to write that letter? Try to be explicit.'

'I don't know, sir, I'm sure.'

Martin got up to re-examine her. 'He'll make matters worse,' Matthew said, and he was right.

Martin's tones became menacing as she muddled on. 'Mrs Flower, I am going to call an expert,' Martin said nastily to his witness, 'who will swear that this letter is a forgery. Are you suggesting that he is mistaken?'

'No, I'll abide by what he says,' said Freda.

'Here comes Ronald,' said Matthew, 'in his new dark chalk-stripe. He should have been a Civil Servant.'

'Detestable man,' said Alice.

'Not a bit of it,' said Matthew. 'You don't know him at all.'

'The jury are whispering together. Are they allowed to do that?' Alice said.

'Yes,' said Matthew. 'It's their court, really. Everything depends on them.'

'I don't like that blonde woman,' Alice said. 'With her dyed hair she shouldn't be on a jury.'

Ronald, as he walked up the steps to the witness box, caught a flash-like impression of the jury, as they leaned across and consulted each other, head to head, and this reminded him of some fresco of the Last Supper. The jury righted itself when Ronald reached his post.

Ronald's evidence, as he compared the precise points at which the handwriting of the letter departed from examples of Freda Flower's handwriting and coincided with examples of Patrick Seton's, provided a perceptible rest-cure for the bewigged minds. The barristers stopped fidgeting with their papers. The judge stopped resting his head on his left hand.

'I have found,' said Ronald, 'from microscopic examination that certain letters have been formed from a starting-point different from those of Mrs Flower's handwriting. The letter "o" for example – although to the naked eye it is completely closed both in Exhibits B and D – has apparently been formed by different hands. In Exhibit B the "o" has been started from the top. In Exhibit D the "o" has been started from the right-hand curve.'

'Exhibit B,' said the judge to the jury, 'is the letter which it is alleged has been forged. Exhibit D is the example of Mrs Flower's handwriting.'

'The effect of trembling in some of the upward strokes of the signature in Exhibit B,' said Ronald, 'is visible under the microscope. This trembling in some of the upward strokes is not present in the body of the letter and suggests that the signature has been traced. The formation of the letter "I" in Exhibits B, C, and D –'

'Just a moment,' said the judge. 'The jury must be clear. Exhibit B is the alleged forgery. Exhibit D is the example of Mrs Flower's handwriting. Exhibit C is the example of the accused's writing.'

'The formation of the letter "I" in Exhibits –'

'He's marvellous,' said Matthew. 'I didn't know Ronald had it in him.'

Ronald was fumbling in his inner pocket.

'Too damned smart,' said Alice. 'You just wait till he's cross-examined. We've got a first-rate barrister in Farmer.'

'What is your conclusion, Mr Bridges?' said Martin.

'That the letter, Exhibit B, is a forgery and that it has been forged by the accused.'

Ronald was fumbling in his outer pockets.

'Now here's our man,' said Alice, as the Defence Counsel heaved himself to his feet.

But Farmer was content to await the conflicting evidence of his expert, he was content to say to Ronald, 'Mr Bridges, have you ever made a mistake?'

'Yes,' said Ronald.

'This opinion of yours couldn't be one of them?'

'I have never, so far as I know, made a mistake in a case of forgery.'

'So far as you know. Thank you, Mr Bridges – Oh, oh, watch out . . .'

Ronald swayed. He fumbled in his pockets for his pills. They were in his other suit, at home. He gave up. He stumbled down the steps and fell two steps before he got to the bottom. There he foamed at the mouth. His eyes turned upward, and the drum-like kicking of his heels began on the polished wooden floor.

'Is this man a medium?' said the judge.

The clerk approached Ronald. Two male members of the jury came out of their places, looking suddenly deprived of any excuse for their presence in the court. It was difficult to get near Ronald. 'Put something between his teeth,' said Martin Bowles, in the tones of a zoophobic veterinary practitioner. 'He's an epileptic.'

The judge rested his head in his left hand. Patrick looked solemnly up at Alice. She was peering over the balcony, looking down at Ronald. Patrick was filled with solace at the sight. I will look down on her, he thought, when she is lying on the mountainside, and the twitching will cease.

'Do you believe in prayer?' said Alice to Matthew when they went down, after the fuss was over, to lunch in the public canteen.

*

217

'He's putting up a marvellous fight,' Alice whispered. 'I've never seen Patrick in such good form. I've never heard him speak up like this. It's as if he was fighting for his life.'

Once or twice Patrick glanced at her from the witness box, for he could get a better view of her from there. The thought of Alice kept him going.

'I know,' whispered Alice, 'he's making the effort for me. It's as if he was fighting for my life. He's not an outspoken man as a rule. It shows what's in Patrick.'

The answers came without hesitation, clear and strong. It might have been the voice of one of those army men who know exactly what they think, and say it. He took courage from his desire to be acquitted, rather than timidity from his fear of being convicted and the practised members of the jury noticed this. Ronald, sitting defiantly in his exhaustion among the witnesses, managed to recall the last time he had heard Patrick speak. That had been at the Maidstone Assizes. Then, Patrick had mumbled.

Freda Flower sat horrified at Patrick's manner.

'I am, in spite of my calling, a man of the world, a practical man ...

'There was never any question of my buying defence bonds ...

'Mrs Flower frequently went into a trance. She is herself an excellent medium with extraordinary psychic powers ...

'It is impossible that she does not know that she possesses this gift ...

'I suggest, without wishing to implicate Mrs Flower further than necessary, that she became incensed when I left her, and dreamed up this story ...

'I prefer to say no more about my private relationship with Mrs Flower, if that is permissible ...

'I made the statement at the police station while still in a state of semi-trance. In such a condition the subject is highly suggestible . . . I signed this statement at the suggestion of the officer in charge. I have no recollection of doing so . . .

'I would describe the statement as a forced confession . . .'

Patrick kept his eyes off Fergusson. He looked from time to time at Alice.

'You would think he'd been saving it up,' Alice breathed. 'Like an athlete that spares himself till the time comes.'

'I deny it,' Patrick said, when asked if he had forged the letter.

His counsel sat down. Martin Bowles coughed and stood up and adjusted his robes.

'Do you really expect the court to believe, Mr Seton, that a widow in Mrs Flower's position would hand you over her life savings of two thousand pounds to use for your own purposes?'

'If you will refer to her letter you will see that she requested me to use the money to further my psychic and spiritual work. She did not ask me to use it for my own purposes. I have used the money to further my psychic and spiritual work as she requested.'

'You have heard the evidence of the Crown's graphologist. I suggest that Mrs Flower did not write that letter, but that you forged it after you had made the statement to the police, in order to discredit the statement.'

'I deny it; and I deny that I made a statement to the police in any circumstances which could be described as free.'

Matthew whispered, 'I wish my sister-in-law could have seen all this.'

'What's it got to do with her?' said Alice.

'Hush,' said Matthew, 'don't talk.'

The judge said, 'In what manner have you used this money to further your psychic and spiritual work?'

'I have spent it on the scientific training of mediums, the purchase of books on psychical research, and in travelling abroad to exchange views on the subject with foreign mediums, and on travelling in this country to extend my knowledge and impart it. Spiritualism is a science, and a science requires financial support.'

'In what does the training of mediums consist?' said the judge.

'A scientific course comprising various exercises of mind and body. An untrained medium is proved by experience to be a menace to society. Properly trained, the medium is a useful and practical vehicle of human aspirations.'

The blonde member of the jury was leaning forward attentively. Seton has got a new customer, Ronald thought, if he gets out of this.

The judge's pen scratched on. The typist in the corner listlessly pounded her silent machine. Martin continued:

'Do you consider it a reputable action to accept money from a widow in Mrs Flower's circumstances to use for your professional advancement?'

The moron, Ronald thought, why doesn't he pin him down on the questions of the forgery and the bonds?

'I was acting under Mrs Flower's instructions. I do not need professional advancement. I employed the money for the professional advancement of others.'

'I suggest that if you spent two thousand pounds between April and August you spent it somewhat rapidly.'

'Mrs Flower said in her letter that she left the details of the disposal of the money entirely to me.'

Why does he go on about the spending? – Ronald sat with the demonic aftermath of his fit working within him. Why doesn't he plug away at the forgery, he has my evidence? Then it occurred to Ronald: He doesn't believe in my evidence, he doubts its validity, and this barrister can't argue a case he doesn't believe in.

'You admit,' said Martin, 'that you accepted two thousand pounds from a woman of middle age?'

And you deny, thought Ronald, that you are swindling Isobel Billows?

'You have said,' said Martin, 'in a reply to a question, "I prefer to say no more about my private relationship with Mrs Flower."'

'That is correct,' said Patrick.

'May I ask why you are so reticent?'

'My lord,' said Patrick, addressing the judge, 'if it is not relevant to the case, I would prefer –'

'I can't see why you need go further into that question, Mr Bowles,' said the judge.

'I submit that it is a relevant question,' Martin said, 'since the jury will wish to know the extent of the influence exerted by the accused upon Mrs Flower.'

'Very well,' said the judge and rested his head on his hand.

'I suggest that your relations with Mrs Flower were of an intimate nature,' said Martin.

'I deny it,' said Patrick with an elaborate air of gallantry.

'And that you used these intimate relations to gain an influence over Mrs Flower?'

And, thought Ronald, on the strength of these intimate relations you obtained control of Isobel Billows's money.

'I deny it,' said Patrick. 'Mrs Flower herself has said nothing of our intimate relations.'

'And,' said Martin, 'you employed this influence to obtain Mrs Flower's savings.'

'I deny it.'

'In your statement to the police of the twelfth August you said –' Martin shuffled and found his document – 'you said "Early in April Mrs Flower handed me a cheque for two thousand pounds for the purpose of purchasing premium bonds and defence bonds. I was tempted and fell. I did not purchase the bonds. I do not know where the money has gone." Now, Mr Seton,' said Martin, 'I put it to you that this is the true and accurate story.'

'I deny it. I was incapable of making a statement. I was in a state of semi-trance, and was in a condition of high susceptibility to any suggestion whatsoever.'

'Do you mean that Detective-Inspector Fergusson hypnotised you?'

For a moment Patrick seemed to sag. His lower jaw receded.

'Are you suggesting that Detective-Inspector Fergusson invented this story?'

'He put the words in my mouth.'

'I did not hear,' said the judge, for Patrick's voice had suddenly failed.

Patrick looked at Alice and revived. 'He put the words in my mouth,' he said out loud.

'How did you get to the police station if you were in a state of partial insensibility?'

'I was taken there in a police car. Two policemen called at my rooms immediately after I had completed a séance.'

'On the morning of twelfth August?'

'Yes.'

'Do you usually conduct séances in the morning?'

'This was a private séance.'

Patrick was allowed to go. The judge looked at his watch. 'Is medical evidence to be called as to the effects of a trance?' he said.

Patrick's counsel said, 'No, my lord, there appears to be no useful source of medical opinion devoted to the nature and effects of the spiritualistic trance specifically.'

Martin Bowles looked confused. Ronald thought, he has slipped up properly. He should have brought in a cataleptist to refute them.

The door from the witnesses' room opened and Ronald looked round to see a fellow-graphologist, sweet old Fairley, emerging. Fairley climbed the steps to the witness box, took off his glasses and exchanged them for another pair. He read the oath slowly, and took his usual leisure throughout.

'So that, in your opinion,' said Patrick's counsel, 'mere inconsistencies in the formation of characters which can only be observed under the microscope do not imply that the characters have been formed by separate hands.'

'I do not say so,' drawled Fairley. 'That would be too large a generalisation. I say only that, in my opinion, the inconsistencies between the formation of characters on the document marked Exhibit B and those on the document marked Exhibit C, taken together with peculiarities common to Exhibits B and D, do not necessarily lead to the conclusion that Exhibit B is a forgery.'

The jury fidgeted.

'You are saying,' said the barrister, 'that the letter which the Crown alleges to be a forged document, need not necessarily be so merely on the evidence afforded by the microscope?'

'Yes,' said Fairley.

'What is the length of your experience in this field, Mr Fairley?'

'Forty-six years,' said Fairley.

Martin got up.

'The methods of forgery detection have changed in forty-six years, have they not?' Martin said.

'There have been developments,' said Fairley.

'You changed your spectacles when you came into the witness box. Do you suffer from any weakness of eyesight?' Martin said.

It's a dirty world, thought Ronald.

'Yes,' said Fairley courteously. 'But I have an excellent optician who provides me with two pairs of spectacles. One pair is for normal use and the other is for reading.'

'And you changed into your reading glasses in order to stand and give evidence in court?'

'I changed into my reading spectacles in order to read the oath, which I take seriously.'

'Oh, quite,' said Martin. 'Did you,' he said 'when you were examining the documents, notice any peculiarities in the formation of the letter "o"?'

'Yes,' said Fairley. 'In Exhibit B the "o" has been started from the top. In Exhibit D the "o" has been started from the right-hand curve.'

'Does that not suggest to you that these letters have been formed by different hands?'

'Not necessarily. There is always the possibility that the writer was at one moment in a disposition to start from the top, and at another time disposed to begin elsewhere.'

'Do you agree that there are other inconsistencies similar to those which relate to the letter "o"?'

'Yes.'

'Do you agree that the peculiar formation of many letters in Exhibit B – the document which is alleged to be a forgery – coincide with peculiarities of formation in Exhibit C – the example of the accused's handwriting?'

'There are many similarities but not enough, in my

opinion, to permit the inference that B and C are the work of the same hand.'

'Did you observe in the course of your examination of the signature the effect of trembling in some of the upward strokes?'

'No,' said Fairley.

'You did not find anything to suggest that the signature had been traced?'

'No,' said Fairley.

'You are aware that an eminent graphologist, Mr Ronald Bridges, has submitted that the effect of trembling in the upward strokes is an indication of tracing.'

'I was not present at Mr Bridges' evidence. But I agree that an effect of trembling in handwriting is sometimes due to a process of tracing. Sometimes it is due to sickness, fear, or old age.'

'You agree that forgers commonly trace the signatures on false documents?'

'Oh, yes.'

'You did not notice an effect of trembling in some of the upward strokes of the signature on the document alleged to be forged?'

'No, I did not observe any effect of trembling.'

'Did you look for it?'

'Oh, yes, it is part of the routine.'

'How does the scientific equipment available to Mr Bridges compare with that available to yourself?'

'We use the same laboratories and stuff.'

Ronald saw how vexed Martin was. He had told Martin that Fairley used private equipment, believing this to be so.

'But you did not notice this trembling effect, while Mr Bridges did?' Martin said crossly.

Oh, shut up, Ronald thought.

'There is room for varying opinion as to what is an effect of trembling,' said Fairley.

'It couldn't be a question of eyesight?'

'The documents are greatly enlarged by the microscope,' Fairley drawled wearily.

'Thank you,' said Martin.

Fairley smirked slightly at Ronald as he left. Ronald winked. A member of the jury noticed this and whispered to his neighbour. They are saying, Ronald thought, that we are in our racket together, regardless of the law. But perhaps that's not what they are whispering.

The door through which Fairley had passed now admitted Father Socket in black suit and clerical collar, the last witness for the defence. As he was shown up to the witness box, the main door on Ronald's right opened, and Elsie came in. She moved in beside Ronald and started to whisper to him. The attendant policeman placed a finger to his lips. Ronald pushed his notepad and pencil towards her. On it she wrote, 'I've come to give evidence against Father Socket.' Ronald wrote, 'You're too late,' and pushed it back.

'Isn't Father Socket marvellous?' whispered Alice.

'Father my eye,' said Matthew.

Father Socket described himself as a clergyman.

'Of what religion?' said the judge.

'Of the spiritualist religion and allied faiths.'

'Spiritualism has already this afternoon been described as a science. Is it a science or a religion?'

'It is a scientific religion, my lord, and has been recognised as such by countless eminent citizens including –'

'Yes, quite,' said the judge, 'I only want to get our definitions clear so that the jury can see what it is dealing with. There has been a great deal of mystification in this case.'

Elsie was scribbling away on the notepad.

Socket's eye was on the jury.

'You remember the morning of twelfth August?' said his Counsel. 'Where were you . . . ? What were you doing . . . ?'

'At Mr Seton's rooms . . . a private séance . . . he was in a trance, a deep trance. I am, if I may say so, something of an authority on the conditions of a spiritualistic trance . . . I left Mr Seton at ten minutes to twelve, he was in a state of complete exhaustion and insensibility to external surroundings.'

Alice looked over from the gallery.

'Elsie's going to make trouble,' she said. 'What is she writing, down there? She wouldn't come and keep me company as a friend, but she's come to make trouble.'

'She should have come up here with you,' Matthew said, 'but never mind, you've got me.'

Elsie folded her note and gave it to the policeman, indicating Martin Bowles.

Father Socket kept his eye on the jury. The blonde woman looked impressed.

'As I left the building after the séance I noticed a police car containing two police officers draw up outside the front door. This was just after ten minutes to twelve . . .' Socket said.

'In your opinion, Mr Socket,' said Patrick's counsel, 'was it likely that by twelve noon, less than ten minutes later, Mr Seton would be in a reasonable and clear state of mind?'

'Certainly not. It is impossible. He would be in a state of semi-trance, perhaps not discernible at a casual glance, but certainly apparent to anyone attempting to question him. He would be in a suggestible condition . . .'

'We've won the day!' said Alice.

Martin was looking at Elsie's two scribbled pages torn from the notepad.

The blonde jurywoman spoke to her neighbour.

Patrick's barrister sat down. Martin got up.

'I suggest,' said Martin to Socket, 'that your evidence is a pack of lies from start to finish.'

The jury seemed offended. Socket's white collar gleamed round his throat. It seemed a tasteless attack.

'It is nothing but the truth,' said Socket, with a look of ministerial reproach.

'I have a witness in court,' said Martin, 'who is prepared to swear that you were not with the accused between the hours of ten a.m. and twelve noon on August the twelfth.'

'Mr Bowles,' said the judge, 'are you wanting to put in additional evidence at this stage?'

'I was about to ask . . .'

The judge looked at his watch. Then he looked hard at Socket.

'Yes, I'm quite sure it was the twelfth of August because it was my birthday, and that's why I took the day off,' Elsie said.

'What time did you arrive at Mr Socket's flat?' Martin said.

'Ten o'clock in the morning.'

'What time did you leave?'

'One o'clock.'

'Mr Socket was present all morning?'

'Yes, he gave me dictation, and he read some poetry.'

She started to leave the witness box immediately she had answered all Martin's questions. It was indicated to her that she had to remain for cross-examination. Patrick's counsel was conferring with Socket in whispers. Presently he straightened up.

'You say you took the day off from your work because it was your birthday?' Patrick's counsel hammered out.

'Yes.'

'Was it not an odd way in which to spend your day off –
going to work as a typist in a voluntary capacity?'

'Well, I was taken in by Father Socket. I thought he was
doing good work and I thought he was a fine person.'

'On what date did Mr Socket dismiss you from his service?'

'He didn't dismiss me. I never went back after I sensed
something wrong.'

'I suggest that Mr Socket dismissed you on or about the
twentieth of July, and asked you not to come again.'

'No, I left two weeks ago because I sensed something
wrong.'

'I suggest he dismissed you, and that you are embittered.'

'Yes, I was embittered all right after I sensed something
wrong,' said Elsie like a needle.

The barrister became irritated. 'You keep saying you
sensed something wrong. What do you mean? – Let's have
it. Did you sense something wrong with your sight, hearing,
smell, touch, taste – which sense did you sense something
wrong with?'

'I sensed it with my common sense,' said Elsie, 'when I
went there and found a man with lipstick and a dressing-
gown that looked like –'

'Miss Forrest, you are an impulsive girl, aren't you?' said
this counsel of Patrick's who now roused himself for work.

'Yes, fairly,' she said, rather put out by his new intimacy
of tone.

'You did not come forward with this evidence at the
proper time. And yet you have seen fit to dash in at the last
minute with accusations against a man whom up to two
weeks ago, according to your own evidence, you thought to
be a fine person. Why is that?'

'Well, I thought about it, and I decided it wasn't my business. Then this afternoon I decided to come along.'

'On an impulse of malice?'

'Yes, if you want to put it like that,' said Elsie.

'You admit to malice against Father Socket.'

'I don't see why he should get away with his sin.'

'You realise, Miss Forrest, that you have not brought a scrap of evidence to this court to support your story – apart from malice?'

'Well, you can take it or leave it,' Elsie said. 'I was with him all morning on August the twelfth.'

'And you have no evidence to support your statement?'

'No,' said Elsie, 'there's only my word.'

Alice said, 'That girl's treacherous. Why did she have to mention the man with lipstick?'

Patrick's counsel told the jury that there could be no end to the calling of one witness to discredit another. He asked them to ignore the extraordinary and, on the face of it, wild accusations of Father Socket's former and, on her own admission, embittered typist, Miss Elsie Forrest. She had admitted to malice.

The extremely dubious evidence of Mrs Freda Flower . . . Everything to show that she was in the habit of trances . . .

The clear evidence of the accused . . . his insistence that the statement was not made while he was in a responsible condition . . . Reflecting, as it did on our ancient liberties . . .

The case of forgery was wiped out by the evidence of Mr Fairley. Particularly to be noted was Mr Fairley's insistence on the effects of variable human moods on handwriting . . .

The jury must rid itself of prejudice against spiritualism.

Patrick's counsel then listed a number of prominent persons, dead and alive, who had adorned the spiritualist movement. He looked at his watch and sat down.

Martin Bowles rose to recite the discredit of all witnesses except his own. 'The letter is undated,' said Martin, 'Why? – Because when he forged that letter he forgot the exact date of the cheque which Mrs Flower had given him, and which he now claims accompanied the letter.' He repeated Elsie's story. He reminded the jury that Fairley was getting on in years, and though must be respected, could hardly compete with a younger mind. He started to ridicule all references to the mediumistic trances which had cropped up in the case – 'foaming mouths, upturned eyes, twitching limbs, and so forth' – but seemed suddenly to be visited by a deterrent thought, which Ronald assumed to be a mental image of himself lying kicking and foaming only a few hours ago under the witness box. Martin switched away from trances and weighed into Patrick and his influence on Mrs Flower.

'You will recall that this man affected a certain delicacy in revealing his intimate relations with Mrs Flower. Yet he did not hesitate to defraud her . . .'

Ronald, heavy with the effects of his fit, sat with his eyes on Martin.

'He did not hesitate to rob her, he did not hesitate to exert his influence by means of those intimate relations with Mrs Flower.'

With Isobel Billows, thought Ronald.

'And yet he stands here and poses as her protector. You observe the irony, ladies and gentlemen of the jury.'

The irony, ladies and gentlemen, thought Ronald.

It was a very disreputable case, said the judge in his summing up, and in some respects a nauseating one. It was his duty to direct the jury to rid their minds of all prejudice against spiritualism as such . . . It was his duty to define both fraudulent conversion and forgery . . . Forgery was . . . Fraudulent conversion was . . .

This was a case which, if there were any substance in it, could have grave and serious implications. Detective-Inspector Fergusson had sworn on oath that the accused had made a certain statement while in a lucid condition of mind. That statement had been produced in court. It contained an admission of the charge of fraudulent conversion. It bore the signature of the accused.

Moreover, Detective-Inspector Fergusson had denied that the accused had at any subsequent time applied to withdraw the statement. The jury should give these facts their weightiest consideration.

'They always stand by the police,' Alice whispered, 'but the jury knows different.'

The judge looked at his watch. Much, however, he was saying, hinged on the question of forgery.

The evidence of the two graphologists tended to cancel each other out and, if he might say so, was less than useless. No prejudice should obtain in the case of Mr Ronald Bridges whose unfortunate collapse in court, he understood, had been due to an inherent disease and was in no way connected with the disedifying trances described by various witnesses.

Mrs Flower appeared to be a very foolish woman. It must be taken into account that she had strongly indicated in her evidence the possibility of having written the letter while in a state of insensibility. The jury would have the opportunity of examining the letter and forming their own conclusions on this point. But while such a doubt was present in Mrs Flower's mind it must certainly receive every consideration . . . The letter was undated. It had been suggested that the accused forgot the date of the cheque . . .

A man was innocent until he was proved guilty. While there was reasonable doubt that the accused was the author of the letter he could not be found guilty.

The jury must be clear that if they brought in a verdict of Not Guilty for forgery they could not logically bring a verdict of Guilty for fraudulent conversion. Everything hung on the question of forgery . . .

The evidence of Mr Socket must be weighed against the evidence of Miss Elsie Forrest, and vice versa. The fact that Miss Forrest had offered evidence at the last moment must not be allowed to weigh against that evidence. She was, on her own admission, impulsive by nature. On the other hand she admitted to a motive of malice against Socket, and this, whether justified or not, must be taken into account.

'Whatever your sympathies in this case,' he said, 'it is the evidence that counts. I will run over the evidence once more . . .'

The jury withdrew at twenty minutes to five. 'We'll have time for tea,' said Matthew. 'They'll be out for at least an hour.'

'The judge was against us,' Alice said, 'but the jury can't find him guilty if there's a reasonable doubt about the forgery. The judge said so himself.'

'Come on,' said Matthew.

She was looking at Patrick and he at her before he turned through the dock door. His face was radiant. The bags packed, the insulin.

'Our bags are already packed,' said Alice. 'We can leave in the morning.'

'The blonde woman was looking pretty nasty about Socket after Elsie had finished.'

'I'll never speak to Elsie again. The whole court was with us after Father Socket's evidence. The whole court. No matter what they say about evidence.'

They sat over their hot canteen tea. 'It's kicking,' said Alice. 'Oh, God, I wish this was over.'

*

Patrick looked up at Alice. It was the only thing, to look and look at Alice. Imprisonment was not the end of the world, he had always found a niche in prisons. But now, this thirst for Alice. She is mine, I have paid . . . She would probably twitch before she died. She had agreed by acquiescence.

The jury were filing in. It was twenty past five.

To make Alice into something spiritual. It was godlike, to conquer that body, to return it to the earth . . .

'On the charge of forgery.'

'Guilty.'

'On the charge of fraudulent conversion.'

'Guilty.'

'I don't believe in God,' said Alice. 'There will have to be an appeal.'

'Quiet, now,' said Matthew.

'It was Elsie mentioning the man with lipstick,' Alice said. 'That did it. I knew!'

'It was a help,' said Matthew.

Fergusson was up in the witness box again. He was reading out a list. At Canterbury in May 1923 . . . three months for larceny. At Surrey Quarter Sessions in 1930, six months for obtaining on false pretences . . . in 1932, six months . . . in 1942, eighteen months and six months to run consecutively for fraudulent conversion . . . Maidstone Assizes, in 1948, three years for forgery and fraudulent conversion. He is described as a spiritualistic medium, unmarried, resident at . . .

'What's this all about?' said Alice.

'They call it the antecedents. It's Patrick's criminal record.'

'I don't believe it,' she said. 'There's got to be an appeal.'

'He can't appeal with that record.'

'The bags are packed,' she said. 'And he's a genuine medium.'

'Just keep still,' Matthew said. 'Nothing matters.'

'A most disreputable case,' said the judge. 'A widow . . . her savings. The distasteful proceedings – I may say without prejudice to any more respectable manifestations of the cult as might exist – the distasteful proceedings of the séance room and the scope it offers for the intimidation of weak people . . . The evidence given by Mr Socket must be looked into: these courts must be kept clean of . . . Mrs Flower has been a very foolish woman.' He glanced towards Patrick. 'Have you anything to say?'

Patrick looked at Fergusson and then at the judge.

'Only,' he said, 'to ask –'

'Speak up, please.'

'Only to say that the lady I am living with is expecting a baby and needs me by her side, and –'

The judge did not look up. 'I cannot sentence you to less than five years.'

'I don't believe in God,' said Alice, clutching her stomach.

Ronald went home to bed. He slept heavily and woke at midnight, and went out to walk off his demons.

Martin Bowles, Patrick Seton, Socket.

And the others as well, rousing him up: fruitless souls, crumbling tinder, like his own self which did not bear thinking of. But it is all demonology, he thought, and he brought them all to witness, in his old style, one by one before the courts of his mind. Tim Raymond, Ewart Thornton, Walter Prett, Matthew Finch – will I, won't I marry her? – Eccie, and himself kicking under the witness box, himself, now, incensed; and all the rest of them. He sent these figures away like demons of the air until he could think of them again with indifference or amusement or wonder.

How long will it take, he wondered to distract his mind, for Matthew to marry Alice? Not knowing at the time that it would take four months – a week before the baby was born – Ronald laid a bet with himself for three months.

It is all demonology and to do with creatures of the air, and there are others besides ourselves, he thought, who lie in their beds like happy countries that have no history. Others ferment in prison; some rot, maimed; some lean over the banisters of presbyteries to see if anyone is going to answer the telephone.

He walked round the houses, calculating, to test his memory, the numbers of the bachelors – thirty-eight thousand five hundred streets, and seventeen point one bachelors to a street – lying awake, twisting and murmuring, or agitated with their bedfellows, or breathing in deep repose between their sheets, all over London, the metropolitan city.